"IT'S HATCHING!"

The egg did not crack. Instead, *something* burned its way out of the sphere, leaving a steaming hole in the shell. The creature looked like a huge, scarlet worm, about half a meter long. Its hide was red and pulpy, like raw meat, except for tiny flecks of mineral matter embedded here and there over its surface. A fringe of tiny tendrils or cilia ran along the bottom of the creature on all sides; it seemed to use the fringe to pull itself slowly across the floor, leaving a trail of scorched grillwork behind it.

So this was a Horta, Nog mused. He wondered how much it was worth. And how much more he could charge for it. . . .

Look for STAR TREK Fiction from Pocket Books

Star Trek: The Original Series

Star Trek: The Next Generation

Star Trek: Deep Space Nine

Star Trek: Voyager

STAR TREK
DEEP SPACE NINE®

DEVIL IN THE SKY

Greg Cox and John Gregory Betancourt

POCKET BOOKS

New York London Toronto Sydney Tokyo Singapore

An *Original* Publication of POCKET BOOKS

POCKET BOOKS, a division of Simon & Schuster Inc.
1230 Avenue of the Americas, New York, NY 10020

This book is published by Pocket Books, a division of Simon & Schuster Inc., under exclusive license from Paramount Pictures.

ISBN: 0-671-88114-0

First Pocket Books printing June 1995

10 9 8 7 6 5 4 3 2 1

POCKET and colophon are registered trademarks of Simon & Schuster Inc.

Printed in the U.S.A.

Historian's Note

Devil in the Sky takes place in the second season of STAR TREK: DEEP SPACE NINE.

CHAPTER
1

Station Log, Commander Benjamin Sisko, Stardate 46384.1:

In hopes of reviving the Bajoran mining industry, left devastated after the Cardassian Occupation, the Federation has arranged, in cooperation with private Bajoran investors, to transport a family of Hortas to Bajor. In theory, the Hortas will use their natural tunneling abilities to find pockets of minerals and ore which the Cardassians either missed or deemed too difficult to extract.

We are currently awaiting the arrival of the Federation cruiser *Puyallup,* en route from Janus VI. I have dispatched a team of officers to welcome the Hortas to *Deep Space Nine.* . . .

THE AIRLOCK DOOR rolled out of the way like a gear in some enormous clockwork mechanism. In contrast to the grim gray walls of the docking ring, the circular door was the dull red color of drying human blood.

Damn Cardassian architecture, Major Kira Nerys thought as she walked briskly through the airlock toward Docking Port 8; *even after so much time on the station, I still haven't grown accustomed to the ugliness of it all. Cardassian aesthetics are on a par with their ethics,* she mused; *that is, they don't exist.*

Kira suspected that Commander Sisko would not approve of such sentiments, at least in public. His Federation was annoyingly reluctant to criticize the cultures of even their most loathsome enemies. Hell, they had even made peace with the Klingons. Sometimes she thought it was a miracle that the entire Federation hadn't been conquered centuries ago. But then, Kira wasn't sure she believed in miracles anymore.

Another airlock door, its gearlike teeth crimson as a Bajoran sea-tiger, opened before her and the Bajoran major found herself in a small waiting area outside the docking port. A triangular display, lit in shades of red and blue, announced the arrivals and departures of various spacecraft. An outdated map of the station, mounted on the wall under a sheet of transparent aluminum, waited to mislead newcomers to DS9. Two of her fellow officers, Lieutenant Jadzia Dax and Dr. Julian Bashir, glanced toward her as she approached them. Although a stark metal bench, of Cardassian design, was bolted to both the floor and the adjoining wall, the pair of officers remained standing. Kira didn't blame them; uncomfortable and uninviting, the bench resembled a torture device better suited to a dungeon than a space station.

Dax gave Kira a friendly smile and nod, while Bashir kept on babbling at the young woman, his hands waving enthusiastically as he spoke. As usual, Kira noted, Bashir was hovering around Dax's lithe, attractive form just like a Ferengi would. Why Dax had never told Bashir just where he could beam himself Kira had never understood.

"As a specialist in multispecies medicine," the doctor was saying, "naturally I find the Hortas fascinating. They were the first silicon-based life-form humanity ever encountered. Not only that, they also secrete a powerfully corrosive acid that allows them to move through solid rock the same way humanoids move through air. They actually *digest* raw iron and other minerals!"

What was Bashir most enthralled with, Kira wondered: Dax's bright blue eyes and gracefully spotted neck—or the sound of his own voice? *Please, Jadzia,* Kira thought silently. *Don't encourage him.*

"Really, Julian?" Dax said indulgently. "That's very interesting."

Oh, no. Kira sighed and shook her head. There was no shutting him up now. Sure enough, Bashir leaned against the bulkhead wall, in what he doubtless considered a suave and dashing manner, and resumed his lecture. A Starfleet medical pouch, strapped over his shoulder, dangled next to his side. "Then, of course," he said casually, his eyes never once leaving Dax's attentive face, "there's the Horta's very unusual reproductive cycle. . . ."

Oh, give me a break, Kira fumed. Typically, however, Dax stood by calmly, with her hands clasped loosely behind her back. Although Dax had a fun-loving side that Kira had learned never to underestimate, the Trill science officer often exuded a sense of effortless serenity that was almost spiritual. Not for the first time, Kira was secretly envious. *Is Dax what Bajoran women were like,* she wondered, *before decades of Cardassian oppression transformed us into refugees and revolutionaries? Could I have ever known that kind of peace?* Kira fingered the silver earring dangling from her right ear. The Bajorans had been a deeply religious people once. Kira liked to think she still was, and yet her spirit was often troubled.

She paced impatiently back and forth across the waiting area. Her dark red boots rapped against the bare, uncarpeted floor. According to the display, the *Puyallup* was now a few minutes late. What the hell could be taking them so long? She had more important things to do than watch another of Bashir's futile attempts to flirt with Dax.

"I've heard," Dax said to Bashir, "that the Hortas only breed once every fifty thousand years." Kira groaned quietly and rolled her eyes. Sometimes she suspected that Dax actually enjoyed playing these games with Bashir. Kira wouldn't put it past her; after all, the Trill genuinely enjoyed socializing with Ferengi.

"That's a common misconception," the doctor explained. "It's true that every five hundred centuries the entire species dies out, except for one Horta who cares for the thousands of eggs left behind, from which, eventually, a brand-new race of Hortas is born. But, prior to these epochal near-extinctions, there are interim generations of Hortas who reproduce regularly."

Frankly, Kira didn't care whether each individual Horta emerged independently from some primordial lava flow, just so they performed as advertised, and found new treasures in Bajor's pillaged mines. She almost said as much, but Jadzia, damn her, gave Bashir another too-perfect smile. "How intriguing, Julian. From a medical perspective, are there any advantages to this cycle?"

"That's a *very* perceptive question, Jadzia!" Bashir gushed. Kira prayed to all the Prophets that the Federation cruiser would arrive soon. She tapped her foot impatiently against the floor, wishing it were Bashir's larynx instead. "Of course, the study of Horta biology is less than a hundred years old, but our best theory is that the cycle is a form of population control. Hortas are basically ageless, indestructible, and have no natural predators. Thus, every fifty millennia, one generation of Hortas disappears to make room for their descendants while the primary Mother Horta, selected through a process we still don't entirely understand, provides a form of cultural continuity." The young doctor leaned toward Dax, caught up by the joys of science, or hormones, or some combination thereof. "Think of it! To be the adopted mother to an entire new generation of beings. Imagine what the sense of responsibility . . ."

"Well," Kira interrupted him, hoping to forestall another dissertation. "I look forward to meeting the Hortas." *And soon,* she prayed. Exhausted already by Bashir's unending chatter, she found herself seriously contemplating the Cardassian-built bench, unpadded metal slats and all.

"You might want to brace yourself, Major," Bashir said. Although addressing Kira, he edged even nearer to Dax. His dark eyes glowing, clearly convinced that the lovely Trill was hanging on his every word, he lowered his voice to a conspiratorial whisper. "Just between the three of us, a Horta is not the most attractive of beings. In fact," he said, winking at Dax and working very hard at being casually, shockingly, endearingly irreverent, "a fully grown Horta resembles nothing as much as an oversized slug made out of molten rock!"

5

Abruptly, the smile disappeared from Dax's lips. The station's science officer remained poised and at ease, but her voice as she spoke was markedly colder than before. "Some of my *closest* acquaintances look like slugs, Doctor, as you may recall." She turned her back on Bashir and gracefully walked away, a three-hundred-year-old symbiont sharing a fresh new humanoid body.

The crestfallen look that came over Bashir's face, as he suddenly realized his faux pas, was absolutely priceless, at least as far was Kira was concerned. Gone was the confident lecturer and ladies' man of mere moments ago. "Jadzia," he stammered breathlessly, "I didn't mean . . . that is, I certainly never intended to . . . you know I have nothing but the highest respect for you and . . . well, if I can explain . . . !"

From the other side of the room, and across as much empty space as possible, Dax glanced back at him over her shoulder. "By the way, Julian, I was excavating planetary cores alongside dozens of Hortas while you were still learning to crawl."

In other words, you cocky young fool, Kira thought, *she's been humoring you all along.* This was getting more entertaining by the moment; she'd have to remember to tell Odo about it later. For the moment, Dax seemed to have rendered Bashir speechless. It wouldn't last, of course, but Kira intended to enjoy the spectacle while she could.

A short chime from her comm badge broke the momentary silence. *Damn,* Kira thought, *just as Bashir was digging his own grave, with Dax maybe ready to throw in a few handfuls of dirt.* The doctor had been saved, quite literally, by the bell. She patted the badge on her left collar. "Kira here."

Commander Sisko's deep voice came over the

comm. "We may have a problem, Major. Our sensors detect another ship on an intercept course with the *Puyallup*. The new ship's not responding to our hails, and it appears to have come from Cardassian space."

Cardassian! Kira snapped into combat mode, all thought of Bashir's infatuations and embarrassments instantly forgotten. Her fists clenched automatically. Glancing at the map on the wall, mentally adjusting for its various inaccuracies, she swiftly deduced the location of the nearest runabout. "On my way," she told Sisko. "I'm taking Dax and Bashir on the new runabout, what's it called, the *Amazon*."

"Understood," Sisko replied. "Be careful."

Kira jerked her head toward the exit and took off at a steady run. She squeezed impatiently past the slowly rolling door as soon as a thin crescent of empty space opened up. Wordlessly, the two Starfleet officers followed quickly behind her. Bashir clutched his medical pouch as he ran after Dax and Kira. The *Amazon* waited in a service bay in the habitat ring, on the other side of the closest crossover bridge. *Take the turbolift,* Kira thought; *that would be faster than on foot.* In her mind, she was already at the helm of the runabout, racing away from the station, ready to engage the enemy once more.

She had no problems with slugs—Horta, Trill, or Terran. Cardassians, on the other hand, were the closest thing to sentient slime she knew.

Phasers fired in her imagination, blasting the slime out of existence. She was ready. She was willing.

If only she could get there in time.

Titan's large, lumpish body made a grinding sound as she tunneled toward the bridge of the *Puyallup*. The latter half of the small cruiser had been packed with lightweight synthetic concrete, the better to simulate the Horta's usually solid environment, but Ttan sensed empty air only inches away. She burned through a narrow partition of concrete and slid down the corridor toward the bridge. Behind her, traces of vapor rose from the freshly created tunnel. As usual, the Nothingness her Federation allies called "an atmosphere" tickled the nerves of her outer carapace and made her feel uncomfortably exposed. *Prime Mother,* she entreated silently, *let the worldstuff of Bajor be firm and hard.*

The doorway opened before her and she entered the bridge. A metallic semicircle large enough to accommodate a three-person crew, the chamber reeked to Ttan of tritanium and duranium. Good, solid construction, if a bit too airily spacious for her tastes. Captain Dawson rose from the command seat and greeted Ttan as the Horta rustled forward, her lower fringes brushing the cool, metallic floor. Dawson was a tall, stocky Terran whose jawline was decorated with a reddish fringe of its own. Ttan believed it was a male, but wasn't quite sure. Humanoids were such peculiar entities: all carbon softness and pointy appendages. If it weren't for their calcium framework, and a smattering of iron and other minerals, they'd bear no resemblance to life as she knew it.

"Prospector Ttan," it (he?) greeted her enthusiastically. "Thank you for joining us. We should be arriving at *Deep Space Nine* shortly."

"Fine Faring to you, Captain." The Federation translator affixed to Ttan's husk gave her a melodious voice with a slight East Indian accent. "And Smooth Voyaging to you as well, Navigator Shirar."

Ttan sensed the presence of the Vulcan navigator before Shirar stepped away from her console and into view. The currents of copper flowing through the navigator were unmistakable.

"Greetings, Prospector," Shirar said. Dark strands of protein fibers, neatly aligned in descending parallel rows, framed the Vulcan's pale features. The points of her auditory organs—"ears," Ttan recalled—were sharp as stalagmites. Previous conversations had made it clear to Ttan that Shirar was female. "I trust your offspring are well."

"Yes, very." Ttan thought proudly of the twenty eggs tucked safely away in a small vault she had carved herself out of the concrete Starfleet had provided. "And many thanks once more for the extra shielding you devised for my pilgrim infants."

Shirar nodded her chin slightly. "Given the importance and relative fragility of your eggs, it was only logical to preserve them in a stasis field independent of regular ship systems."

"Not, I hasten to add," Captain Dawson said, "that we anticipate any danger to your children. Still, it always pays to be careful, especially where little ones are concerned. I have three of my own, you know."

Three eggs? Ttan briefly reconsidered Dawson's gender. Then the captain called her attention to the large viewscreen at the opposite end of the bridge. The visual display, which occupied nearly the entire forward wall, revealed a vast and terrifying blackness in which distant stars seemed to race past them like sparks thrown off by struck flints.

The Emptiness Beyond the Emptiness. Ttan had experienced space before, but still that vast and endless void, so different from the subterranean home of her people, both thrilled and intimidated her. It was so *open*. How could any Horta survive without the reassuring, all-surrounding press of rock about

9

her, and where, she wondered, had she found the courage to cross this immense absence in order to carve new tunnels on a distant world? Ttan felt a surge of pride and anticipation. What an opportunity to burn her mark into the Stone of Memory. And maybe, just maybe, centuries hence, she or one of her children might become the Prime Mother of the next Renewal? Ttan would never be so immodest as to admit such an ambition to any other living being, but if she truly strived and succeeded at the great task before her . . . well, she could always dream, couldn't she?

"Approaching DS9," an eager young voice announced. A Benzite, Ttan realized, recognizing the distinct odor of chlorine from the artificial breathing apparatus affixed under the ensign's chin. Although he was basically humanoid in shape, and clad in a standard blue Starfleet uniform, the Benzite's face and hands were protected by a pale blue chitinous covering with glistening silver undertones. His ears, located higher on his skull than either Dawson's or Shirar's, were also deeply recessed and less ornate than other humanoids'. Ttan was proud that she could identify them at all. With his smooth, hairless shell, the Benzite somehow seemed more convincingly alive than the other humanoids on the *Puyallup,* although of course Ttan was far too tactful to say so.

"Go to impulse, Ensign," Dawson instructed.

"Yes, sir!" the Benzite responded, expelling a gust of carbon trichloride. Seconds later, the ever-present dilithium aftertaste Ttan had learned to associate with warp travel dissipated from the bridge. The streaking stars before her slowed in their fiery trajectories past the ship. They were almost there, she thought in wonder. Bajor: her new home and her children's future birthplace.

The fibrous mineral filaments around her base rustled with excitement as she edged nearer the viewscreen. Captain Dawson stepped beside her. He stroked the fringe under his own chin.

"Let me show you one of the more interesting local sights," he said cheerfully. "Ensign, lateral view, medium magnification."

"Yes, sir," the young Benzite responded from his post. Instantly, the image on the viewer shifted, revealing what appeared to be a moon or planetoid much closer to the ship than the faraway stars. The moon was large and irregularly shaped, marked by a chaotic pattern of gray-brown peaks and shadowy craters, divided by intersecting veins of some rough, reddish material. Unlike most other moons, this object could not be described as a globe; unknown forces had deformed its mass, flattening its eastern hemisphere and causing the other half to stretch and protrude along random stress lines, like a human skull that has been smashed against a hard surface, with its shell distorted but barely holding together, and bits of soft tissue jutting out through the cracks. The moon's coarse and mottled exterior suggested eons of violent volcanic activity, resulting in a cracked, scarred, and pitted terrain that had obviously never known the patient polishing of wind or water. In many ways, Ttan noted, the huge floating rock bore a distinct resemblance to a Horta. She wondered if that was why Dawson had invited her to the bridge.

If the captain had observed the similarity, he did not comment on it. "What you're looking at," he said, "is the most distant of Bajor's moons. They call it The Prodigal, because it has an unusually wide and elliptical orbit which brings it within sight of Bajor only once every five years. More importantly, from our point of view, its orbit should bring it near *Deep Space Nine* in a couple of days. If you're still on the station then, the view should be spectacular. Something about the moon's composition causes it to glow whenever it comes into close proximity with what we now know to be the entrance to the wormhole. Tourists and sightseers from all over the Federation are flocking to DS9 to witness firsthand 'The Illumination of The Prodigal.'"

"Previously," Shirar noted, "the station was not located so close to the moon's path, nor were the Cardassians inclined to accommodate outside observers during the Occupation. A better opportunity to view the spectacle has not been available for generations."

A tempting prospect, Ttan thought, but she suspected that she would prefer to travel on to Bajor itself as soon as possible. Indeed, her stop at the station seemed more of a Federation formality than anything else. As DS9 was beyond transporter range of the planet's surface, a Bajoran shuttle had been hired to convey her eggs and herself on the final leg of their long journey. *Soon,* she recalled eagerly, *my children and I will burrow into the comforting denseness of a brand-new world.* She wondered what Bajor would taste like.

Suddenly, the Benzite ensign sat up straight in his seat. A puff of chlorine escaped his breathing tube. "Captain! Unidentified vessel dead ahead and approaching fast." His hands moved briskly over the face of his console. Ttan heard his chitinous fingers click lightly against the controls. "They're powering up their phaser banks."

"Shields up!" Dawson ordered. "Red Alert!" He hurriedly regained his seat at the center of the bridge.

Shirar resumed her post as well, to the left of the Benzite's station. "Brace yourself, Ttan," the captain said.

Alarms blared liked screaming babies. Ttan fought her instinctual response to tunnel to safety; she would only destroy the delicate circuitry below the bridge. Instead, she wedged herself into the space beneath an unmanned computer station and the floor. Despite her best intentions, a trickle of acid dripped from her hide, scarring the surface of the floor. *My eggs,* she thought desperately. *My children!*

Dawson fired off commands to his crew. "Navigator, take over piloting. Ensign, hostile onscreen."

The Benzite brought their attacker onto the monitor. The onrushing ship had a hammerhead prow that promised no peaceful intentions. The craft's muted, reddish brown exterior made it difficult to spot against the darkness of space—until a flash of phaser fire lit up the screen.

The first blast struck like an earthquake. The *Puyallup* shook around her; she could feel the vibrations as, even shielded, the ship's hull shuddered under the blast's impact.

"Shields down forty-three percent, Captain." Shirar announced from her post. "Forty-three point seven seven seven nine, to be precise."

"Round numbers will suffice," Dawson said dryly, his voice admirably cool. Beneath the crimson facial filaments, however, his hide had gone pale. Ttan sensed the iron coursing through his veins. "Weapons systems?" he asked.

"Inoperative," Shirar replied. "Executing evasive maneuvers." Unlike Dawson, Ttan noted, the Vulcan's internal fluids were not moving any faster than before the attack.

"Dammit," the captain swore, as the *Puyallup* took a sharp turn away from their attacker. "We're hopelessly outgunned." His fist pounded the armrest of his chair. "This was supposed to be a passenger run, nothing more!"

Another bolt struck the Federation cruiser, rocking the floor from side to side. The illumination in the bridge flickered. A shower of green sparks exploded from the console in front of the young Benzite. He fell from his seat and lay twitching only a few yards away from Ttan. The thin blue shell covering his flesh was splintered in several places. A thick orange liquid leaked through the crevices. Mercury mixed with platinum, Ttan realized. She regretted that she had never learned the ensign's name.

"Shields down one hundred percent," Shirar warned. Her eyes did not leave her console display. "Warp engines off-line."

"Open hailing frequencies," Dawson ordered, staring in horror at the fallen Benzite. "Find out what they want."

"No response, Captain," the Vulcan said.

The main viewer remained locked on the hammerhead ship. Its prow grew larger and nearer by the second, until it seemed to fill the screen. "Send an SOS to *Deep Space Nine*," Dawson said. "Tell them we need assistance . . . now!"

Crammed into her hiding place, Ttan felt an unusual sensation suffuse her entire being, as though she were instantly dissolving into vapor or less. White static, loud and crackling, seemed to come between her and the rest of the bridge. Still, just before the *Puyallup* faded completely away, she heard Shirar say, "They're activating their transporter. . . ."

My children, my children, Ttan's soul cried out as she was snatched by the Void.

"The unidentified vessel has fired upon the *Puyallup,*" Dax announced from the conn station aboard the runabout. Seated beside her, Kira piloted the *Amazon,* pushing the ship as fast as it would go on impulse power, just short of warp speed. Behind Dax and Kira, Dr. Bashir gripped the armrests of his seat with white knuckles as the runabout banked sharply to the right.

"Unidentified vessel, my foot," Kira snarled. She knew a Cardassian sneak attack when she saw one. She glanced down at her monitors; they were only seconds away from the battle. A small, tight smile lifted the corners of her lips. She imagined strangling the Cardassian attackers with their own ropy neck tendons. It wasn't enough that they had repeatedly robbed and pillaged this system during their long occupation . . . no, they had to keep coming back for the scraps as well!

Not this time, she vowed, as they came within sight of the conflict. In the distance, she saw the scarred and blackened hull of the small Federation cruiser, drifting in space. The command saucer was still intact, she noted with relief, but both warp nacelles bore the marks of direct phaser strikes; the cruiser wasn't going anywhere on its power. Beyond the *Puyallup,* her attacker, of recognizably Cardassian design, hovered a little short of striking distance. Not a full-size Galor-class warship, Kira noted with relief, and only slightly larger than the runabout itself. She increased the magnification on the viewer. The Cardassian ship was curiously unadorned, bearing no military insignia or markings. A rogue pirate, she speculated, or some sort of covert mission? Knowing the Cardassians, she suspected the latter.

"I'm still detecting life signs on the *Puyallup*," Dax informed her. Despite the runabout's wild flight, every strand of Jadzia's long brown hair remained tucked neatly in place. *How* does *she manage that*, Kira wondered, despite herself. "Humanoid, that is. I'd have to recalibrate for Hortas." Suddenly, Dax's violet eyes grew wide. "Major, the attackers beamed something away from the *Puyallup*."

Thieves! Kira thought, shifting course slightly to bring the runabout above and away from the besieged cruiser. The last thing she wanted was to put the *Puyallup* in a cross fire. The bumpy flight smoothed out quickly as she slowed to combat speed. "Lieutenant Dax, activate shields and weapons systems. Prepare to fire on command."

Even as she spoke, a ray of crimson energy leaped from the prow of the Cardassian ship to strike the battered transport. For a second, Kira's heart stopped as she feared she was too late, that the Federation ship would fly apart, killing everyone aboard, an instant before she could try to defend them. *Those bastards*, she cursed the Cardassians; clearly, they intended to leave no witnesses behind. *If they've destroyed the Hortas*, she thought angrily, *I'll see them reduced to interstellar ash*.

Plasma flames, green and incandescent, rippled across the surface of the *Puyallup*, and the entire ship turned cartwheels in space, but the cruiser held together, if only for a few moments more. Kira breathed a sigh of relief. The Prophets had given her another chance.

To hell with warning shots. "Microtorpedo. Now!"

she ordered. Dax's fingers flew across her control pad. Kira watched with grim satisfaction as the torpedo darted straight for the enemy's bridge. A photon blast exploded against the Cardassian's shields, rocking the raider's ship. "The other torpedo. Now." That was the end of her torpedoes, but Kira wasn't going to let up now. The *Puyallup* probably wouldn't survive another blast, so she didn't want to give the Cardassians a moment's rest. Besides, she still had her phasers.

The second torpedo detonated against the underside of the Cardassian vessel. Their shields held once more, but the force of the explosion caused the enemy ship to lurch and dip momentarily, like a fixed buoy riding out a sudden wave. And was that the Cardassians' emergency lighting blinking off, then on? Kira couldn't tell for sure, but she hoped as much. Seconds later, the ship lifted away from the *Puyallup*. Was it going to take the battle to the *Amazon?* Kira held her breath. "Enemy's shields at eight-five percent," Dax said calmly. "Energizing our phaser banks."

Then, to Kira's surprise and disappointment, the Cardassian raider rotated horizontally until the rear of the ship faced the runabout. Warp engines flashed like prismatic lightning before her eyes and the Cardassians took off in retreat. "Heading?" she asked Dax quickly.

"The Cardassian border. Away from DS9."

Everything in Kira's blood urged her to pursue the Cardassian ship, to hunt them down and make them pay for this unforgivable attack, to recover what they had stolen from the Federation and Bajor. She contemplated the wounded cruiser, its once gleaming hull now burned and twisted. The *Puyallup* floated out of control, at an angle almost 360 degrees away from its original orientation; she hoped, for the survivors' sake, that the artificial gravity had not been shorted out by the Cardassians' blasts so that everyone would stay rightside-up aboard the ship, regardless of its shifting position in space. But were there any survivors? Even as she wondered, the Cardassians were getting farther and farther away.

"Damn," she muttered under her breath. Then, more firmly: "Hail the *Puyallup*. Find out if they require medical assistance." She swiveled her seat around to address Bashir. The young physician met her gaze steadily. "Get ready, Doctor. I think you're going to be busy." Kira turned toward Dax. "Lock a tractor beam on the cruiser. We'll tow it back to DS9 later; for now, hold it in place."

Dax had already established a comm link with the *Puyallup*'s captain. Kira was relieved to hear that, apparently, someone was still alive over there. Still, she stared with cold fury toward the sector into which the Cardassians had warped away. *This isn't over yet,* she promised herself. *Nobody invades the Bajoran system and escapes with impunity, not while I'm alive. Especially not the Cardassians.*

"Major?" Dax interrupted Kira's vengeful musings. "Bad news. The Mother Horta was beamed off the *Puyallup*. She's been kidnapped."

CHAPTER
2

SISKO'S OFFICE had once belonged to Gul Dukat, the former Cardassian commander of *Deep Space Nine,* who obviously hadn't been interested in making his visitors comfortable. Seated behind an imposing black desk, his head and shoulders framed by a cat's-eye-shaped window that looked out on the surrounding stars, Benjamin Sisko observed his staff standing at attention before him. Not for the first time, he reminded himself to get some more chairs.

Dr. Bashir, flanked by Dax and Kira, continued to debrief the commander on the crisis involving the *Puyallup.* "To our knowledge, there are no casualties so far. Ensign Muluck was severely injured, but his situation seems to have stabilized. Nurse Kabo is looking after him now; I've given her detailed instructions on the care and treatment of Benzites." Sisko noted orange stains on the sleeves of Bashir's uniform: Muluck's blood? He wondered how much emergency, hands-on care the Benzite had required, and if Muluck would still be alive if not for the young doctor's efforts. "Captain Dawson and Lieutenant Shirar received only concussions and minor fractures. They've been released from the infirmary." Bashir hesitated before continuing. "Captain Dawson wants to take part in any rescue mission, but, as medical officer, I don't think that's a good idea."

Sisko agreed. While he sympathized with Dawson's desire to fulfill his responsibilities toward Ttan, neither he nor Lieutenant Shirar sounded like they were in any shape to take on the raiders. Better they should supervise repairs on the *Puyallup,* which, no doubt, had other vital missions scheduled.

"What about the Horta eggs?" Sisko asked. As a father himself, he felt a pang at the thought of the unborn Hortas being destroyed or orphaned.

"All twenty eggs are unbroken and appear to be unharmed," Bashir said. "I must admit, though, that prenatal examination of Hortas is something new for me. Horta eggs look like smooth silicon nodules; they can—and have—been mistaken for lifeless mineral deposits."

Those nodules are going to hatch, Sisko thought. *What then? Twenty newborn Hortas separated from their mother? That could be a problem.* Still, there were more pressing issues to deal with now, like the fate of the Mother Horta. . . . He made a mental note to have Chief O'Brien secure the eggs in an unused cargo bay.

On second thought, he corrected himself, these eggs are guests, not freight. Better make that an empty suite on the habitat ring.

Dax stepped forward, a data padd in her right hand. "The eggs were protected by a contained stasis field, Benjamin. I suspect that this field shielded the eggs from the brunt of the attack, and may have prevented the raiders from beaming away the eggs as well."

"Raiders?" Kira said. "Cardassians, you mean." Placing her palms firmly on the surface of Sisko's desk, she leaned toward him. He recognized the fiery look in her eyes; Kira was out for blood. "Commander, this is a shameless Cardassian incursion against Bajor and the Federation. We *have* to retaliate."

Sisko spoke slowly, choosing his words with care. "I've spoken with Gul Dukat. He insists that the Cardassian military government knows nothing about the attack on the *Puyallup*—or the present whereabouts of the abducted Horta." Kira snorted, and Sisko waved a hand to head off her objections. "Yes, yes, I know. I don't believe it either. Without proof, however, I can hardly launch a full-scale armada against the Cardassians, even if I had the ships, which I don't."

"But we have to do something!" Kira insisted.

"And we will, Major," Sisko said firmly. "The Horta, Ttan, was under Starfleet protection. A rescue mission is our top priority, but first we have to figure out where she's been taken." He rested his chin on his clasped hands. "So, assuming the Cardassians are responsible, why would they kidnap Ttan?"

"To sabotage the Bajoran economy?" Bashir speculated.

"Unlikely," Dax said. She consulted her padd. "The Horta mining project was an experimental affair, confined to one site on the southern continent. Although promising in theory, it wasn't yet a proven success, let alone essential to the Bajoran recovery."

Kira pulled back from Sisko's desk, but her entire body still shook with indignation. "Since when did Cardassians need a reason to rob and kill?"

"Point taken," Sisko said diplomatically. "Still, it's clear that this attack had a purpose, and that purpose was specifically to snatch Ttan. So, again, why does someone steal a Horta?"

"Mining," Dax said. "That must be it. The Hortas are the greatest natural miners in the known galaxy. The human-Horta mining alliance on Janus VI is the most productive—and profitable—source of raw ore and rare elements in the entire Federation."

Yes, Sisko thought. That made sense. Slave labor and greed; even Kira had to agree that those were plausible motives for a Cardassian operation. "What we're looking for then is a Cardassian mining installation. That's where we'll find Ttan." Sisko rose from his chair, his decision made. "Dax, check the station's computer. Find out the coordinates of the five nearest Cardassian mining operations, in order of proximity to DS9. Kira, rearm the *Amazon* and assemble a security team." Sisko paused for a second before continuing. "Take Wilkens, Muckerheide, Parks, Jonsson, and Aponte." He saw Kira's eyes widen as he named his choices, all Starfleet personnel, but she said nothing, for now, and he chose to ignore her expression.

Later, he thought. He was not fool enough to think that the confrontation had been permanently postponed. "The goal here is to rescue Ttan and, hopefully, return her unharmed. Fast in and fast out."

"Commander," Bashir began. "Request permission to accompany the rescue party. Ttan may already be injured, and I've been reading up on Horta first aid."

"What about Ensign Muluck?" Sisko asked. He glanced again at the bloodstains on Bashir's wrists.

"Nurse Kabo can care for him now. My presence is not required."

"I think I should go along too, Benjamin," Dax added. "I've probably had more experience with

Hortas than anyone else on the station. In fact, one of my granddaughters lives on Janus VI."

Sisko nodded. He wondered briefly whether Dax was that woman's grandmother or grandfather. "Kira," he said, "Bashir and Dax are with your team. Prepare to depart within the hour." He looked them over. "Be careful, all of you. That will be all."

The office doors slid shut behind Dax and Bashir as they exited. Not surprisingly, Kira lingered behind. *Okay,* Sisko thought, slowly stepping out from behind his desk, *let's get this over with.* "Is there something else, Major?" he asked flatly, his voice giving nothing away.

"Permission to speak frankly, Commander?" Kira asked.

"Go ahead," he replied, surprised and impressed that she had actually requested permission.

"The security team you assigned, they're all Starfleet. No Bajorans, aside from me. What's the story?"

"Does there have to be a story?" Sisko said.

"The majority of the station's security forces are Bajoran. The Horta had been invited by Bajorans for a Bajoran project. The attack on the cruiser occurred in Bajoran space." Kira's voice grew more forceful with each point she recited. "And yet, there are almost no Bajorans involved in the rescue mission. Oh, I think there's a story, Commander, and I'd like to know what it is."

She is my first officer, he thought. *She deserves an honest answer.* "I don't want this situation to escalate, Kira. Because of your history, Bajorans and Cardassians are a volatile combination. For that reason, I'm reluctant to send a team of armed Bajorans into Cardassian territory."

"You don't trust us to behave?" Kira asked sarcastically.

"I trust *you,*" Sisko emphasized. "But your mission is to bring back Ttan, not start a war or avenge old wrongs. We have many fine Bajoran security officers, but I'd rather use Starfleet personnel on this particular mission. Sorry."

Kira's eyes blazed, but she kept her voice even. "I disagree strongly. Bajorans have a large stake in this mission, and we shouldn't be treated like trigger-happy children."

"Fine," Sisko said. "Your objections are noted. But we'll do this my way."

"Understood," Kira said. She turned and walked out the door, her spine straight as a spear. "I'll be under way shortly." The double doors closed behind her with a whish of air.

"Good luck," Sisko said. He took a deep breath and settled back into his chair. After a moment's thought, he tapped his comm badge. "Chief O'Brien. Report to Ops in about fifteen minutes. I want to talk to you about some eggs."

Dax returned to Sisko's office before O'Brien arrived. A black equipment pouch was at her side, held on by a strap over her shoulder. Her blue eyes observed Sisko with warmth and concern. "You wanted to see me, Benjamin?"

"Yes." He glanced at the intricate Saltah'na clock resting on his desk. "Find any likely coordinates?"

Dax sat down on one corner of his desk. They'd known each other too long to worry about Starfleet protocol, at least in private. "The closest Cardassian mining colony is an L-class planet in the Xoxa system, about twelve hours away at warp three. There are other possibilities, but they're much more distant. Of course, they could have taken Ttan to a new mine we know nothing about, or maybe even an archaeological dig."

"I've thought of that," he said. He'd even considered the possibility that the Cardassians might have some insane idea of using the Horta in a military operation; after all, one Horta had managed to kill several armed humans during the Federation's first encounter with their species. Fortunately, that initial misunderstanding had been straightened out quickly, close to a century ago.

"The Xoxa colony sounds like our best bet, though," he continued. "We'll have to try there—and hope for the best." He looked again at the bronze Saltah'na clock he'd constructed some time ago, while under the influence of an alien matrix; almost three hours had passed since the Horta had vanished from the bridge of the *Puyallup*. Thank goodness her children were safe, at least. "Jadzia, do we have any idea when those eggs are likely to hatch?"

"According to the immigration files in the *Puyallup*'s data banks, not for a week or two," she said. "Horta births are no more predictable than human delivery dates, of course, but I think you've some breathing space before the children emerge. And don't forget, the eggs are also confined in a stasis field, which should keep them dormant for the time being."

A mental image came to his mind, of over a dozen baby Hortas, like huge corrosive earthworms, awaking without their mother. If they were to hatch, what was he supposed to feed them? Raw rhodinium ingots? *Kira,* he thought, *get Ttan back* soon. "Is the away team ready?" he asked Dax.

"Almost. The runabout's being refitted with a larger

passenger module, as well as additional torpedoes. Julian's getting together some special medical supplies. The security team is armed and ready. Kira will page me when she's ready; it should be soon." She gave Sisko a searching look. "Benjamin, what did you really want to talk about? I haven't got much time."

"It's Kira," he said. "You know how hot-blooded she can be, especially where Cardassians are concerned."

"That's to be expected," Dax responded. "She's fought the Cardassians her whole life, seen friends and allies victimized by them time after time."

"Of course," he agreed. "Frankly, there's no love lost between me and Gul Dukat. But I don't want this hostage situation to erupt into a shooting war, not with DS9 so close to the border and Starfleet so far away." Sisko paused. The polished gears of the Saltah'na timepiece rotated notch by notch. "I just want you to keep an eye on things, and a cool head about you. Kira and Bashir are good officers, but they can both be impetuous, Julian because of his youth and Kira because, well, she's Kira. Together, on a risky search-and-rescue beyond the Cardassian border . . ." Sisko permitted himself a pained expression. "Without stepping on Kira's authority, do what you can to keep this mission from getting more complicated. I've known you longer than anyone else on this station, so I know I can count on you."

"Even in this new body?" she asked. Sisko smiled. Sometimes he still visualized her as the rascally, silver-haired man she'd been when they first met.

"Even if your next host is a Ferengi," he declared.

Dax grimaced, as if imagining a particularly unappetizing meal. "Please, Benjamin, let's not get carried away." Then she grinned at him mischievously. "I mean they're a nice species to visit, but I wouldn't want to *be* one."

A chime from her badge interrupted them abruptly. "Kira to Dax," the major's voice said. "Meet me at Landing Pad Two."

Dax tapped her chest. "On my way. Dax out." She hopped off the desk and checked the tricorder in her pouch. "Don't worry, Benjamin. It won't do us any good."

Sisko watched her hurry out of his office, through Ops to the nearest turbolift. "Take care of yourself, old man," he said as the lift carried her away.

And take care of Kira and the others.

CHAPTER
3

IN THE PASSENGER COMPARTMENT aboard the *Amazon*, Major Kira strode up and down before the assembled rescue team, looking each member over with a critical eye. *If Sisko had any sense,* she thought angrily, *this would have been an all-Bajoran mission.* She would have made a bigger fight for it if time hadn't been so pressing. She couldn't risk delaying any further; rescuing Ttan had to come first.

The five Federation security officers, three male and two female, all human, kept their backs straight and their eyes focused on the bulkhead in front of them.

Kira hid a private smile. *My reputation precedes me,* she thought with a trace of pride. *If I said "boo" I think they'd die of heart attacks.*

She prided herself on maintaining a reputation as a tough-as-nails Bajoran officer. She did her best to reinforce that impression every chance she had, and this was no exception. If they came under fire, these men and women had to be ready to follow her orders without question or hesitation.

She began to relate the events leading up to the Horta's capture. As she did, her mind raced ahead to thoughts of actual combat against the Cardassians. She still had a lot of old scores to settle—even if she had to take an all-human security team to do it.

At least Sisko had made some sensible choices in assigning members to the team. Ensigns Duane Wilkens and Ian Muckerheide had hair the color of copper. The pair made a good security team; Kira had seen them help Odo break up the brawls that invariably started at Quark's Place. Ensign Delia Parks was blond, with her hair pulled in a tight bun behind her head. *Another good choice,* Kira thought. Parks was bright, ambitious, and could double as pilot or navigation officer, if necessary. Tall, pale Ensign Sven Jonsson had the creamy color of kaafa milk. He was all rippling sinew and speed: Kira had once seen him drag a pair of drunken Klingons off to the brig. Last but not least came Ensign Natalia Aponte, with her space-black hair and dark good looks. Ensign Aponte had always been something of an enigma to Kira. She always seemed to be watching everyone and everything around her, almost as though she expected something strange and out-of-place to happen. Sometimes it made Kira uneasy, but now she welcomed such watchfulness. Nobody would sneak up on them with Aponte on watch.

Kira finished the briefing with, "Any questions?"

"Sir," Ensign Jonsson said.

"What is it, Ensign?"

"Shouldn't we have environment suits?"

Good question, Kira thought. "Dax?" she called. "I'll let you answer that."

"No," Dax called from the conn station, where she was running the last of the diagnostics. "Cardassian mining plants are almost always in M-class environments. Otherwise, they're not cost-effective."

"What if they dropped Ttan off somewhere only a Horta could live?" Jonsson persisted.

"Not bloody likely," Kira said. "Cardassians are control freaks. To them, a Horta will be merely a new tool. Believe me, they'll find a way to put her to use in one of their mines. Any other questions?"

Nobody spoke up. Good; they were wasting time.

"Strap yourselves in," Kira said. She watched as they scrambled to do so.

Turning, Kira stalked forward to where Dax, at the conn, had been running diagnostic tests. To make a bad situation worse, Kira thought, Bashir was watching over Dax's shoulder and chattering about the excitement that lay ahead. If she had Bashir breathing down her neck the whole trip, she'd go crazy.

"Major," Dr. Bashir said. "Do you think we'll face any real fighting?"

"Don't worry, I'll keep you out of it," Kira said. She turned to Dax and asked, "What's our status?"

"Everything checks," Dax said. "Ops just cleared us for takeoff."

"Doctor?" Kira glanced at Bashir. "Are you ready?"

He grinned and pointed to a small black bag on the floor beside him. "All I could possibly need. Thanks to Dr. Leonard McCoy's pioneering medical research on the Hortas, I'm even prepared in case Ttan has been injured."

"Very well," Kira said. "Take your seat with the others in the back. We lift off in one minute."

Kira cut Bashir off when he opened his mouth to protest. "That's an *order,* Doctor." The last thing she needed was him bouncing around the cabin while they left DS9.

"It may be a bumpy flight again," Dax added. "We'll need you to keep an eye on the crew."

"Right!" Bashir said, brightening. He picked up his bag and headed aft.

Dax said, "All humanoids have their foibles, Major."

For a second Kira wondered if Dax was telepathic, too. "Am I that obvious?" she asked. *If so, I'm going to have to work on my professional look,* she thought.

"You hide it well. But yes." Dax gave her a little smile.

"Why do you . . . you know . . . encourage him?"

"I must admit there is a part of my host that does find him . . . attractive."

"Attractive? *That?*"

"Perhaps, if you got to know him better . . ."

Kira snorted as several dull thuds reverberated through the runabout. It had to be the docking clamps being released, she thought. Leaning forward, she scanned the readouts before her. Engines were powered up; artificial gravity engaged; weapons systems active. Hopefully it wouldn't come to ship-to-ship fighting; a Cardassian battle cruiser would blow them to atoms. No, they'd have to be fast in and fast out, she thought, like Sisko had said. She allowed herself a tight smile. And just like the old days, when she left there would be a few less slime-devil Cardassians to worry about.

Kira activated the thrusters, nosing the runabout up and away from DS9 in a series of gentle surges that the artificial gravity couldn't quite mask.

"Docking ring cleared," Dax said.

Kira said, "Going to impulse power." She watched the viewscreen as the runabout turned smartly and accelerated away from the space station. DS9 dwindled to a speck, then vanished. Still she accelerated. There was no telling what tortures they were putting Ttan through.

"Heading one-nine-eight degrees, mark four," Dax said.

That's where the Cardassians attacked the *Puyallup,* Kira realized after a second of mental calculations. "Why aren't you setting a course for Xoxa?" she demanded.

"Chief O'Brien had a better idea," Dax said. "I didn't have time to tell you. He recalibrated the *Amazon's* sensors to pick up ionized particles caused by subspace distortion."

"You know the wormhole plays havoc with subspace—"

"True. But I think we can get there quickly enough to pick up some residual traces. And the farther we get from the wormhole, the cleaner the trace we'll find."

"It's worth a shot, I suppose," Kira said slowly. *But I'd prefer it if you'd tell me first next time,* she mentally added.

"If it doesn't work, we've only wasted half an hour. If it *does . . ."*

"If it does," Kira finished for her, "we've saved ourselves a lot of unnecessary worry . . . and possibly a huge mistake." *That's what counts in the end,* she thought.

Ttan felt a great nothingness all around. Her cilia spun helplessly; her sensory organs registered only the faintest traces of oxygen, nitrogen, and carbon dioxide; she felt as though she were falling into a bottomless void. There were no familiar tastes of minerals, no comforting surfaces to burrow into.

She tried to fight it, but the same panic that had overwhelmed her the first time she'd seen the sky over Janus VI struck her. She began to scream in terror, a high-pitched keening sound that went on and on and on. Her cilia whirled helplessly. Acid squirted uncontrolled from her glands.

"Stop that, Horta!"

With the voice came light, and the light revealed a huge cavern. Ttan found herself suspended halfway between floor and ceiling, spinning slowly in a counterclockwise direction. The walls of the cavern consisted of thick metal girders. The floor underfoot looked like sheet-metal plating . . . like the floors in the Federation ship that had been taking her to Bajor.

Ttan managed to regain control of herself. Acids from her body had already begun to etch designs into the floor and wall plates, she saw with some embarrassment. Prime Mother, had she really lost control of herself like some day-old hatchling?

She realized she had to be in another ship, this one without the concrete hold specifically designed to accommodate her. She was suspended in midair by some sort of tractor beam. That explained the sensation of falling, the lack of comforting surfaces into which she might burrow.

"Creature!" the voice bellowed.

Ttan managed to focus on the room's other inhabitant: a humanoid wearing shiny black clothing with only its head, neck, and hands exposed. It stood in an open hatch regarding her. Its pale skin had a strangely corded look, as though thick ropes of muscle connected its small head to its body.

"Creature!" it bellowed again. "Answer me!"

"I am called Ttan," Ttan said. The Universal Translator attached to her back spoke for her, adding an almost imperceptible tremble to her voice.

"Ttan," the humanoid said more softly. "You will listen to my instructions and obey them. I am Gul Mavek, and you are now a guest aboard my ship, the *Dagger*."

"Why have you done this?" Ttan demanded. "Where are you taking me? What has happened to my children?"

"No questions, Ttan. We have some tasks for you to perform—very special tasks. If you do them well, you will be rewarded. If you cooperate, you may even gain your freedom . . . and the freedom of your children."

"Please, I must know—!" Ttan began.

But the humanoid had already stepped back. As the hatch rolled shut, darkness fell.

Once more Ttan began to scream.

CHAPTER
4

BAJORANS, Sisko had privately concluded, could be distinguished from other humanoid races by the creases on their noses—and the chips on their shoulders. The deputy secretary for the Council on Ecological Controls, currently on the main viewer in Ops, was giving him no reason to change that opinion.

"No! Absolutely not," the deputy secretary declared, only his head and shoulders visible on the oval screen. A blond young man with perfectly groomed hair and blindingly white teeth, Pova had the self-righteous air of someone suddenly thrust into a position of power—and enjoying it far too much. "Under no circumstances are you to transfer the Horta eggs onto Bajoran soil."

"But, Secretary Pova," Sisko said diplomatically, "it was my understanding that the Hortas had been invited to Bajor for the express purpose of mining below the planet's surface."

"That enterprise," Pova began, "was the work of a consortium of private individuals, who irresponsibly

35

launched their reckless endeavor without securing the approval of the provisional government. Now that this unfortunate abduction has called the entire project to our attention, we cannot in good conscience stand by and allow alien life-forms to be introduced to our planet's delicate ecology."

Sisko suppressed a weary sigh. He kept his back straight, his posture confident, despite this frustrating turn of events. He did not know whether the Bajoran officials had truly been unaware of the Horta mining project, but obviously the political tides had shifted for the time being, with the more conservative elements gaining power. This was not uncommon; the provisional government, established hastily after the Cardassians abandoned the planet, was a loose coalition of competing factions that seemed to change its policies every time there was a full moon. And Bajor had several moons. . . .

That political instability, he reminded himself, was one of the main reasons Starfleet was here in the first place. He considered calling Vedek Bareil, who was probably the Federation's most influential friend on Bajor. But, unlike the departed Kai Opaka, Bareil's power was limited—and his spiritual authority hardly granted him jurisdiction over mining policies.

Sisko took a deep breath and tried again to reason with the secretary. "Perhaps the correct procedures have not been observed," he conceded, "but the fact remains that I have twenty eggs, each containing a sentient being, that will surely hatch long before they can be taken back to Janus VI. They may be *orphans,* Pova, and, biologically, they're not suited to life on a space station." Again, Sisko visualized an entire brood of baby Hortas, burrowing out of control. Who would be worse off in such a situation, the Hortas or

Deep Space Nine? "They belong on a planet, deep underground, not stuck out in space."

Clearly, Secretary Pova was not a sucker for orphans. "That is a problem for the Federation," he declared. "My first priority must be the environmental sanctity of Bajor. The eggs stay where they are."

"If we send them by shuttle to Bajor now," Sisko argued, "it doesn't have to be a permanent solution."

"No." Behind Pova, the deputy secretary's office looked impeccably clean and perhaps newly painted. If only Bajor were within transporter range of DS9, Sisko mused grumpily; *I'd beam the eggs directly onto Pova's desk.*

"They may have lost their mother, Pova." *Just like Jake lost Jennifer,* Sisko thought, feeling a pang of sympathy for the unborn Hortas. He wondered if Ttan had a mate or family back on Janus VI, and hoped he wouldn't have to send them word of her death.

"You are wasting my time, Commander," Pova said. "Our decision is final. The Hortas will not be allowed on Bajor."

Until the coalition government changes its mind again, Sisko thought, *but how long will that take? This isn't over yet, Pova,* he vowed, while calmly stating, "I suspect that we will discuss this matter again, Secretary. For now, I'll let you get back to your work. Sisko out."

Pova's image vanished from the screen, replaced by a view of the surrounding space. At Sisko's orders, the main viewer was to be directed toward the Cardassian border until Kira's return, except when needed for other purposes. The wormhole, unexplored at the moment, could not be seen. Sisko relaxed his shoulders and leaned forward, bracing himself on a guardrail upon the upper tier of Ops. He glanced around the operations center. A relief crew manned all important stations, including four officers at the operations table alone, but Ops still seemed empty without Dax or Kira. On Sisko's left, Miles O'Brien fussed with a trapezoidal display grid at the engineering station; *Deep Space Nine* never seemed to run out of minor malfunctions for O'Brien to fix.

O'Brien looked up from his repairs to give Sisko a sympathetic look. "Not being terribly cooperative, was he?" O'Brien said, with a nod toward the screen.

"No. I think we're on our own for the duration. Have the eggs been secured?"

"Yes, sir. An unfurnished suite on level fifteen. About all that was available, what with the crowds coming in for that Illumination business." O'Brien strolled over to where Sisko was standing. "If you don't mind me asking, any word from Major Kira and the others?"

Sisko shook his head. "While they're in Cardassian space, they have to maintain strict communications silence." His knuckles tightened around the guardrail. "It's a sensible precaution. All we can do is wait—and take care of those eggs."

"Well, you know what they say anyway: Don't count your Hortas until they're hatched." O'Brien's broad grin faded as Sisko stared at him with a blank expression. "Er, that was meant as a joke, sir."

"I know, Chief. Carry on." Sisko marched into his office and let the doors slide shut behind him. *Damn Deputy Secretary Pova,* he fumed, *and his whole Council on Ecological Controls! Quark would have been easier to deal with; at least you can bribe a Ferengi.* The thought of those twenty young Hortas being rejected by the very planet their mother might have sacrificed her life to salvage infuriated him, and raised uncomfortable associations with his own motherless son. *Suppose,* he couldn't help speculating, *Jennifer and I had both died in that battle at Wolf 359, and Jake's fate had ended up in the hands of some self-important bureaucrat?* Sisko promised himself that he would do everything in his power to protect Ttan's children until Kira brought the mother Horta safely home.

Thank goodness, he thought, that Jake at least was safe and far from trouble.

"You must be crazy!" Jake Sisko whispered emphatically. "Odo will catch us for sure!"

Nog brushed away Jake's objections with a wave of his hand. "You're paranoid about Odo, you know that? He can't be everywhere."

"Yes," Jake replied, "but he could be *anything.*"

The two teenagers crouched behind a gray rhodinium support beam outside Suite 959. It was early in the day and this section of the habitat ring was sparsely populated; only a few tired traders, staggering back to their ships after a long night of gambling and carousing at Quark's, had passed by Jake and Nog in the last half hour. A Bajoran security officer swung by the suite periodically for a routine check. According to Nog's calculations, she wouldn't be due back for at least twenty minutes. Jake wasn't sure he trusted Nog's calculations. He'd seen some of Nog's homework assignments. . . .

"Look," Jake argued, "what's the big deal with a bunch of eggs anyway?" Even with both of them kneeling, Jake was a head taller than the young Ferengi. To blend with the shadows, Jake had put on his darkest blue jumpsuit. Nog, shameless, wore a bright orange shirt with purple trousers. The wrap behind his ears glittered with metallic fibers.

"Ah, but these are *Horta* eggs!" Nog's eyes gleamed with the same excitement he usually displayed for gold-pressed latinum—or anything recognizably female.

"So?" Jake asked.

"Well, er, that is . . ." Nog seemed reluctant to abandon his dreams of profit merely for lack of any solid justification. "The Cardassians wanted them, right? So they must be worth something!"

"But it's stealing," Jake objected. He hated having to be the wet blanket all the time, and certainly amusements on DS9 were few and far between, but it felt like he and Nog were crossing some sort of line with this particular caper. His conscience nagged at him, with a voice that suspiciously resembled his father's.

Of course, stealing was no big deal to a Ferengi. Even now Jake could see Nog blinking his eyes at his friend's objection, and struggling to wrap his brain around the idea that "So what?" was not a workable response.

"We're only going to *borrow* it," Nog said instead. "Besides, it's only a bunch of eggs, no one is going to miss one."

"I thought these were the extra-special Horta eggs," Jake said, mimicking Nog's greedy fervor with pinpoint accuracy. *Hah,* he thought. *Got you there.*

Nog was unimpressed by logic. "Consistency is a hu-man virtue," he said, drawing out the first syllable in "human" so that it sounded vaguely obscene. "C'mon, are you with me or not?"

Jake briefly considered rapping his head against the girder. How did he get sucked into these messes? But he knew why. A) he was bored. B) Nog was his only real friend. Despite the combined efforts of his conscience and common sense, he couldn't convince himself that some weird alien egg was more important than either A or B. "Okay, I'm in. Let's get this over with."

"Yes, yes, yes!" Nog muttered gleefully. The boys rose quickly to their feet, bolted out from behind the girder, and nearly collided with a large Bajoran security officer.

She was at least six feet tall, with firm muscles (and an impressive figure) visible beneath her brown uniform. A stern expression seemed to have frozen on her face. "Shouldn't you boys be in school?" she said. It sounded more like a statement than a question.

Nog's jaw dropped. His mouth quivered soundlessly, making him look like a trout caught on a hook. Was he speechless with fear, Jake wondered, or simply overwhelmed by his close proximity to the woman's imposing curves? Probably a bit of both. *I'm going to kill him,* Jake thought, *assuming we get out of this alive.*

"School doesn't start for another hour," Jake explained hurriedly. "We were pacing out the circumference of the habitat ring . . . for geometry class. Extra credit." Actually, Nog hadn't attended Mrs. O'Brien's school for days, but Jake saw no reason to go into that. "We were at five hundred and fifty steps so far, right, Nog?" He elbowed his friend, none too gently. "Right?"

"Oh yes," Nog sputtered. "Five hundred and sixty for sure!"

The security officer eyed them skeptically. The wrinkles on her nose seemed to deepen. "You were rushing pretty fast to be doing such careful counting."

"We count better when we run!" Nog volunteered. Jake groaned inside.

"Like you said, we don't want to be late for class," he added. *Please,* he thought, *don't call my dad. I still haven't lived down that business with Odo's bucket and the oatmeal.*

The officer stared at them in silence for what seemed the length of a transgalactic voyage—on impulse power. A thin layer of sweat glued Jake's shirt to his back. Nog's hands nervously protected the lobes of his enormous ears.

"Very well," she said finally. "Be on your way."

"Yes, sir, officer, ma'am!" Jake said, almost bursting with relief. He grabbed Nog roughly by the arm, and, taking long careful strides, tried to pace away from Suite 959 as rapidly as he could. "Five hundred and fifty-one, five hundred and fifty-two, five hundred and fifty-three . . ."

"Five hundred and sixty-four," Nog said beside him, "five hundred and sixty-five . . ."

Oh, leaking radioactive wormholes, Jake cursed silently. Looking back over his shoulder, he saw the officer watching them depart, her hands on her hips, a suspicious scowl on her face. "Human steps equal one-point-five Ferengi steps," he called back by way of explanation. He hoped he didn't sound nearly as stupid as he felt.

Finally, they rounded a corner and left the security woman behind. Jake collapsed against the corridor wall. His heart was pounding. The sweat on his back cooled to a chilly film. *If this was a bad holo,* he thought, *I'd be fainting now.*

Nog, on the other hand, seemed positively invigorated now that they were safe. "Eluding prosecution!" he crowed, bouncing off the floor in an impromptu victory dance. "There's no greater thrill!" He grinned at his reluctant accomplice. "A school project! Extra credit! That was sheer brilliance . . . almost as good as what I was going to say. As you sure you aren't part Ferengi?"

"Positive," Jake replied, forcing himself to remember that Nog meant that as a compliment. Slowly, his heartbeat returned to normal.

Nog pointed his ears in the direction they had come. "Okay," he said enthusiastically. "I can hear her bootsteps. She's going the opposite way." Without even asking Jake's opinion, he dashed back toward the suite. Halfway there, he paused only long enough to look back at Jake. "What's keeping you?" he asked, appearing genuinely puzzled. "Hurry!"

I don't believe this, Jake thought. *I don't believe* me. Breaking into a jog, he caught up with Nog outside the suite door. The Ferengi was busy affixing a white crystalline patch to the lock beside the door. Jake didn't need to ask where the patch came from; like most Ferengi, Nog wore his pockets on the inside of his clothes. "Something you 'borrowed' from your uncle?" Jake asked.

"Actually, I got it from a cat burglar in exchange for some Eeiauoan pornography." He shrugged dismissively. "I'm not into felines."

The crystal patch sparkled as it swiftly flashed through the entire spectrum from white to black, trying every intermediate shade in between. It operated completely silently, which made sense, Jake realized, given the sort of jobs it had probably been designed for; that this device had once belonged to a professional thief did not make Jake feel any more comfortable about this whole stunt. "Look, Nog," he started to protest.

Too late. On its third cycle through the spectrum, the patch halted on a hue somewhere between rose and pink. It blinked three times; then the two halves of the sturdy door slid back into the adjoining walls. Nog rubbed his palms together and scooted inside the bay. With a sigh of resignation, Jake followed him.

Low-level illumination activated automatically upon their entrance, and Jake found himself in a vaultlike chamber about half the size of his and his father's personal quarters. Alien graffiti defaced the walls, and the floor was scratched and in need of repair. No wonder, Jake thought, the suite was empty except for the eggs, which he spotted right away.

They were lined up like bowling balls on top of a black, triangular platform about three feet tall. "Careful," Nog said, "there's some type of stasis field." To demonstrate, he brought his hands near the eggs; a sudden burst of crackling blue energy repelled his grasping fingers. Nog seemed more amused than concerned by the shielding, Jake noted as he drew closer to their target. Keeping at least a foot away from the invisible field, he stared at the eggs while Nog, scurrying around on his knees, inspected the field generator. The eggs all looked identical: completely spherical, slightly smaller than an old-fashioned basketball, with a glossy metallic sheen. He had trouble placing the exact the color of the eggs in the dim light; they were somewhere between violet and copper, depending on what angle he looked at them from. Was there actually some sort of organism growing inside? It was hard to believe; the spheres looked more like geological curiosities than something alive.

Then again, he'd bumped into some very unusual life-forms during his travels with his father. Humanoid races were most common, but Jake had no illusions that all beings fit the Terran mode. The universe —even just the Federation—was full of strange and exotic entities, like those "nonlinear" intelligences his dad had discovered in the wormhole. Or Q, who looked human, but sure wasn't. Or *whatever* they were that had impersonated Buck Bokai, Lieutenant Dax, and that troll during their first year on the station. Or, for that matter, Constable Odo.

Thinking about the station's security chief reminded Jake of how much trouble they could get into if they were caught. He glanced nervously around the empty suite; thank goodness it was so barren, he thought. There were no stray objects that could be the shapeshifter in disguise—unless he was one of the eggs themselves!

"C'mon," he whispered to Nog. "What's the problem?"

"No problem," Nog replied. He ran his stubby fingers over a control pad located under the rim of the platform. "There! Try it now."

Half expecting an energy shock, Jake reached hesitantly for an egg. Nothing happened. He met no resistance. His hand stroked the smooth, metallic shell; it was surprisingly cool. He grinned despite himself. This was too easy! Obviously, the field was intended to shield the eggs from shocks, not . . . borrowing.

Nog sprang to his feet and scampered, his freckled face beaming, around the unprotected eggs. "Take that one!" he suggested. "No, no, *that* one! Wait a nano, maybe this one here . . . !"

"Nog," Jake said patiently. "They're all the same." He realized, with a jolt of recognition, that he sounded a lot like his father talking to Dr. Bashir. "Choose one and let's go."

"But which one?" Nog whined, torn by greed and indecision. "Maybe we should take a couple more . . . ?"

"No way!" Jake said.

"But . . ." Nog's eyes darted back and forth between his friend and the eggs.

"No," Jake said firmly. He removed a piece of toweling that he'd tucked into his boot earlier. There was only so far he could be pushed, even by Nog. He had to draw the line somewhere. Picking one at random, he carefully lifted an egg from the platform and wrapped it in the soft white towel. For a second, he thought he felt something move within the egg, as though its center of gravity had suddenly shifted, but he chalked it up to nerves. That Bajoran woman could be back at any minute!

The stolen egg left an empty, circular recess in the top of the platform, an incriminating gap that caught Jake's eye like a silent accusation. He looked away from the depression. "We're out of here," he told Nog. "Now!"

The Ferengi hesitated for a moment, staring at the remaining eggs as if he could absorb the entire haul into his eyes. He ran his tongue over his rough, uneven front teeth.

"Nog!"

With a pained expression on his face, Nog turned from the eggs and ran with Jake back into the corridor outside. Jake looked up and down the hall while Nog hastily removed the crystal patch from the locking mechanism. There was no one in sight, thankfully. By the time the suite doors slid shut again, the boys were already several meters away. Clutching the swaddled Horta egg close to his chest, Jake walked quickly toward the nearest turbolift, with Nog struggling to keep up with him.

You know, Jake thought, *maybe human steps do equal one-point-five Ferengi ones.*

Nog was nearly out of breath by the time they reached the turbolift. He snarled under his breath. Why did humans have to have such long legs anyway? It seemed an unfair advantage, and unfair advantages by rights belonged to the Ferengi. Then again, he didn't really mind that human females had those astoundingly endless legs. Too bad they felt obliged to cover them up. Take that Lieutenant Dax, for instance. Thinking about her, out of uniform (and not into anything in particular), made his lobes tingle. Suppose she and he were marooned on . . .

"Say, Nog," Jake said, knocking him out of a promising fantasy, "I thought of something. Did you reactivate the stasis field around the eggs?"

Deficits, Nog cursed silently. He'd forgotten all about that field. "I thought you'd done that," he said hastily, embarrassed. To err was Ferengi, he reminded himself; the trick was to shift blame fast enough.

To his surprise, Jake didn't argue the point. "I guess," his friend said with shrug, "it was going to be pretty obvious that an egg was gone, even if we'd put the field back the way we found it. And it's not like we're expecting an earthquake or something anytime soon. The eggs will be perfectly safe, right?"

"Right!" Nog said automatically. Jake was obviously indulging in that odd human habit of "rationalizing" his actions in order to "appease his conscience." Nog didn't really understand this, but he recognized it when he saw it. Sometimes humans just had to be talked into pursuing their own best interests. *Good thing,* he thought, *that Jake has a partner like me to set him straight.*

The turbolift deposited them on the Promenade. As Nog had planned, there wasn't much traffic among the shops and stalls at this hour. Although night and day were, naturally, abstract concepts on DS9, most people stuck to Starfleet time for convenience's sake. It was handy, especially on the Promenade, to have regular hours for business—and pleasure. This early in the morning, most establishments were, depending on their bill of fare, closed, shutting down, or just setting up shop.

Technically, Quark's was open twenty-four hours a day, but the bar was nearly deserted when they arrived. Only a handful of diehards and new arrivals occupied the tables, consuming replicated meals or trying unsuccessfully to get drunk on heavily diluted synthehol. (The strong stuff, Nog knew, wasn't served until serious gambling got under way.) A skinny, lime-green Asominian, whose species required sleep only once every twenty years, was flirting shamelessly with a Dabo girl.

Quark himself was nowhere to be seen. Nog wasn't surprised. His uncle seldom woke before noon, and then spent an hour or two in a holosuite. A distant cousin, Chram, manned the bar during the morning shift. Tufts of gray hair sprouted from the bartender's large ears. *When I'm that age,* Nog promised himself, *I'm not going to be working for my richer relations.* He gave Chram a wave as he led Jake back into the storerooms. Chram glowered at him in return; the older Ferengi was not a morning person.

In contrast to the glitz and glamour of the public Quark's, the rear of the bar was a maze of boxes, compartments, and closets, generously equipped with odd nooks and crannies. After all, as Nog had been taught several times, you never knew when you might need a private meeting place for . . . whatever. He guided Jake to a broken-down refrigeration unit stuck between a crate of bootleg Cardassian wine and a stack of anti-Bajoran propaganda disks. Several gallon bottles of kamoy syrup, all covered in dust, rested on top of the crates.

"Since the Cardassians left," he explained, "there hasn't been much call for any of this stuff. My uncle's waiting for a good time to dump it—at a decent profit." He tapped the controls on the freezer, then gave it a slap on the side. The lid sprang open with a noisy pop. "The egg will be safe in here. Hand it over." Inwardly, he congratulated himself on maneuvering Jake into carrying the stolen egg on his person this whole time. Puzzling as it could sometimes be, this human tendency to trust came in very handy.

"Here," Jake said, slowly unwrapping the egg. "Boy, am I glad to get rid of this."

And am I ever glad to take it, Nog thought.

Layers of toweling came away, revealing the gleam of the Horta egg underneath. For the first time, Nog started to wonder what exactly a Horta was, and what he was supposed to do with the egg. He stroked his right ear thoughtfully. No matter. There was profit here somehow; he *knew* it.

His fingers itched for the egg. What was taking Jake so long? He wanted that egg now!

Instead of handing it over right away, his human friend gazed quizzically at the semiexposed sphere. "Funny," Jake said. "It seems warmer than before." He peeled away the last layer of cloth and his palm came into direct contact with the shiny metal shell.

"Oww! Damn! Oww!" Jake blurted suddenly, yanking his hands away from the egg. With horror, Nog watched his prize drop onto the hard molybdenite floor.

"You . . . you hu-man!" he cried out angrily. The egg crashed down with a ringing clang that made Nog's lobes shrivel. It rolled away toward the back of the storeroom. Jake waved his fingers wildly about, then started blowing on his palm.

"It burned me!" Jake said, showing him the reddened flesh on his hand. Nog gave the burn, which didn't seem *that* serious, only a second's look before chasing after the egg. *Please,* he thought, *don't let it be broken.* The egg came to a stop against a cask of Klingon war games. Nog reached out for it anxiously. "Wait!" Jake yelled from behind him. "Be careful!"

At the last minute, Nog yanked his hands away. He disliked pain almost as much as he craved profit. Bending over the egg, he searched its surface with his beady blue eyes for any crack or disfigurement.

At first, the sphere seemed unharmed. *Praise the bottom line,* Nog thought gratefully. Then the egg began to shake. Nog's eyes widened. "Jake, get over here. Something's happening!" A high-pitched grinding noise emerged from inside the egg. As the two boys looked on in amazement, one side of the sphere began to glow with a faint red radiance. Thin trails of vapor rose from the glowing portion of the shell. "It's going to explode!" Nog exclaimed, backing away frantically on all fours. "Run!"

Jake grabbed onto Nog's foot, halting his escape. "No, Nog, no! Don't you see? It's hatching!"

What? Of course! "I knew that," Nog said defensively. "Can't you hu-mans recognize a joke when you hear one?"

"Sssh!" Jake said. "Here he comes!"

The egg did not crack. Instead, *something* burned its way out of the sphere, leaving a steaming hole in the shell. The creature looked like a huge, scarlet worm, about half a meter long. Its hide was red and pulpy, like raw meat, except for tiny flecks of mineral matter embedded here and there over its surface. A fringe of tiny tendrils or cilia ran along the bottom of the creature on all sides; it seemed to use the fringe to pull itself slowly across the floor, leaving a trail of scorched grillework behind it. So this was a Horta, Nog mused. He wondered what it was worth. And how much more he could charge for it.

Before he could calculate a price, however, the newborn Horta crawled (oozed?) back toward the now-empty egg. Jake and he watched as it burned a new hole through the shell and disappeared inside the egg. "What . . . ?" he started to ask, but then the entire egg glowed with the red light as before, and proceeded to dissolve before their eyes. White fumes rose and evaporated as the hard metal shell melted into the baby Horta itself, which seemed to absorb every bit of matter that wasn't boiled away. In a second or two, there was no shell left, only a wriggling red thing that emitted a teeth-jarring vibration from no orifice Nog could detect.

"What's the matter with it?" he asked Jake desperately. "What do we do now?" And how, he agonized silently, was he supposed to hide this burning little monster from his uncle?

Jake didn't look as confident as Nog would have liked. "I think it's hungry," he said.

CHAPTER
5

"WHEN CAN WE EXPECT some excitement, ladies?"

Feeling bored, Julian Bashir leaned both arms on the back of Major Kira's chair and peered over her head at the console. As near as he could tell, Kira and Dax appeared to be running a series of sensor sweeps of the space around the ship, but he couldn't swear to it. Kira's hands danced across the controls almost more quickly than he could follow, and she wasn't taking time to explain each step as she went along the way Chief O'Brien usually did. It didn't surprise him, considering the time-critical nature of their mission.

Kira said, "You're crowding me, Doctor."

"Oh, sorry." *She's on edge,* he told himself, straightening quickly. The Bajoran equivalent of adrenaline must be surging through her veins, priming her body for battle-readiness . . . and making her a little irritable. Doubtless he could find plenty of information on the effects of Bajoran adrenaline back on DS9. He'd have to look the subject up when they got back. There might be a paper in it—especially if the Bajorans made it into the Federation and began serving on Starfleet ships. He grinned a little. There was a certain fame to be had by being the first to file a new medical paper—just look at the way Leonard McCoy's name was plastered all over the Horta reports as the "pioneering surgeon" who first operated on a Horta.

"No problem," Kira said curtly. "Bajorans just have a very definite sense of personal space."

"You can look over my shoulder, Julian," Dax said. "It doesn't bother me."

"Why, thank you, Jadzia!" *She must have forgotten my slug remark,* he thought, *or at least put it from her mind in the tumult following Ttan's kidnapping.* He felt his heart skip a beat. Something about her excited him more than any other female he'd ever been around. He'd heard Chief O'Brien muttering about "crushes" and "puppy love" under his breath more than once, but Julian knew it was more than that. This was the real thing. If only he could get her to notice him . . . and if only he could manage to not say something stupid.

Leaning on the back of Dax's chair, he moved his head down until he caught a faint whiff of scent from her hair, a subtle perfume mingling what smelled like Andorian wildflowers and flowering plankton from Cilas XII. Beautiful, like she was, he thought. He breathed more deeply.

Kira brought the runabout around and accelerated again. Julian toppled forward and barely caught himself in time to keep from hitting the back of Dax's head. Accidentally insulting her was bad enough, he thought. He didn't need to fall on her when she wasn't looking.

He shot a quick glance at Kira, but she seemed completely occupied at the controls. Julian frowned. She appeared a little *too* occupied, he decided. She should have at least taken a quick glance when he almost fell; she must have caught his sudden wild movement from the corner of her eye.

Julian felt the engines' vibrations deepen through the deck underfoot. Glancing at the monitor, he watched the runabout speeding forward. He couldn't tell if the course change had been necessary. If he didn't know better, though, he would have said Kira made the ship lurch forward on purpose . . . or was he being too paranoid?

Then the truth hit him and he had a hard time keeping from laughing. Kira was jealous of Dax! Why hadn't he seen it before? Clearly she didn't want him leaning on the back of her seat because she couldn't concentrate with him so near. Women had told him he was handsome before—indeed, he'd been something of a ladies' man at the Academy—but he'd had no idea he could so thoroughly penetrate even Kira's mask of icy professionalism. After the mission was over, he'd have to find a way to let her down gently. Much as he admired her command talents, Kira wasn't exactly his idea of a perfect date.

"Where are we now?" he asked. It would be best to try to keep Kira's mind on the work at hand.

"On the last known course the Cardassian raider took," Dax replied instead. "We're at half impulse power. I'm running a sensor sweep for subspace distortion."

A small light began to flash across Kira's monitor. Julian found himself leaning forward to see, and when Kira shot him a glance, he gave her what he considered his most reassuring bedside smile. *Don't break her heart now,* he thought. *Let it wait till the end of the mission. That's the professional thing to do.*

"I have it," Dax said, pointing at what looked to Julian like a smear of pale gray on her monitor. "This pattern has to be bled from a warp coil generator. Major?"

"It's very diffuse," Kira said slowly.

"The wormhole might account for it," Julian ventured, though he didn't feel at all sure of himself. This stuff was way out of his league.

"No," Dax said, "there's definitely *something* there. Let me try a few computer enhancements. . . ."

Julian watched as the three-dimensional representation of space around the runabout blanked on Dax's monitor, then redrew several times in what he found a dizzyingly quick succession. Each enhancement showed more detail in the diffused ion cloud.

"Allowing for normal drift and distortion from the wormhole," Dax said, "let's run a backward simulation. . . ."

After another dizzying sequence of images, the diffuse spray of ions suddenly drew together into what Julian recognized as a distinct trail of ionized particles. Dax had been right, he saw now. There couldn't be any mistaking it. A starship had been through here, and not that long ago.

"Bingo," Dax said.

"What?" Kira demanded.

"An old Earth expression," Julian said, a little proud that he had recognized such an archaic word. Forsooth, his classic Earth poetry classes were paying off at last. "It means we've found it."

"I can see that!" Kira snapped. "Strap yourself in, Doctor. We're going to warp speed in ten seconds."

Ten seconds? Julian thought. Turning, he darted into

the rear of the runabout. The five members of the security team hadn't yet ventured from their seats. He scanned their faces and noticed looks ranging from amusement to fascination. They must have been listening to every word they said up front, he realized-. . . and watching his every move. He swallowed. *I hope they didn't see me smelling Dax's hair*. Then he gave a mental shrug. *Well,* he thought, *this was my day for putting my foot in it*. Hopefully there wouldn't be *too* many hot rumors surrounding Dax and him when they got back home.

He dropped into his seat and buckled himself in. He knew they were in a hurry, but ten seconds was cutting it awfully close for comfort.

He watched as the stars on the forward monitor over Dax's head turned to streaks; then suddenly they were moving faster than light. He started to unbuckle himself, but Kira called, "Better stay seated back there, guys. We may have a few more sudden course shifts coming up."

"Right," Julian muttered unhappily. He looked back and found the five members of the security team all watching him. Ensigns Aponte and Wilkens definitely seemed to be smirking. He had to find something to occupy them or they'd all end up grinning behind his back through the entire mission.

"Well," he said slowly, his thoughts racing to find something to do. "I looks like we're stuck back here for a while. Anybody bring a deck of cards?"

Kira risked a quick glance over her shoulder, found Bashir talking animatedly to the five ensigns, and chuckled softly to herself. They were undoubtedly the largest audience the doctor had had for quite a while.

They should keep him busy for the time being, she thought. At least until he ran out of those boring Starfleet Academy stories of his.

"Don't you think that was a little cruel?" Dax said in a low voice. "He could have come back up here."

"Cruel, but entirely justifiable," Kira replied. "The way he was smelling your hair made my skin crawl."

"He smelled yours first."

Kira found herself speechless. The thought of that —that—that pedantic fovian *worm* smelling her hair —it made her sick to her stomach. She'd have to find a way to tell him, in no uncertain terms, to stay well away from her when they got back after this mission.

"The ship made a turn," Dax announced. "Coming up. Log course change in five seconds."

"I see it," Kira said.

"They must have thought the wormhole would hide their new course," Dax went on. "Our new destination is . . . the Davon system? Computer confirms. The Davon system. Estimated time of arrival: twenty-two hours."

"The Davon system," Kira mused. There weren't any Cardassian mining camps there. Or none that she knew about, anyway.

"I don't think I'm familiar with it," Dax said.

"I am," Kira said. "It has a total of six planets, four gas giants and two sun-scorched rocks in tight orbits around the sun. It was disputed territory until twenty-two years ago, when Starfleet ceded it to the Cardassians in a border treaty."

"I think I did hear something about that," Dax said. "There weren't any desirable planets, so it was easier to give it up than make a fuss over it."

"Just like Bajor," Kira said. She tried to keep the

bitterness from her voice and knew she didn't quite succeed. "Just like Bajor."

Ttan heard it as much as felt it when a series of jolts shook the *Dagger*. She began to struggle again, trying to get free, but the tractor beam seemed to work against her every movement, pinning her in midair. She would have given anything to be free just about then. She had to find her eggs.

The jolts stopped as suddenly as they'd begun. Ttan strained to hear, but no new sounds reached her. The hold remained as eerily silent as a mined-out pocket of duranium ore. *Will I never be free?* she mentally cried out. *Will I never see my children hatch?* She began to despair.

What seemed hours later—she had lost all sense of time and had no idea how long it had actually been—a new series of jolts ran through the *Dagger*. This time the far wall began to fold down into a ramp, admitting a flood of brilliant white light.

Ttan was still spinning very slowly. As she came around to face the ramp, she peered into the brightness. Several dozen figures moved out there. As she watched, half a dozen humanoids sprinted into the hold and took equidistant positions around her. They all held massive energy weapons of some kind, which they pointed at her body.

"What do you want?" she demanded. "Where are my children?" The Universal Translator repeated her message. None of the humanoids replied.

As she continued to spin, Ttan studied their faces. She wasn't certain, but though they dressed in black like Gul Mavek and had the same corded necks, she didn't think any of them were him. If she'd been free, she would have gladly melted him alive for what he'd done to her.

"What do you want?" she demanded again. "Tell me! *Tell me!*"

"Ttan," she heard Gul Mavek say, "I am the only one who can help you." He climbed the ramp and stood looking at her, his hands on his hips. "You are my guest. You will follow all instructions with precision and care. Do you understand?"

She shot a stream of acid at him. He leaped backward in time to avoid it, and the acid began to smoke and hiss as it ate away the metal plating.

A whining noise filled the air, and a dull, unpleasant itch hit Ttan from all sides at once. The humanoids were shooting their weapons at her, Ttan realized.

"Stop, stop!" Gul Mavek cried. "Cease fire!"

The phaser rifles grew silent. Ttan continued to spin in midair, a little faster now, facing first the back of the hold, then the side, then the front ramp again. If the weapons had done any serious damage, she didn't feel it yet. Luckily her people were resistant to phaser fire.

She watched Gul Mavek's head twitch and his hands clench into fists, signs she knew represented great anger or frustration. However, the humanoid's voice remained a calm, studied neutral when he spoke again.

"Ttan," he said, "that was a mistake. I am your only friend here."

"You are not a friend!" she cried.

"I am," he said. "I am the only one who will talk with you as an equal. I am the only one who can release you from the tractor beam. And I am the only one who can let you see your children."

"My eggs—" Ttan said.

"Yes, your eggs. They, too, are on board my ship, Ttan. We haven't counted them yet, but we have them all. All of the unbroken ones, anyway."

"What?" Ttan shrieked, her insides suddenly twisting up with fear. "My eggs—" She began to struggle frantically against the tractor beam. "My eggs—"

"There were plenty of eggs left," Gul Mavek said. "I don't believe we counted all the whole ones. I can find out how many are still intact, if you want. How many were there supposed to be?"

"Twenty," Ttan sobbed. She went limp. "Twenty beautiful children. Oh, my poor, poor young ones—"

"Wait," Gul Mavek said. "I will be back with the exact count." He turned and strolled down the ramp at a leisurely pace, as though he had all the time in the world.

Spinning, Ttan felt a confused jumble of anger, hurt, and despair. Her cilia quivered. She felt numb in all of her extremities. *How many dead?* she wondered. *How many still alive?*

How could they have allowed harm to come to her eggs? How could they let her children perish so casually, so callously? When humans first came to Janus VI, thousands had been destroyed, but that had been an accident. The Federation hadn't realized the silicon nodules *were* eggs. As soon as they found out, they had moved to protect the young Hortas, to help the Prime Mother feed and care for them. And in return the Hortas had helped the Federation. It was unthinkable that a sentient being could let harm come to children . . . any children.

Ttan twitched when Gul Mavek appeared at the head of the ramp again. He folded his arms behind his back and watched her silently.

"Yes?" Ttan cried. "Yes?"

"Your eggs . . ."

"Tell me!"

"I had them removed from the ship for safekeeping. It seems that nineteen of the twenty are still intact—"

Ttan felt a keen pang of hurt at the one loss, but then relief flooded through her when she realized how many more were still alive and whole. It almost caused her to miss Gul Mavek's next words.

"—for the moment," he finished.

"What do you mean?" Ttan demanded. "If you harm my children—"

"You are in no position to make threats," Gul Mavek said. "If you threaten me or any of my men again, I will have another egg destroyed."

Ttan all but gasped in horror. "You can't—"

"And," Gul Mavek continued, "after that I will have another destroyed, and another, and another, until they are all dead. Every last one of them, Ttan. Unless . . ."

"Unless?" Ttan said, a small hope rising within her.

"Unless you cooperate," he said. "If you perform one small task for me today—one small, almost insignificant task—I will let you see your eggs for a few moments this evening."

Despairing, Ttan could only say, "Anything you ask, I will do."

Aboard the *Amazon*, Julian Bashir tried to concentrate on the mess that his tricorder had become. *It hates me*, he thought, though he knew that was irrational. Machines didn't hate anybody. Only this one certainly seemed to have it in for him. He'd spent twenty minutes taking it apart and now, an hour and a half later, it wasn't any closer to being fixed.

His vision began to blur, and he rubbed his eyes with the back of his hand. What he wouldn't have given to have Chief O'Brien's skills right now. He took a sip of replicated coffee and grimaced at the bitter taste.

Enough stalling. He forced himself to concentrate on the tiny computer screen set into the wall. A trickle of sweat ran down this back, and suddenly he began to get a neck ache. He knew it was from staring up at the monitor too much. The colorful schematic of the tricorder's inner mechanism the monitor displayed started to blur again.

"Blast," he said, and slammed down his electron probe. This wasn't the simple recalibration he had expected. "Blast it all!" He rubbed his eyes again. It didn't look like he'd ever get the tricorder working again.

He glanced a little wistfully over his shoulder at the other pull-out table, where the five ensigns were busily playing poker with cards and chips the onboard replicator had made. Not that he gambled much; he simply hadn't realized how little there was to actually *do* aboard the *Amazon* until now. With a little over warp four as the runabout's greatest speed and another sixteen hours of travel still ahead, he would have welcomed a decent science library, a holodeck, or even a visit to Quark's infamous holosuites to pass the time. Without them, poker would have to do.

He watched as Ensign Aponte dropped three blue chips into the pot. Everyone else folded, and Aponte raked in her win with a gleeful laugh.

Julian hated that sound. He'd lost steadily through the hour he'd played, and Aponte's laugh had started to get to him. On impulse, he'd decided to take a break from the game, have a snack, and try his hand at recalibrating his tricorder to pick up silicon life-forms. He'd thought it might change his luck.

Instead, things had rapidly gotten worse. He turned back to his pull-out table and stared helplessly down at the circuits in front of him.

Bad as they were, what remained of his snack—half of a replicated ham sandwich and a rapidly chilling cup of the worst replicated coffee he'd ever had—looked more inviting than the tricorder, so he stalled by taking a couple of bites and sips. *It should be easy,* he told himself. *You're a surgeon. You fix biological machines every day. How can one tricorder be so hard?*

Finally he couldn't put it off any longer. He set his sandwich down, selected a probe, and tried to push a primary connector back in place. Instead, he touched a scanner trip circuit by mistake. Blue sparks hissed and spat into the air, and he jerked his hand back to avoid being burned.

"Blast!" he said.

"Having a problem, Julian?" Dax asked. Julian jumped. He'd been so wrapped up in the tricorder problem, he hadn't seen her wander back into the passenger section. He had to get his act together, he thought, or she'd never respect him.

"A problem, um, yes," he said, then winced inwardly at how pathetic that sounded. "I was trying to recalibrate my tricorder to pick up silicon-based life-forms. The changes I need to make are all listed in the manual, but somehow I've got them all muddled."

"So that's what you call it."

Julian felt himself growing flustered. Somehow, that seemed to happen rather frequently when he was around Jadzia Dax.

"I can do yours next, if you want," he offered.

"I'm afraid mine is already done," Dax said. She

unclipped it from her belt and set it on the table. "I cleaned and recalibrated it two hours ago; then I did Kira's."

"Then do you think you might—" He gestured helplessly at the tangled mess of wires and data chips before him. He didn't have the nerve to meet her gaze.

Dax laughed lightly. "Of course I'll help put it back together." She slid into the seat opposite him, took the probe gently from his hand—her touch was cool as silk and sent a shiver down his spine—and began snapping pieces of the tricorder together. "It will give me something to do for the next few minutes."

"Are you bored, too, then?"

"A little."

Julian felt some of his confidence return. "Would you care to join the poker game with me? I'd be glad to give you some pointers, if you've never played before."

"Actually, one of my previous hosts was a mathematician and an inveterate gambler. He enjoyed playing the odds so much, I'm afraid that—with very few exceptions—I've grown tired of all games of mathematical probability. Except for Ferengi, it's hard to find real competition. There's something not quite fair, I feel, about always being the winner. It puts a strain on relationships."

"Ah," Julian said, biting his lip. He'd walked right into it again. "That's very thoughtful of you, Jadzia."

He watched her smooth, feminine hands fit piece after piece of the tricorder together. Every now and then she made a small adjustment with the probe. Almost before he could blink, the tricorder was back together.

"That's it?" he asked, amazed.

"That's it," Dax said. "You might want to try it out, of course, to make sure."

He flipped it open and saw the display panel come to life. The readout now matched the manual's—right down to the split screen for carbon-based and silicon-based life-forms. It worked perfectly. He met her gaze.

"Thank you," he said, sincerely meaning it.

Dax rose. "Any time, Julian." She paused. "I'm going to get some sleep. I strongly suggest you do the same."

"Yes," he said. "Right away. I just want a few more hands of cards first." *Only sixteen hours,* he thought, *and we're there.* He wondered if he was going to make it.

As Ttan moved down the ramp from the *Dagger,* she felt strangely giddy, as though she weighed next to nothing. They were in some kind of underground chamber, with crude stone walls far to either side and a smooth stone floor beneath her. Light came from brilliant glowing panels set overhead, to either side of what looked like a glowing forcefield of some kind. Through the forcefield she could see distant stars.

She gave an experimental hop, pushing off the floor with her cilia, and to her surprise soared several meters forward, almost striking Gul Mavek's back. The guards bellowed warnings to their leader, snapping up their weapons. Ttan paused, hardly daring to move. She had noticed that they had increased the power settings on their weapons.

Gul Mavek, though, merely paused and regarded her with a strangely serene expression. "The gravity here is roughly a third of what you are used to," he told her. "You will adapt quickly, as have we all." He turned his back and led the way down the ramp to a stone floor.

As oddly light as Ttan felt, it was good to have a planet around her. Already she tasted traces of ferrous oxide, calcium, and other minerals through her cilia. If not for her eggs, she would have burrowed deep into the rock underfoot in seconds. Not even the phasers could have stopped her.

As long as Gul Mavek held her eggs, though, she knew she would do whatever he asked. *Nineteen children still alive,* she thought. *Nineteen chances for immortality. I must not fail them.*

They crossed an underground docking bay to a large cargo lift—little more than a rhodinium box with antigrav units underneath it.

Gul Mavek boarded first, then Ttan, then the guards. After one guard rolled a gate across the front of the lift, they started down.

Through the gate Ttan watched as they descended past level after level. The first ten looked identical: square and white, with doors opening to either side. A few humanoids in uniforms that matched the guards' moved through them on errands. The eleventh through twentieth hadn't been finished, with walls and floors of a gray-green stone that glistened as though wet. Ttan knew that look: these tunnels had been carved out with heavy-duty phasers.

At the twentieth level the lift came to a halt and the gate opened. Gul Mavek stepped out.

"This way," he said.

Ttan emerged more slowly. Here, this far underground, she felt at ease for the first time since she'd left Janus VI. The rock walls around her, the comforting closeness, the cool touch of stone—she had come home.

Gul Mavek turned left without a second's hesitation. Ttan followed, and the guards brought up the rear. They traveled in silence for several minutes before Ttan began to feel vibrations in the stone under her. She wasn't certain, but it felt like it came from heavy machinery somewhere ahead.

At last they rounded a corner and entered another large cavern. Some kind of large mining and smelting operation was under way here. On the far side of the cavern, a seemingly endless line of dust-covered cargo bins easily ten meters long and five meters wide floated in on antigrav lifts, dumped tons of gravel into a pile, then floated back out. Huge robot-driven bulldozers shoveled the gravel onto a conveyor belt, which carried it into an immense box that radiated heat in waves—probably a smelting furnace, Ttan thought. She'd never seen one quite like this before, but she knew the general principle. Inside, the gravel was reduced to its composite minerals, then put back together into ingots of pure latinum or rhodinium or carbonite or whatever else it had been programmed for. She couldn't see where the ingots came out of this one, though.

"As you may have already guessed," Gul Mavek said, "Davonia is a working moon. We have found traces of latinum on this level. I want you to find the main deposit for us."

Moon? Ttan wondered. Where in the Great Plan had they brought her?

"As you command," she said through the translator.

"And Ttan—you have twenty minutes to find it and report back. Either that or you won't see your children again tonight."

"But—" she began.

"Nineteen minutes and fifty seconds," Gul Mavek said.

Ttan whirled and hit the rock wall. It melted before her, surrounding her, filling her body with the delicious tastes of iron, nickel, and three billion years of water seepage and geologic stability. *Latinum, latinum,* she thought, searching frantically for the right taste. She had to see her eggs, had to know her children were safe. *Where is the latinum—*

CHAPTER
6

As USUAL, Quark was claiming to be the injured party. Odo didn't believe it for a second.

The security chief sat in Quark's bar, his table conspicuously free of drinks or refreshments, while Quark himself paced and scurried around him, waving his hands in the air and putting on a fine display of Ferengi indignation. "I don't believe this!" he barked, spraying saliva past his rodentlike teeth. Quark wore a lime-green jacket over a garish, multicolored blouse that looked like it had been decorated by a mob of hyperactive, crayon-wielding two-year-olds. "I come to you as a law abiding citizen, a community leader, victimized by crime, and you won't even lift one gelatinous finger to do your duty! It's an outrage, a scandal. Just what do you think your job is anyway?"

"To keep an eye on you," Odo answered, gazing impassively over the bar. He declined to look in Quark's direction. The more agitated Quark became, the less interested Odo seemed.

The bar grew more crowded as lunchtime approached. Odo spotted an unusual number of strangers amid the regular customers. A large family of Tellarites stuffed their porcine faces on Quark's overpriced buffet. The eldest Tellarite, typically nearsighted, squinted at a plate of Vegan truffles before snorting his approval and tipping the entire plate above his waiting mouth. At another table, a pair of hairless Deltan women glibly fended off the attentions of over a dozen Argelian men. A small party of Betazoids sat at the bar, carrying on a silent telepathic conversation, much to the annoyance of Morn, the hefty alien who usually occupied one or more of those seats. Scanning the room, Odo also spotted Klingons, Caitians, Tiburons, P'alblaakis, and many other new arrivals, all presumably drawn to DS9 by the imminent flyby of The Prodigal. Odo allowed himself a moment of nostalgia for the bad old days of the Occupation; the Cardassians might have been tyrannical butchers, but at least they never turned the station into a tourist trap.

You'd think, he thought, *Quark's greedy little heart would be filled with glee at this boom in business.* Instead, the Ferengi kept on ranting about some alleged inconvenience.

"Contrary to your deranged opinion," Quark declared, "I do not steal from myself."

"You would if you could," Odo snorted in disgust.

Quark ignored the gibe. "In the last two hours, three plates, five mugs, and one entire chair have disappeared from the premises. Do you think they simply evaporated?"

"I believe the Ferengi still practice an archaic scam known as 'insurance.' Are you insured, Quark?"

"Look," Quark said, lowering his voice. "You and I both know that if I were after insurance money, I'd lose more than a few plates. This is petty theft, and not worth my effort."

True enough, Odo thought. Although he hated to admit it, Quark had a point. "I suppose," he said slowly, making eye contact with Quark for the first time this encounter, "there's no reason why a major criminal cannot be afflicted by a minor one."

"Exactly!" Quark crowed. "Hypothetically speaking, of course. You'll find the thief, then?"

"Actually," Odo said. "I'm wishing that this robber were more ambitious. It would appeal to my sense of justice."

The Ferengi started to protest, but was interrupted by the beep of Odo's comm badge. Rising to answer the call, Odo immediately recognized the urgent tone in Sisko's voice and turned his back on Quark so he could listen to Sisko in privacy; then he realized that Quark's enormous, eavesdropping ears were still too close for comfort. Very well . . .

Odo's bottom half, from his waist to his feet, dissolved into a translucent orange goo that flowed upward, forming a soundproof cone over Odo's head and upper torso. Glancing over his shoulder, through the glassy sheen of the cone, he saw Quark chewing his bottom lip in frustration. Odo permitted himself a thin smile, but his expression turned grim as Sisko quickly informed him about Ttan's abduction. An unfortunate matter, he concluded, that could pose a threat to the station's security should the raiders return for the other Hortas.

"Understood," he signed off. Regaining humanoid form, he rose from his seat and strode out into the Promenade. He had to organize his security team, prepare them for the possibility of an imminent Cardassian assault. This would have to happen, he groused, when the population of the Promenade was already swollen beyond reason. Quark hollered at him from the doorway of his bar: "Wait! What about my plates?"

"Look after them yourself," Odo said brusquely. "I have more important things to do."

"I have another chair," Nog whispered. Beneath his protruding brow, Nog's eyes darted furtively about the storeroom as he wrestled the chair past stacks of (mostly contraband) supplies. Crouching on the floor, his knees resting on the scorched metal grillework, Jake watched his friend approach.

"I don't think chairs are going to cut it much longer," he said glumly. Quark's broken freezer had been absorbed by the Horta in a matter of minutes. "We're going to need tables next."

In fact, all that was left of the first chair was one shining blue leg that was even now dissolving beneath the Horta's tendrils. The stolen alien was growing at an alarming rate, and so was its appetite. Twice as large as before, it no longer looked so raw and newborn. A layer of dark, stony armor had formed over its crimson hide, spreading outward from the mineral flecks it had been born with. Only veins and fissures in the armor revealed the redness underneath, like rivers of molten lava breaking up through faults in a planet's surface.

"Tables!" Nog exclaimed. "How am I supposed to sneak tables out of the bar? My uncle is already looking suspicious. If he wasn't so busy with all those moon watchers, he'd be onto us for sure!" He handed the new chair over to Jake, who shoved it toward the voracious Horta. He was careful not to get his hands too close; so far, the little monster seemed more interested in metal than flesh, but Jake didn't feel like taking chances. His palm still stung where the egg had burned him.

"Nog, I think maybe it's time to tell my dad about this."

"No!" Nog said. "My uncle will kill me. Besides, it's ours. We borrowed it fair and square." Feigning confidence, and failing miserably, he tried to reassure Jake. "Look, as long as we keep feeding it, it's not going anywhere. You stay here and I'll . . . I'll go find a buyer right away."

"Hey, wait a sec!" Jake complained, as Nog backed away, then turned and ran out of sight. *No way is he sticking me with this,* Jake thought, leaping to his feet and chasing after his friend. The Horta had another chair to eat. That would keep it busy for a while, he told himself. Or so he hoped.

Suddenly, the food stopped coming. The Horta finished off another sumptuous scrap of chair and waited for something new to eat. But nothing appeared, and even the carbon-smelling creatures who had been caring for her disappeared abruptly.

She let out a grinding cry, but received no response. She was alone and hungry. The chairs and cups and other morsels, while delicious, had not satisfied her hunger. She felt, on the very fringes of her senses, something else, a promise of food and fulfillment that was exactly what she craved. And it was nearby.

Snuffling along the storeroom floor, she came at last to a solid rhodinium wall and proceeded to burn a path straight through it. The lights in the storeroom winked on and off as severed circuits were replaced by backup systems.

The Horta left a steaming tunnel behind her as she

left the storeroom for unknown territory. The food she wanted called to her. If only she could find it.

Maybe this way . . .

Clad only in a diaphanous white gown that barely veiled the tantalizing feminine body underneath, the Vulcan priestess slipped quietly into the young crewman's quarters. Ensign Marc Tomson sat upright in his bunk, his heart pounding, as the beautiful Vulcan drew nearer. Only the small reading light over his head illuminated the room, penetrating the filmy gauze stretched tautly over the woman's breasts. Marc shifted uncomfortably upon his bunk, naked beneath a single thin sheet.

"T'Leena?" he asked breathlessly. "Why are you doing here . . . I mean, what are you coming . . ."

Damn, he thought. *I sound like an idiot.* "Computer, freeze program."

Her arms outstretched toward him, her lips glistening moistly, the figure of T'Leena suddenly became as motionless as a marble statue. Not breathing, not blinking, she froze in place as though trapped in a single instant of time. Marc took a deep breath and wiped the sweat from his forehead.

Oh well, he consoled himself. The great thing about holosuites was you could keep rerunning a fantasy until you got it right. And he had been fine-tuning this particular scenario ever since his last term of duty on Vulcan, several months back. All those irresistible, unapproachable Vulcan women . . . ! Still, DS9 had its attractions as well, including Quark's holosuites.

Anxious to begin again, he leaned back on the bunk and rested his head on the pillow. "Computer, resume program from beginning."

T'Leena disappeared, then rematerialized at the

entrance of his quarters. The door slid silently shut behind her, leaving them alone together. She crept through the shadows toward him, into the revealing glare of the reading light.

Marc swallowed and cleared his throat. "T'Leena," he tried again. "What are you doing here?" (*That's better,* he decided. His voice sounded deeper, more confident.)

"I do not know. I do not understand." She knelt beside the bunk and placed a warm palm upon Marc's cheek. Her hair, blacker than space and more lustrous, fell about her bare shoulders. "It is not logical. It is not Vulcan."

"But . . ." Marc prompted her.

"You make my cool green blood burn like a stream of fiery emeralds, Marc Tomson. My time is years away, but when I look on you I feel the passion of the *pon farr.*" With total Vulcan honesty, she stared at him, puzzled but unashamed by her strange desires. God, she was gorgeous, Marc thought. Even though he had carefully scripted all her dialogue, he was still overwhelmed by the experience of hearing it from her own lips.

"Wha . . . what do you want from me?" (*Take it easy,* he thought. *Don't rush things. We're almost there.*)

T'Leena rose to her feet and reached behind her neck to untie the straps of her robe. The sheer, translucent fabric fell away from her body, drifting with agonizing slowness to the floor. "I want to *meld* with you, Marc Tomson. I want to explore infinite pleasures in infinite combinations. I want to teach you the ancient secrets of Vulcan love. . . ."

"Yes!" Marc blurted. He couldn't stand it anymore. Sweat streamed down his back. The bunk itself seemed to be growing hotter by the second. He grabbed the hem of his blanket and tossed it aside, exposing . . .

A steaming, wriggling mass of brown-and-red rock burning its way up through the mattress and between his legs.

Marc screamed in panic. He half-jumped, half-tumbled out of the bunk, colliding with T'Leena. They fell in a jumble of naked limbs onto the hard tile floor. Forced to improvise, the holographic Vulcan tried to embrace Marc while continuing her prepro-grammed declaration of love.

". . . Every seven years is not enough, not for you. . . ."

Marc barely heard her. All fantasies and fervor had been driven out of his head by the sudden, shocking appearance of the thing in the bed, replaced by an instinctive urge to escape. Ohmigod, he thought. I'm completely defenseless. His uniform and communica-tor lay in a heap on the other side of the floor. His phaser was back in his real quarters; Constable Odo didn't allow weapons on the Promenade.

Frantically, he tried to disengage himself from the amorous Vulcan priestess. Acidic fumes seared his nostrils, and he struggled to look over his shoulder to see what the alien creature was doing, but T'Leena's teeth held on to his ear. An awkward thunk behind him suggested that the thing had dropped off the bunk onto the floor. Maybe it was oozing toward him this very minute.

"Computer," he shouted, "end program!" He bare-ly got the words out before T'Leena thrust her tongue into his mouth.

Tongue, T'Leena, and darkened room vanished instantly, and Marc found himself sprawled on the floor of the holosuite. Blinking against the sudden, brighter lighting, he heard a heavy, thrashing sound nearby. He sprang to his feet and scrambled away from the sound. Only when he was at least a yard away did he turn around and look toward the empty space where the simulated bunk had existed heartbeats ago.

His fantasy might have dematerialized, but the monster remained. Tentatively, like a puppy learning to walk, it zigzagged across the floor, leaving a trail of charred and sizzling tile behind it. A high-pitched screeching, like plates of rusty metal being scraped against each other, emerged from the creature, hurting Marc's ears. The creature's hunger, and corrosive nature, were all too obvious.

He glanced quickly in the direction of his clothing, wondering if maybe he could make a run for them. Then the alien, perhaps agitated by the sudden change in the holosuite's appearance, lurched toward the only remaining object in the room: Marc.

The young ensign raced out of the suite as fast as his feet would carry him. Oh god, he thought, how am I ever going to explain *this* to the Commander?

Shrieks and laughter broke out in the lounge. Behind the bar, Quark looked up in time to see a human male, quite naked, stumble down the stairs from Quark's upper floors. Blushing redder than an Dumesite man-lobster, the human navigated through the bar and ran out into the Promenade. Despite the young male's haste, Quark recognized him as the ensign who had rented Holosuite #5.

Humans! Quark shook his head. Sometimes he thought he'd never figure out the sexual customs of *Homo sapiens*. No Ferengi would ever flee from a holosuite unless in pursuit of something more profitable. Still, this incident only confirmed his faith in one of the oldest and most sacred of the Rules of Acquisition:

Always get payment in advance.

The baby Horta was quite confused. This chamber had appeared very interesting at first. There had been more of the carbon beings, like the two smaller ones who had first fed her, as well as solid structures that looked and smelled as if they were real. But then the snacks disappeared and so did the creature who smelled like copper. And the other carbon person, the one that secreted sodium chloride in an aqueous solution, had run away, just like her feeders.

The Horta howled in frustration and hunger. Where was Mother? Where was the food she craved?

Despite her cries, she felt no trace of her mother's presence. She could sense the food, however, somewhere in this strange, unsettling world she had awakened into. Below, she realized; it was still farther below.

Sinking into the floor, she left the empty holosuite behind.

CHAPTER
7

JADZIA DAX made a point of being awake and at the conn when the *Amazon* entered the Davon system. If they came across any other vessels, she would be at the controls. She could still hear Benjamin warning her to keep things from getting any more complicated than they had to be—and she had no intention of letting him down.

She felt the thrum of the engines change as she brought the ship out of warp at the very edge of the system. Hopefully they were beyond the range of any sensors the Cardassians had set up. She put a receiver to her ear to scan privately for subspace radio transmissions, but instead of the usual whir and crackle of static and the mumble of distant voices, she heard a loud hiss . . . a hiss that grew louder by the second. When it became painful, she yanked the receiver from her ear, wincing. It had to be a Van Luden radiation belt. Nothing else made that sort of sound.

"You should have awakened me," Kira asked, dropping into the seat beside her. "What's our status?"

"There's a Van Luden radiation belt nearby," she said. An uncomfortable ringing tone sounded in the back of her head.

"Where? I don't see . . ." Kira began, bending over the sensors. "Got it! Fifty thousand klicks ahead and closing."

"That's precisely the cover we need," Dax said. "If we can't hear them, they can't hear us . . . including the noise from our warp coils."

Against her better judgment, she had to let Kira take control of the ship. The ringing sound had begun to throw off her sense of balance. There was no sense in jeopardizing everyone if her ability to pilot the runabout was impaired. She shook her head slowly, trying to clear the sound away. If it didn't stop soon, she'd have to call Julian.

"That's fine as long as we're out here," Kira said. "But it doesn't help us find that Horta. See if you can spot any Cardassian ships."

"I told you," Dax said, "there's too much white noise from the radiation belt." Wasn't Kira listening to her? "We're going to have to get farther away from it if we're going to pick anything up." She shook her head again. Finally the ringing sound began to fade.

"I didn't mean for you to take a sensor scan, I meant for you to physically go look using your eyes."

"What?" The idea sounded crazy, but Kira didn't look like she was kidding. For a second Dax wondered if the static had affected her hearing. "You want me to go and look out the ports?"

"That's right," Kira said. "Eyeball space around us. You Federation types are too used to technology. What would you do if the sensors were down? So you don't see more than a few thousand klicks in any direction. Sometimes that's all you need."

Dax found herself nodding. It could work. "A very insightful, if primitive, answer. I'll see what I can spot."

Rising, she headed astern. At each viewport on the starboard side she paused and gazed out for a few seconds, studying the darkness of the void around them. Slowly her hearing returned to normal, and she relaxed a bit. That was one less thing for her to worry about.

The Van Luden radiation belt hung tantalizingly near, a shimmering yellow veil of light across the horizon that she found curiously appealing. There wasn't anything quite so beautiful as the wonders of deep space, she thought. Perhaps that's what had drawn her to the sciences—and ultimately to the fringe of the known universe.

As she continued around the runabout, she passed the spot where the card table had been folded into the wall for the night. Julian and the others had sacked out on the floor, on sleeping pads taken from ship's stores. Gingerly, she stepped around them. Julian, she thought, looked positively charming in his sleep, with his perpetually furrowed brow now smooth and relaxed. She smiled almost maternally at him. He was such an endearing child in so many ways.

She hadn't spotted anything when she reached the rearmost viewport, so she started back along the port side, repeating the process. Once more the Van Luden radiation belt stretched seemingly to infinity ahead of her, drawing her eye like a moth to its flame. She found a curious hollow feeling in her chest looking at it, and she knew when she got back to DS9 that she'd have to look up whatever studies Starfleet had done on it during the time this system had been in Federation space.

Two viewports from the front of the ship, a subtle movement caught her eye. She squinted, straining to see. Yes, there it was . . . a small black circle moving across the glow of the radiation belt.

"Kira," she said. "There's something coming slowly at us from port side."

"Where?" Kira demanded.

Putting the radiation belt from her thoughts, Dax hurried back to her seat. She leaned forward, located the speck on her monitor, and pointed. "There. See it?"

"I'm bringing us closer," Kira said. "Moving to an intercept course."

Dax felt a faint tremor run through the runabout's deck plates as the *Amazon* came about. She leaned forward, watching closely as the black shape grew from the size of a pinhead to the size of a dinner plate to the size of a small ship—

No, not a ship, she decided with relief. "It's an asteroid," she said. "The radiation belt isn't as clean as you thought, Kira."

"Hang on!" Kira said.

"What are you doing?" Dax demanded. They were still on a collision course with the asteroid, she realized.

"One second more . . ." Kira whispered.

"Decelerate! *Kira!*" Dax cried, her alarm growing. "Pull up—you're going to hit it!" The crater-scarred surface of the asteroid now loomed like an immense pockmarked wall ahead of her, filling the wide viewscreen.

"Relax, I know what I'm doing," Kira said. She fired docking thrusters at the last possible moment. "I've done this a thousand times."

Dax braced herself for collision. Kira was certifiably insane. Dax knew it now. Nobody flew on manual this close to an asteroid.

Kira fired the thrusters once more, easing them to a crawl. Finally, with a jarring bump, the runabout's nose touched the asteroid's surface. Slowly Kira applied the thrusters again.

"You're going to push it," Dax said in awe. She'd never seen such a move before, and the sheer daring of it amazed her more than she would admit.

"Very good," Kira said. "Hold on!"

A heavy thrumming noise filled the cabin as the runabout's engines strained against the asteroid's mass, but Dax had the distinct impression they were making progress. She glanced down at the ship's relative-velocity gauge. It showed an almost exponential increase in speed. When Kira switched from thrusters to impulse engines, they were positively racing.

They rapidly cleared the Van Luden radiation belt. When Kira cut the engines and used the thrusters to move back fifteen meters from the asteroid's surface, Dax breathed easily for the first time. Now at least they had a little room to maneuver. She didn't like cutting it so close.

Kira began flicking switches. The interior lights went out, along with most of the instruments. "We don't want them to pick up our energy bleed," she said. She leaned back and looked at Dax. "We should be clear of the radiation belt's interference. Try the sensors again."

Dax blinked. "You continue to amaze me, Kira," she said.

"Like I said, it's an old trick. There are a lot of

asteroids around Bajor. We used to sneak whole strike forces into orbit this way. Are you picking anything up?"

"Not yet." Dax finished the readouts from the first two planets and moved on to the third. For a gas giant, it had a suspiciously high energy reading. She took a more detailed scan, but found nothing unusual. If not the planet, she thought, perhaps the moons . . . There, on the innermost moon—that had to be a forcefield. Smiling triumphantly, she brought up a subspace scan. They were definitely broadcasting, and the transmission was being beamed back toward Cardassia.

"I've found them," she announced. "There's a small base on the third planet's innermost moon. And I'm picking up a Cardassian transmission." She looked at Kira. "The computer can't read it. That transmission is security scrambled."

Kira smiled wolfishly. "Bingo, as you might say. Too bad Cardassian codes are such a devil to crack; I'd give a lot to know what they're saying right now."

"So would I," Dax said. "Let's see what our records have to say about that moon. I loaded the Starfleet survey of all the local systems before we set out, just in case we needed them."

She called up a readout on the Davon system and skipped ahead to the proper planetary body. "The gas giant is fourteen AUs from the sun," she read aloud. "Its innermost moon showed real promise for mining exploitation. The preliminary survey team found traces of phlaginum, uranium, and several other heavy metals—and latinum. They didn't find any large deposits, but the Davon system was handed over to the Cardassians before a real survey could be done."

"Latinum," Kira mused. "The Cardassians use it as much as the Federation does. This has to be the place they've taken Ttan."

"It's a good possibility," Dax agreed. The mathematician part of her symbiont would have wagered heavily on it, she knew.

"Anything else?" Kira asked.

"Not in the report." She made a second sensor sweep of the moon. Knowing how paranoid Cardassians tended to be, she suspected a few traps lay in store for them. This time she spotted an orbiting security satellite. It had been on the far side of the moon during her first scan. They would have to stay out of its reach—doubtless it had quite a few nasty weapons at its command. Now it was just a matter of calculating their approach.

She brought up the survey again. "The innermost moon has a seven-hour orbit around the planet," she said. "The third moon is much faster . . . one point seven seven hours. It laps the first moon every two hours, give or take a few minutes."

"I know what you're thinking," Kira said. "As soon as the moon with the Cardassian base is behind the planet, we head for the third moon."

"That's in roughly twenty minutes," Dax said, rising. She could already feel the start of an adrenaline rush. "I'll wake the others."

Ttan burrowed frantically through the rock wall, searching for the elusive taste of latinum. The trace elements she associated with the crystal were present everywhere she went. She hit a vein of quartz that seemed to run deep into Davonia's core and veered away; it wouldn't be here, she thought. It would be surrounded by nickel and iron, by pergium and cobalt.

Perhaps it lay deeper, she thought, tunneling downward. The rock surrounding her felt cool against her skin, like a healing salve after the endless hours of falling she'd felt aboard the *Dagger*. Fifty meters below the level where Gul Mavek and his soldiers waited, she found a pocket of pergium. Latinum crystals—some as big around as a human hand—lined the node.

Success! she thought. At once she turned and headed for the spot she had left Gul Mavek.

She burst through the wall behind Mavek's men. They scrambled out of her way, keeping their weapons trained on her. She ignored them and surged forward to stand before Gul Mavek.

"Well?" he asked mildly. "What did you find, Ttan?"

"Latinum, as you requested."

"Where?"

She told him. "Now, let me see my children!"

"I think not," Gul Mavek said. "You took longer than you were supposed to. Perhaps tomorrow, if you prove more . . . cooperative."

Ttan shrieked in rage, in betrayal. She barely managed to contain her anger. She wanted to leap on Mavek, to burn him with her rock-chewing acids until he let her have her children back.

He seemed to sense her reaction. His lips turned up in what Ttan had come to know was a humanoid gesture of amusement.

"You realize, of course," he said, "that if anything happened to me, all of your eggs would be destroyed *at once.*"

Ttan said nothing for a long moment. At last she said, "Yes."

"Go with these guards," he told her. "They will take you to a place where you can rest. Remain there until I send for you. If you cooperate, perhaps I will even let you see your children tomorrow."

He turned and strode up the tunnel, leaving her there alone. Ttan felt the same hollow helpless rage that the last Prime Mother must have felt when humans first burst into the sacred Vault of the Ages and destroyed hundreds of eggs.

Only these are my *eggs,* she thought. *These are* my *children.*

If anything happened to them, she swore she would see Gul Mavek dead, even if it meant the loss of her own poor life.

Kira leaned forward, trying to quell the anxious fluttering in her stomach. This was the first place where something could go wrong, she knew. Her palms had begun to sweat.

As she watched, the inner moon disappeared completely behind the gas giant. Now the window of opportunity opened for them. She exchanged a quick glance with Dax, who nodded with more cool self-assurance than Kira felt.

"Here we go," she muttered. She activated the thrusters and moved them out from behind the asteroid.

An alarm light began to flash on Dax's console. "What is it?" Kira demanded, a thousand possibilities—all bad—flashing through her thoughts.

"We're being scanned!" Dax said.

"Get me the coordinates!" Kira snapped. A strange

calm descended over her. It was just like the old days, back in the Resistance, dodging and burning through Cardassian traps.

"There is a small device sheathed in duranium about fifty thousand kilometers away. Twenty degrees, mark four."

"Got it!" Kira said. She altered course. It had to be a bullet-probe, she thought. The Cardassians used them around Bajor—each one activated when it sensed the runabout's power emissions.

"I'll see if I can beam it aboard," Dax said. "Perhaps I can deactivate its—"

"No!" Kira said. She armed and fired the runabout's first torpedo. "It's mine!"

She braced herself. On her monitor, she watched a glowing white ball of plasma energy home in on the bullet-probe. When the torpedo detonated, throwing off ring after ring of brilliant energy, the resulting force waves rocked the runabout like a leaf on a Bajoran ocean. It felt glorious. Kira had almost forgotten how alive you felt during a battle.

She turned proudly. "Got it!"

Dax sank back in her seat. "I'm not sure that was such a good idea, Kira," she said. "As soon as the Cardassians discover their probe is missing, they'll know something is wrong."

"It's not a problem," Kira said. "I'll change the asteroid's course so they think it caused the damage." She nosed the runabout toward the asteroid once more. That should take care of everything, she thought.

"And you've lost one of our torpedoes."

"They're meant to be used," Kira said, a little annoyed. She was getting tired of having to justify her every move to Dax. "That's why we brought them, remember? Besides," she said, "if you'd brought that thing aboard, it would have destroyed the ship. Bullet-probes blow up if you tamper with them. Believe me, I know. I've lost several friends that way."

"Ah," Dax said. "In that case, thank you, Kira."

"No problem," she lied. "No problem at all." She fired the thrusters again, and the runabout touched the asteroid with a soft thud. Slowly she applied thrusters once more, shifting its course toward the wreckage of the bullet-probe.

"I only want a little more teamwork, okay?" Dax said. "This is supposed to be a rescue *team.*"

Kira took a deep breath. Sometimes the three-hundred-year-old symbiont in Dax made Kira feel like an unruly child being gently lectured by her grandmother. "All right, I'm sorry. I acted instinctively."

Dax smiled. "Those may well be the instincts we'll need to keep us alive."

"They've worked for me all these years," Kira muttered.

With the asteroid now on its new course, she pulled the runabout away and steered for the third moon. She had no intention of wasting time now. If Dax wanted teamwork, she'd give it to her by the book—whatever book Starfleet used.

Dax said, "I estimate our arrival in thirty-two minutes at this speed. That will give us forty minutes before the moon with the Cardassian base clears its primary, and fifty-two minutes before it's in trans-porter range."

"Good."

Kira's thoughts raced ahead. *Teamwork.* If that's what they wanted, that's what she'd give them. At times Dax—and for that matter Sisko—seemed to think all Bajorans were gun-crazed loners out for personal glory. If she played things close to her chest, what of it? The fewer people in a command chain, the fewer links that could break. All Bajorans had learned that lesson in the Resistance.

Let them think what they wanted, she finally decided. She knew exactly what she was doing and called it taking responsibility. That's what came with rank on Bajor. And if some Cardassian bastard happened to come between her and Ttan . . . well, a team could kill just as well as an individual.

CHAPTER
8

HABITAT SUITE 959:

The little Horta had no name as yet, but she was growing restless. For months, her world had been dark, snug, and sustaining. Now that snugness seemed cramped and confining, and the remains of the hard shell around her no longer satisfied her appetite. She yearned for more, and somehow she knew that what she wanted lay *beyond*.

Acid seeping from her pores, she flexed and pushed against the boundaries of her world. Suddenly, the barrier dissolved away and, to her amazement, everything was bigger and more open than before. She wriggled forward, drawn by instinct and the lure of this strange new universe. Already she sensed exciting, different tastes and sensations on the air; the high black plateau that supported her tantalized her tendrils with intriguing mineral flavors that only heightened her hunger. Her secretions freed the flavors from the floor, melting and loosening them so that her avid tendrils could suck them up.

There was motion all around her, too. Other beings —beings like her—emerged from their own eggs. The dark and open space surrounding her was filled with the crimson glow, and smoky fumes, of burning shells. But above the odor of the fumes, and the delicious taste of the platform, she sensed something even better, something irresistible, something distant but enticingly nearby.

With her brothers and sisters joining her, the newborn Horta began to burrow downward into the platform itself. Beyond the exterior casing, she found other delicacies inside the pedestal: crystalline lattices and minute, often microscopic appetizers made of various combinations of different elements and alloys. Though intriguing, these intricate confections were, she quickly discovered, more frustrating than fulfilling; her hunger was such that she wanted to feast on something rich and substantial, not nibble on tidbits that she digested almost as soon as she detected them.

Her hatchmates tumbled past her, jostling her on all sides, their cries echoing her own hunger and excitement. By the time she reached the floor of the suite, less than ten minutes after escaping the confines of her egg, the entire platform had been devoured by the Hortas. Only a smoking triangle of blackened residue marked the former location of the eggs' resting place.

But where to go now? The little Horta found herself distracted and disoriented by a bewildering array of tastes and sensations. Where to dig next? What to consume? On the tip of her tendrils she still felt the lure of a nectar more savory than anything she had sampled so far, but her senses were confused by her alien surroundings and she could not locate her treat so easily. Gravity itself seemed somehow unnatural in this place. And she was so hungry, and there were so many other things to eat . . . !

All around her, the Horta's siblings sounded just as confused. They spread out in every direction, shunning the open air to burrow instead into the walls and floor. The heat of their various passages released still more tangy odors into the environment, stimulating the Horta's appetite and masking, almost but not entirely, the diffuse traces of the food she craved most. She smelled polymers and plastics, processed metals and compounds, isotopes and rare earths. It was more stimuli than any newborn Horta could hope to cope with; it was both too much and, strangely, not enough.

All at once, the Horta felt an absence, and a yearning, that had nothing to do with the hunger of her body. Someone should have been here for her, she realized, to guide her and care for her and protect her. A sense of loss came over her then, as if she'd been hatched with it: Mother. Where was Mother?

The floor beneath her vibrated as the Horta howled for her Mother, a desperate cry that sounded like an emergency siren blaring. But no one answered, and after a seemingly endless minute the little Horta felt the feeding urge rise up again within her, so she trusted her instincts and did what any Horta would do when puzzled and provoked and left to her own devices. She dug deep into the substance of *Deep Space Nine,* devouring everything she encountered.

She tunneled beneath the floor, adding to the craters left behind by her departing hatchmates. She burned through open conduits and solid apparatus. Strange energies tickled her hide as she interrupted the directed flow of electrons and ionized particles. The Horta barely noticed the radiation; she was only interested in *solids,* and there were so many new flavors to relish, one after another. She couldn't tunnel fast enough.

Keiko O'Brien's classroom was crowded that morning. She suspected that many of the tourists now visiting DS9 had decided to use her school as a free day-care center. Students from over a dozen different species sat at their desks, behind their tray-sized personal computers. A hubbub of speech, growls, squeaks, and chirps filled the room, as the kids exchanged jokes and gossip in the last few minutes before the class commenced. (Homework and notes, Keiko knew, had been exchanged earlier, out on the Promenade.) Jake Sisko was absent, she noted. Probably off hanging around with that Ferengi pal of his. She wondered if she should mention this no-show to Jake's father. She'd hate to bother him about it; certainly, Commander Sisko had enough things to worry about without her bringing up his son's poor choice of friends. Maybe Miles would have some idea about how to broach the subject. She resolved to discuss the matter with her husband as soon as he came home.

In the meantime, she had a class to teach. She squinted at the padd in her hand to check on today's lesson plan. "Good morning," she said cheerfully, giving her students a friendly smile that also served to silence the general chatter. "Yesterday we discussed the moon that will be passing by DS9 in a day or so. Does anyone remember what that moon is called?"

Seated at a desk in the front row, little Molly raised her hand. Keiko wasn't surprised; her daughter always raised her hand, whether she knew the answer or not. Only three years old, Molly was technically too young to be attending school already, or even to understand most of what went on in the class, but she enjoyed sitting in on her mother's lessons, and reliable baby-sitters were, like so many other amenities, in short supply on the station. Thankfully, Molly usually behaved herself, playing games and drawing pictures on her computer.

Keiko grinned at Molly, but called on a ten-year-old Bajoran girl in the third row. "The Prodigal," Yelsi answered proudly. A ceremonial earring peeked out from behind the girl's dark brown pigtails.

"Good," Keiko said. She addressed the rest of the class. "Now, can someone tell me why it's called that?" A fuzzy-faced Tellarite youth, his bristly yellow mane indicating the approach of puberty, raised a three-fingered hand. "Yes, Gann?"

"It's from an old Bajoran fairy tale," he said with a smirk. Keiko saw Yelsi, and the other Bajoran children, fix venomous stares upon Gann.

Oh, no, Keiko thought. Ever since Bajoran fundamentalists bombed her classroom, supposedly for offending their religious sensibilities, she had become cautious whenever the subject of Bajoran culture and beliefs came up; worse, she hated feeling that way. True, that particular incident had turned out to be merely a cover for an assassination plot against a rival religious leader, but Keiko was all too aware that the underlying issue, of Bajoran spiritualism versus Federation science, remained unresolved, and liable to explode again at any moment. Still, despite her concern, she tried not to censor herself—and hoped she was succeeding.

"Now, Gann, you must know that's an unnecessarily disrespectful way to describe Bajoran . . . religion." She started to say "mythology," but caught herself in time. *I'm speaking from the heart,* she assured her conscience, *and not trying to appease the Bajorans.* "This moon is named after a figure from ancient writings that many Bajorans hold sacred. How would you like it if one of the other students made fun of the Tellarite *Scroll of Eternal Feasting?*" Gann looked uncomfortable; he stamped his hooves in embarrassment. "We have to remember, the wormhole is a wonderful opportunity to bring together people from different civilizations all over the galaxy. But if we're to take full advantage of this opportunity, we must be open-minded about people who look or think differently than we do. Tolerance and understanding are what *Deep Space Nine* is really all about.

"The Vulcans have a saying," she started to say; then, without warning, the floor beneath her *rippled.*

Keiko had put on sandals that morning, ones with heavy rubber soles. Yet she felt a sudden surge of heat beneath her feet, intense enough and sudden enough that she jumped backward, dropping her padd in surprise. The padd crashed with a bang on the classroom floor, only centimeters away from where the floor began to glow red like a burning ember. Keiko watched in horror as the padd sizzled and melted away. The smell of burning plastic and crystals stung her nostrils. Smoky white fumes rose from the floor.

Some sort of plasma leak, she guessed. A momentary flare of anger almost burned away her fear. She had always hated *Deep Space Nine. This place is a death trap,* she thought; *I knew this was going to happen someday. Miles,* her brain screamed. *Where are you? You promised me we'd be safe.*

The padd crumbled into smoking ashes. The floor dissolved before her eyes, and a writhing, shapeless mass of rocklike tissue lurched upward into the room. It had no head, no limbs, no features that Keiko could identify, but the front half of the thing lifted up off the floor, stringy fibers dangling from its exposed underside, and it swayed back and forth, as if questing for something.

Gann squealed like a Terran hog. Yelsi shrieked in fright, her cries quickly joined by several other kids, male and female and none of the above. The children leaped from the seats, sometimes overturning their desks in the process, and ran for the exit, pushing and shoving and crawling over each other in their wild flight from the monster that had burst into their presence. A froglike Wollowan boy, propelled by his powerful hind legs, bounded over the heads of his classmates, nearly colliding with the ceiling. "Wait! Don't panic. Remember our drills," Keiko shouted after them, but it was a futile effort. Her students could not, or would not, hear her over their shouts and stomping feet. A harsh metallic keening came from the invader, adding to the cacophony.

So much for interspecies tolerance, Keiko thought bitterly. She couldn't blame them, though. She was terrified, too. She looked frantically for Molly. To her surprise, her child was still sitting at her desk, eyeing the creature with undisguised fascination. Molly seemed to regard the lumpy monstrosity as no more terrifying than a caged slime-devil at the zoo. *Well,* Keiko thought with dark humor, *at least I know someone was listening to my high-minded lecture.*

The creature wriggled hesitantly toward the almost-abandoned rows of desks, toward Molly. Every muscle in Keiko's body wanted to dash forward, grab her baby, and run, but the alien, its craggy hide pulsating to some internal rhythm, moved directly between her and Molly. So far, it wasn't making any obviously threatening movements; in fact, as nearly as she could tell with such an inhuman entity, it seemed disoriented, possibly confused by its surroundings. Keiko forced herself to stay still. She didn't want to provoke the thing by making any sudden moves.

Overcoming her initial shock, and perhaps inspired by Molly's fearless example, Keiko tried to analyze the situation rationally. *This must be one of the Hortas that Miles told me about,* she realized. They were supposed to be peaceful, she knew, but this one appeared out of control. "Keep calm," she whispered. *Odo should be here in a few minutes. And Miles too,* she hoped.

The Horta slid closer to Molly's desk. Keiko's heart seemed to climb up her windpipe. "Don't move, honey," she said hoarsely, praying her voice would not upset the Horta. "It won't hurt you, I promise." *Please let me be telling her the truth,* she thought. They had survived so much, endured so many dangers both here and on the *Enterprise.* She couldn't bear it if she lost her daughter now.

Unlike her mother, Molly acted totally unafraid. As Keiko gasped and clutched her throat, the toddler hopped off her chair, her small computer clutched in her tiny little hands, and trotted to meet the Horta. *It's sentient,* Keiko thought over and over like a mantra. *It's not going to eat her.* But the still-smoking hole in the floor, and the charred remains of the padd, did nothing to allay her fears.

Molly stopped only a few steps away from the Horta. Its corrosive hide had left a trail of scorched rhodinium flooring. The Horta also paused, apparently contemplating the small, fragile humanoid in its path. Keiko found herself unable to breathe.

"H is for Horta," Molly said sagely. Keiko recognized the line from one of Molly's favorite story chips.

She held out her computer and dropped the light-weight metal construct onto the floor in front of the Horta. It rattled lightly against the metal tiles. "H is for Hungry."

A sound that might have been a mew escaped the Horta, and it instantly fell upon the computer, melt-ing it into a mineral gruel that its tendrils eagerly sucked up.

Understanding, and an overwhelming sense of re-lief, flooded over Keiko. Of course! Miles had said that the only Hortas left on the station hadn't hatched yet. This must be a baby. And how do you handle an upset newborn? You feed it.

Molly's computer had already been devoured en-tirely, and the young Horta was flailing its "head" and making that keening sound again. Keiko hurried to join Molly, and together they proceeded to offer the voracious creature computer after computer. Keiko winced inwardly as she watched her precious teaching supplies disappear into the nonexistent maw of the Horta. First the bombing, now this. Starfleet's budget office was not going to like this.

Still, if it kept the Horta happy, and Molly safe, Keiko was willing to feed it the entire classroom, desks, chairs, and all. She hoped Odo got here while there was still a shred of a school left.

"B is for Breakfast," Molly supplied happily. Keiko nodded and handed her another computer.

Odo thought he was ready for anything. Then everything happened at once.

One minute, he was sitting in his office, a forbidding expression on his waxlike face, staring at the screen on his desk as it gave him a quick, condensed education on the subject of Hortas. Odo grimaced when he read about the murders committed by the first Mother Horta over eight decades ago, then conceded that there had been extenuating circumstances in that case. Ever since, he discovered, the Hortas had proven a remarkably law-abiding people.

Aside from the Starfleet officers who had accompanied Kira on her mission, Odo had deployed his security force all over the habitat ring. No one was off-duty. Many were working extra shifts. Odo alone manned the security office at present; fortunately, only a few drunks and pickpockets occupied the adjoining cells, and the drunks were still sleeping off the effects of Quark's noxious potions.

A color illustration of an adult Horta appeared on the screen. He rotated the image, observing it from several angles and directions. He rather admired the Hortas' lack of bilateral symmetry; it struck him as a much more comfortable shape than the humanoid form he'd been forced to assume for most of his life. He looked longingly at the shining steel bucket sitting unobtrusively in one corner of his office. He had remained solid for well over twelve hours now, and it would be relaxing to let go for a few minutes, but, no, not with a potential emergency in the offing. He took comfort, however, in knowing that DS9 couldn't be more prepared in the event the raiders returned.

Then, preceded by hoots and hollers from the Promenade, a naked human male came running into the office. Odo recognized him as one of Sisko's men, assigned to the wormhole research team. "And just what do you think you're doing?" Odo snarled, standing up behind his desk. His right arm stretched across the room and snatched up a blanket from the nearest empty cell. "Here, put this on. You look ridiculous."

Wonderful, he thought sarcastically. On top of

everything else, a case of indecent exposure. Humans! Sometimes he thought they deserved whatever Quark pulled on them. Justice was still justice, though, regardless of the victim. And Quark was Quark.

The ensign looked pathetically grateful for the covering. "There's a monster," he stammered. "I mean, an alien intruder aboard, sir. Nonhumanoid and . . . hot! It *burned* through the wall at Quark's!"

Odo's eyes glanced back at the illustration on his screen. A Horta? Sisko had said that none of the Hortas had hatched yet. Still, this couldn't be a coincidence; something was not right. His muscles molded themselves into a state of maximum alertness. He fine-tuned his reflexes.

"When? Where?" he demanded. "Give me the details." His hand hovered over his comm badge, ready to open a line to Sisko in Ops.

The ensign appeared inexplicably reluctant to elaborate. "I was off-duty, you see. And, well, there was this woman on Vulcan. . . ."

Odo grabbed hold of the young man's shoulders, sorely tempted to shake a quick and concise answer out of this chattering human. Before the youth could say another word, however, Odo heard screams from the Promenade. Screams of terror.

"Stay right here," he ordered the ensign. "Don't move an inch." Leaving the man standing there, clutching haplessly onto the blanket wrapped around his absurd human body, Odo rushed into the wide corridor outside his office—and found himself faced with a scene of utter pandemonium.

Everything indeed seemed to be happening at once. A pack of hysterical children ran shrieking down the Promenade. The overhead lights flickered off and on. Sparks erupted from panels on the floor and walls.

Odo wished he had a sense of smell, so he could detect smoke if a fire broke out. Merchants and souvenir seekers poured out of shops and doorways, unsure what was going on, but adding to the tumult and chaos. Extending his torso to see above the crowd, Odo scanned the Promenade. At first, he couldn't spot the root of the panic, only confused and frightened people. Then, as if seeing one opened your eyes to the rest, he saw Hortas everywhere he looked.

They dropped from the ceiling, smashing through awnings and flashing outdoor signs, only to land apparently unharmed. The spray from a falling Horta, the acid trailing behind it like the tail of a comet, set a cloth banner ablaze. They emerged from the walls, leaving gaping cavities in the skeleton of DS9. They burst from the floor, sending bystanders sprawling and crashing into each other. Odo heard yells and shouted obscenities and even the unmistakable sound of angry fists ramming into flesh and bone. An avian trader flapped her wings helplessly, her talons stuck in the gooey protoplasm of a hysterical Gelloid. His security officers tried to reach the Hortas, but found themselves hampered by a mob of allegedly rational beings fighting to get away from the madness that had exploded in their midst.

"Get these people out of here!" he ordered his team, shouting to be heard above the roar. "Clear the Promenade!" Damn, he cursed. Where was he supposed to put all these people? Was there any place on DS9 the Hortas couldn't reach?

The maze was made of gold-pressed latinum. Sheets and sheets of the precious material, stacked up like bricks to form gleaming walls that stretched at least a meter above Jake's head. Latinum as far as the eye could see, he marveled; this had to be one of Quark's personal simulations.

"Computer, halt program," Jake said, but the transformed holosuite did not respond. No doubt Nog knew how to turn off the labyrinth, but finding Nog was the problem. Three possible pathways lay before Jake, and he could not see more than a couple of meters down any of them. "C'mon, Nog!" he shouted. "You can't hide from me forever!"

"Ferengi invented hiding!" Nog's voice called out from somewhere in the depths of the maze. Guessing at his friend's location, Jake ran down the right-side corridor, between two looming latinum partitions. The overhead lights, reflected off the gold plating, made Jake's eyes water, forcing him to remember that Ferengi eyes were much less sensitive than a human's. He zigzagged through the maze, turning left, then right, then left again. Rounding another corner, he found himself confronting a dead end. SUCKER! screamed the graffiti phaser-burned into the wall that blocked him. Cursing under his breath, Jake was in no mood to appreciate Quark's attention to detail.

God only knows what that Horta's up to, he thought, while I'm wasting my time in this stupid maze. He tried to retrace his steps back to the maze's entrance, but soon realized he was hopelessly lost. All this latinum looked the same to him.

"Nog!" Jake yelled angrily. "I'm already going to kill you. But, if you don't show your greedy face in the next five minutes, I'm going to kill you even worse . . . starting with your ears!"

An involuntary gasp of horror, sounding surprisingly nearby, came from a turnoff just ahead of Jake. He sprinted toward the noise and caught a glimpse of a stunted figure darting around another curve in the maze. Forget it, Jake thought; you're not getting away from me this time. He chased Nog through a twisting, S-shaped path, undistracted by the sight of enough gold-pressed latinum to buy DS9 several times over—if only it were real.

Nog ran as if pursued by the entire Romulan Empire. Not for the first time, however, long human legs triumphed over the Ferengi's natural talent for fast getaways. Jake grabbed on to the neck of Nog's jacket and yanked him back hard. Pulled off his feet, Nog flew backward into Jake. Both boys crashed onto the floor of the maze, smacking their flailing knees and elbows into the hard latinum wall.

Ouch, Jake thought, smarting from the pain. Why couldn't Ferengi build mazes out of shrubs or foam like everybody else? Holding tightly on to Nog, he placed the Ferengi in a firm headlock and refused to let go. "I thought you were looking for a merchant to sell the Horta to," he challenged.

"I lied, of course. What did you think?"

Caught off-guard by the utter candor of his friend's dishonesty, Jake wasn't sure how to respond. His grip on Nog loosened a little. "Well, what are we going to do about the Horta then?" he asked eventually.

Nog did not reply. He seemed mesmerized by the stacks of latinum directly across from them. "Hey, snap out it!" Jake said. He stood up slowly, hauling Nog onto his feet as well. "Let's go. We have to find that Horta."

"Uh, Jake," Nog said nervously, still staring at the wall of the maze. "I don't think that's going to be a problem."

"What?" Jake followed the path of Nog's gaze and saw that the white light shining off the holographic latinum seemed even brighter than before. This was more than a reflection, he realized; the wall was actually glowing. Before his eyes, the wall flashed white, then red, until the light faded to reveal a lumpy, pulsating mass of steaming rock lurching toward them.

"Let me go! Let me go!" Nog shrieked, tugging on Jake's arms with desperate fingers. Shocked by the sudden appearance of the Horta, Jake released Nog from the headlock. His arms dropped limply to his sides. Nog ran around behind Jake, placing his human friend between himself and the Horta.

"How did it find us?" Jake asked aloud. And now what was he supposed to do?

The Horta inched closer. Jake guessed it was confused by the holographic walls. Probably not as tasty as the real thing, he thought. "Down, boy," he said in what he hoped were soothing tones. "Back off. Play dead."

The Horta came within a few centimeters of Jake's boots, and Jake jumped backward, bumping into Nog. The newborn Horta had obviously never attended obedience school.

Cowering behind him, Nog let out an alarmed scream. Turning around quickly, Jake saw *another* Horta burning its way through the maze. He couldn't believe it. How could there be two of them? Could their stolen Horta have reproduced already? There was no other explanation. Unless . . .

We never reactivated the stasis field around the other eggs.

A sudden chill rushed over his body as the full

implications of what he and Nog had done sunk in. Maybe there were more than two Hortas loose. Perhaps neither of the Hortas in the holosuite was the one they'd left downstairs in Quark's storeroom. If that was true, then all the eggs must have hatched—and it was all their fault.

"Nog, get us out of here now."

"Huh?" Nog's terrified gaze jumped back and forth between the two approaching Hortas.

"Shut off the stupid maze, Nog!"

This time he got through. Nog stopped trembling and pulled himself together. "Computer," he said loudly. "Program code: Midas. Stop and save."

The labyrinth vanished, replaced by an empty blue chamber marked by a gridlike arrangement of lighted yellow strips. The Hortas howled in protest, sounding like overloaded phasers about to explode. Jake and Nog took advantage of their puzzlement to run through what was now clear and open space to the closest exit. The minute the door slid open, Jake heard the shouts and confusion below.

He knew what they meant, too. "The Hortas," he groaned at Nog. "They're loose, all of them, and they're eating the station!" An awful sense of guilt suffused his thoughts; despite the screams from the Promenade, he felt more ashamed than frightened. "We have to do something!"

"Hide?" Nog suggested helpfully. "Steal a runabout and escape?" They stepped out onto an empty walkway. Jake breathed a sigh of relief as the door to the holosuite shut behind them, cutting them off, if only for the moment, from the pair of Hortas within.

"No," he said. "We have to help somehow, do what we can to make up for this disaster!"

Nog shook his head. "I don't like that idea. It sounds too . . . hu-man." His expression brightened for a minute. "Do you think there's any looting going on?"

"It's our fault," Jake insisted.

"So," Nog replied. "Nobody knows that . . . do they?" He looked around apprehensively, ending with a wary glance at the entrance to the holosuite.

Clenching his fists in frustration, Jake took a deep breath and tried again. "It's matter of responsibility, Nog."

"You mean, survival," his friend corrected him.

"Responsibility."

"Survival."

This is getting us nowhere, Jake concluded. "Look," he said, "I'll make you a deal." Nog stopped peering around and gave Jake his full attention. Jake wasn't surprised. There wasn't a Ferengi in the galaxy, he knew, who could resist bargaining. "If you help me fix this mess, I won't insist we confess to starting it."

Nog's jaw dropped at the very prospect of admitting their guilt. "You wouldn't!"

"Try me," Jake said. He fixed his face in as grim and Odo-like an expression as he could muster. Nog's jagged overbite gnawed on his lower lip as he considered his options. The Ferengi's eyes narrowed to a squint, as if searching for microscopic loopholes in the bargain.

"You won't tell anyone?" Nog said finally. "Not even your father?"

"Not even your uncle," Jake assured him.

Nog held out his hand. "Deal!"

From the Promenade came the sound of breaking glass and the smell of smoke. Grabbing his friend's outstretched hand, Jake pulled him toward the stairway. *Maybe Odo needs volunteers,* he thought hopefully, *or Chief O'Brien.*

He'd find some way to make things right. He had to.

"Commander!" O'Brien announced in Ops. "I have power outages all over the station. Something is disrupting the microwave junction nodes."

Now what, Sisko wondered. He sat on a stool by the operations table, analyzing a map of Bajor and trying, unsuccessfully, to find a safe haven for the Hortas when they hatched. He wanted to find a site so isolated, or environmentally secure, that Pova's council couldn't conceivably object. So far, he hadn't found one. "Is this the usual brand of DS9 malfunction," he asked, "or anything more serious?"

"It looks bad, sir." O'Brien scowled, clearly puzzled by the incoming data. "I can't be sure, but it's almost like there's something, maybe more than one something, chewing their way through the hull, and messing up everything in their path." He looked over at Sisko. "You don't think the Cardies left us with mice, do you?"

"The Hortas," Sisko realized instantly. But how? They weren't supposed to hatch for weeks. And what about the stasis field? Never mind, he told himself. That wasn't important now. "We have twenty Horta babies on the loose, Chief. Frisky, hungry, Horta babies."

"Bloody hell," O'Brien muttered.

"Can you track them?" Sisko asked.

O'Brien looked embarrassed. "I'm trying, sir, but it's not easy. These accursed Cardie sensors aren't equipped to deal with beasties made out of silicon. I can reconfigure the parameters—over the central computer's dead circuits if I have to—but the Hortas are already eating away at the station's internal monitors. God knows what sensors will be left by the time I get them on the right track."

Sisko scowled. He shoved himself off the stool and onto his feet. This sounded like a disaster in the making. He knew he had to take action immediately. "Can you give me any sense of their progress, Chief?"

"Judging from the damage reports," O'Brien told him, "they're spreading out from Habitat Suite Nine-five-nine and making pretty good time." He examined every screen at the engineering station. "Hmmm. Nothing in the docking ring yet." He stared at Sisko with an anxious expression on his ruddy features. "Commander, I think some of them have already reached the Promenade."

In other words, Sisko translated, *DS9 is facing a full-scale Horta invasion.*

"Seal off all the turbolifts and walkways between the Promenade and Ops," he ordered. "See if you can contain them—without harming them." O'Brien had a small child of his own; Sisko knew he could count on Miles to keep the safety of the baby Hortas in mind.

Now, he thought, *all I have to do is keep the rest of us intact as well.*

Sisko tapped his comm badge. "Odo. Sisko here. We have a problem. . . ."

"Tell me about it, Commander," Odo replied sarcastically before informing Sisko of the rioting on the Promenade. He didn't waste words either; he had work to do. Signing off, he observed with satisfaction that his team was managing to impose a semblance of order on the frantic exodus from the scene. Bajorans, Ferengi, humans, and the rest cleared out of the

Promenade, without actually killing each other. Good, he thought. Let the deputies handle crowd control. He'd deal with the Hortas personally.

The Hortas looked like they were having a grand time. At least three Hortas were ransacking the mineral assay office, knocking over the shelves and consuming the rare ores and gems. "Like kids in a candy store," Odo grumbled, before turning his gaze elsewhere.

A single Horta, tendrils vibrating with excitement, attacked a snack kiosk. It ignored the mouthwatering display of glopsicles, preferring to consume the kiosk itself. Despite himself, he thought the Horta showed surprisingly good taste.

Two more Hortas dined sloppily at the Replimat, dissolving the small dining tables of the outdoor café. A Bajoran priest fled from his temple, the hem of his scarlet robe smoking around his ankles. "The altar!" he shouted, torn between fear and fury. "A devil is eating the altar!"

Yet another Horta wriggled out of the doorway of the schoolroom. Remembering the screaming children, Odo began to move in that direction. Lieutenant Moru, his second-in-command, got there first; Odo watched the tall Bajoran woman, a veteran of numerous battles and emergencies, escort Chief O'Brien's wife and daughter out of the building and away from the Promenade. From where he was standing, they appeared unharmed. Satisfied that Ms. O'Brien and the child were in good hands, he twisted his head in the opposite direction, rapidly assessing the disaster.

So far, Garak's clothing shop had escaped the Hortas' appetite. The Cardassian himself lurked in the shadows of his doorway, a thin smile on his pallid lips. No doubt he was mentally taking notes for the report he intended to send to . . . whomever. Odo directed his attention toward the haberdasher/spy. "They don't seem to like your wares, Garak," he said suspiciously.

Garak threw out his hands, all bemused innocence. "I deal only in the finest natural fibers. Nothing inorganic or synthetic."

"Convenient," Odo observed.

Garak shrugged, then adjusted the shoulders of his well-cut tan suit. "Perhaps I can interest you in an 'I Saw The Prodigal' T-shirt?" he said with a smirk.

"Get out now or I'll have you dragged away."

"Don't trouble yourself, Constable," the Cardassian said unctuously. "I know when I'm not needed." He crept slowly toward an exit.

Odo snorted in disgust. Someday he'd deal with that viper, but not now. Especially since he saw a pair of Hortas burning their way toward Dr. Bashir's infirmary. Odo nodded, his decision made; that was where to begin. Glopsicles and mineral samples were one thing. Medical supplies took priority.

As for Quark's Place . . . well, he'd check on that eventually, in his own good time.

Rom stood, his knees shaking, atop the bar counter. Quark sat on Rom's shoulders, and wished he had a stronger and taller brother.

Below, a rampaging young Horta sampled the furniture of Quark's establishment. Right now, it was nibbling away at the gaming wheel in the casino section. Mostly plastic and cheap Bajoran timber, the wheel quickly bored the Horta, who turned its corrosive attention to an automated chip dispenser that, ordinarily, cashed all manner of currency for a mere thirty percent service charge. Quark had based the technology on the Federation's Universal Translator —with modifications.

Heavy money bags filled with sheets of gold-pressed latinum were slung over both Quark's shoulders. A belt packed with precious jewels and rare, antique coins was wrapped around his waist. Quark felt Rom shudder under the weight. "Careful, you dolt!" he snapped. "And don't step on those cocktail napkins, and watch out for that puddle of spilled bubble juice!"

"Yes, brother," Rom huffed. Except for the Horta, he and Quark were alone in the bar. The rest of the staff and customers had fled upon the creature's first appearance. Even Morn had deserted his customary place at the bar to escape the monster. Too bad, Quark thought; the massive barfly could have lifted me higher and longer than Rom. Quark briefly considered firing his Dabo girls for running out on their jobs. Then again, he scolded himself privately, that's what I get for hiring reptiles. He'd dock their pay instead.

Quark's beady eyes tracked the Horta's progress across his bar. He'd identified the creature at once, of course; very little occurred at DS9 that he didn't find out about. Still, he thought Ttan's offspring had been safely stored in stasis. Watching the hungry infant make a meal of a sturdy circular table, he was reminded of the eternal wisdom of an old Ferengi adage: Children should be worked and not seen.

"How much longer must we stay like this?" Rom whined.

"Until the beast is sated or absent," Quark said harshly. He wanted to keep his profits as out of reach of the Horta as possible. Although it pained him to watch the damage to his business, the loss of his furnishings was of minor concern; most of his supplies had, after all, "fallen off a cruiser" and would be easy enough to replace. But if the Horta developed a taste for latinum . . . By the treasure of the Nagus, it made his ears ache just thinking about it.

Before his eyes, an entire case of commemorative "Prodigal" medallions (manufactured on the sly in Dr. Bashir's personal replicator) disappeared into the Horta's unrecognizable maw. Frustrated, Quark dug his heels into Rom's ribs.

Quark didn't trust banks, having managed more than one shady savings institution in his youth, but right now he wished he had socked more of his earnings away in an unlisted account in the Orion system.

A brown-suited security officer rushed in from the Promenade. One of Odo's men. His eyes gaped as he spotted the Horta on the loose, and the tower of Ferengi balancing on the bar. Maintaining a safe distance from the Horta, he shouted over the bubbling sound of melting barstools. "All civilians are to leave this area immediately. Constable Odo's orders."

"Whatever you say," Rom blurted far too readily. Quark smacked Rom's bulging cranium. He had no intention of abandoning his business to the Horta, or carrying all his precious commodities into an unruly mob of refugees. Why, there might be thieves and pickpockets at work, including a few he hadn't employed yet.

"Leave us alone, Vu Kuzas, or I'll tell your wife—and your entire temple—about your visits to my holosuites. Not to mention your gambling debts." The Bajoran turned visibly pale, and backed toward the exit.

"Uh, you have been officially warned," he said. "My responsibility is discharged." With that, he slipped out of sight, looking a good deal more a shaken than before. The nice thing about religious cultures, Quark gloated, was the endless opportunities for blackmail they gave you.

Such pleasant thoughts were interrupted by a shaking underneath him. Peering down, Quark saw that the Horta had begun to consume the very bar they were standing on. Clutching on to Quark's knees, Rom edged away toward the far end of the counter. Quark felt a rush of alarm as well; he tried to calm himself by mentally filling out insurance claims, but his lobes felt as if they were filled with ice water.

Odo, he thought angrily. *Where in recessionary hell are you?*

"Intruder alert," the computer announced. "Hostile life-forms attacking station functions. Initiating elimination procedures. . . ."

"Computer, halt all defensive procedures on my command," O'Brien snapped. The sleeves of his black-and-yellow uniform were rolled up past his elbows. Hunched over his station in Ops, he waited for the inevitable argument from the station's stubborn main computer, and just when he'd finally gotten a sort of lock on the runaway Hortas. "Bloody-minded Cardassian programming," he muttered; O'Brien wasn't sure exactly what the computer had in mind, but he knew he wasn't going to like it. DS9 itself hadn't got used to doing things the Federation way, which made its computer the bane of O'Brien's existence, and the last thing he needed to deal with right now, especially with Hortas rampaging through the Promenade. O'Brien was only too aware where his wife and child would be this time of day: right in the middle of the disaster.

Molly, Keiko, he thought. *Be careful.*

He glanced over his shoulder at the commander's office. The door was shut, but he thought he could hear Sisko arguing loudly with someone. O'Brien guessed that some Bajoran politician was still refusing to take responsibility for the now hatched and on-the-loose Hortas. Which dumped the problem back in O'Brien's lap, and the computer's.

"Warning," its artificial voice insisted, "station under attack. Safety protocols require that unauthorized life-forms be terminated immediately. Activating transporter now. . . ."

"No!" O'Brien barked. My God, the thing actually wanted to beam the Hortas into space. Forget it, he thought. No one was throwing those little snappers out into the vacuum while he had anything to say about it. "Computer, listen to me. Those are not invaders. They are, er, unruly guests. You will not take any potentially lethal action against them, understood?"

The computer fell silent for a heartbeat or two. O'Brien imagined he could almost hear the machine riffling through its files, looking for a loophole. His face grew red. "Understood?" he repeated.

"Warning," the computer said. "Dangerous parasitic infection aboard station. Health and quarantine regulations require immediate sterilization. Activating transporter. . . ."

"Damn it," O'Brien cursed. He pounded the console with his fist. "Cease sterilization procedures this minute!"

"Authorization of station's medical officer required to override public health regulations."

"What?" he sputtered. For a second, he was taken

aback. What was he supposed to do now? Dr. Bashir was light-years away, and probably knee-deep in Cardassian soldiers by now.

"Resuming sterilization procedures," the computer declared—with what O'Brien could have sworn was a trace of smugness in its tone. "Activating transporter. . . ."

"Computer, stop at once," O'Brien ordered. His ruddy face began to turn pale. His heart pounded.

"Attempting to lock on to sources of infection. . . ."

Oh, Lord, O'Brien thought. He never thought he'd be praying for Julian Bashir, of all people, to suddenly reappear. Those poor baby Hortas . . . ! O'Brien felt terrible, and the worst part, he guiltily acknowledged, was that, deep down at the bottom of his soul, one selfish part of him felt relief at solving the Horta crisis so easily. They were more than unruly guests, after all. For all he knew, they were threatening his family at this very minute.

But they didn't deserve to die in space.

"Computer," another voice suddenly interrupted. "This is Commander Benjamin Sisko. Stop transporter. Halt sterilization. This is a High Command Executive Override." O'Brien looked up and saw Sisko standing outside his office. He had been so caught up in his battle with the Cardies' merciless software that he hadn't even heard the commander emerge.

"Acknowledged," the computer said curtly. "Warning: Infestation continues to spread."

"Oh, shut up," O'Brien said. That had been too close for comfort; he'd been only minutes away from becoming an accomplice to automated infanticide. He got shaky thinking about it. His bones felt like gelatin, and he wanted desperately to slump into a chair somewhere, but not while the commander was watching.

"Problems?" Sisko asked. He walked toward O'Brien's station. From the look on Sisko's face, O'Brien could tell his debate with the Bajorans had gone badly.

"Nothing I can't handle," he said briskly. "With a little bit of help, that is. Thanks, sir."

"Any time," Sisko replied. He peered at a screen on O'Brien's station. Raw data, etched in shades of scarlet and turquoise, streamed across the monitor, Cardassian and Federation symbols mixing to form a technical pidgin unique to DS9. "How are we doing with our main problem, the Hortas themselves?"

O'Brien hastily moved his meaty fingers across the screen, trying to make up for the time he lost fighting the computer. Unfortunately, the situation had not miraculously improved during the debate. "I'm sorry, sir. A few are spreading through the habitat ring, but the rest are tearing up the core. They're difficult to track in the first place, what with their silicon-based biology and many of the internal sensors burning out. I'm not ashamed to say I wish Lieutenant Dax were here; she might be able to make better sense of these readings then I can."

That's putting it lightly, O'Brien thought silently. *I'm an engineer, not a science officer, let alone a specialist on strange alien babies. Hell, I can barely figure out my own tyke sometimes. Give me something I can handle, like a defective warp coil or an unstable transporter pattern.*

"Just do your best, Chief," Sisko said. "Can't we confine them somehow?"

"I'm trying, Commander, but they're worse than

termites. They get everywhere. I've set up shields in all the connecting tunnels, but they're burning into the cargo aisles and the turboshafts and who knows what else. They don't even need to use any of our passageways; they can make their own. And I'm not sure the forcefields even stop them." O'Brien shrugged wearily. "To be honest, the best way to track them is to look for the trail of damage they leave behind."

As if to second O'Brien's report, the screen suddenly indicated a loss of temperature controls in Crossover Bridge 2. O'Brien quickly rerouted the heating units to a backup system on Level 17. "Any luck with the Bajorans, sir."

Sisko shook his head. "Not yet. Pova is adamant. No Hortas on Bajor. I've tried to go over his head, but, so far, the director herself isn't returning my calls."

"Too bad Kai Opaka isn't there for us anymore," O'Brien commented.

"Yes." Sisko's gaze momentarily turned inward, and O'Brien recalled how close the commander and Bajor's departed religious leader had been. Maybe I shouldn't have brought her up, he thought. Then Sisko shook off his reverie and looked directly at O'Brien.

"Hopefully, Odo and his people can protect the Promenade—and prevent them from climbing to Ops. Frankly, I'm more worried right now about the Hortas left on the habitat ring, where the weapons towers are. If the Cardassians stage another raid, those are our primary means of defense. Take a team of security people and engineers and protect the towers. I'll hold down the fort here."

O'Brien nodded and headed for the turbolift. He paused and looked over Ops. The command center was fully staffed, and O'Brien recognized most of the personnel on duty: Sanger, Eddon, N'Heydor. All good people, but he couldn't help wishing that Kira and the others were on hand during this mess. Assuming they were still alive . . .

"Computer," Sisko said behind O'Brien. "Estimated location of alien life-forms."

"Infestation spreading throughout Promenade," the computer answered. It didn't actually say "I told you so," but O'Brien thought he could hear the words in its cool electronic voice.

"On my way," he said loudly, picking up his pace. Thoughts of his wife and daughter haunted him. He wanted to beam to the Promenade as fast as he could; instead, he headed for the weapons towers.

Watch out for them, Odo, he thought. *Please.*

Contracting his elongated torso to normal humanoid proportions, Odo jogged toward the infirmary. Unlike the two Hortas, who dawdled along the way, continually veering off to check out the colorful sights and smells of the Promenade, Odo was not so easily distracted from his goal. He reached the entrance of the infirmary ahead of the Hortas, and faced the oncoming creatures. Despite their short attention spans, they definitely wanted to explore the medical center. Odo wondered what sort of vitamins or radioactive isotopes Bashir had in there that were so damn attractive to Hortas.

He watched the Hortas as they headed toward him, their rough carapaces quivering like miniature mountain ranges shook by tremors, their fringes of brownish filaments rustling against the floor. They were smaller than the adult Horta shown on his screen, looking less than a meter across. Younger, less mature.

If their mother were here, Odo thought, *I wouldn't be in this fix.*

Then again, there was no reason she couldn't be.

He let his substance loosen, abandoning his face and arms and legs. He became a large pile of golden jelly, glistening and translucent. Then the jelly darkened, solidifying, and a reasonable approximation of a Mother Horta appeared under the flickering lights of the Promenade. The shape, Odo decided, was every bit as comfortable as he had imagined.

The baby Hortas seemed to approve as well. High-pitched screeching, like tuning forks gone mad, penetrated the noise generated by many Hortas running amok. Odo had no idea what, if anything, they were trying to say. *This could be trouble,* he thought, *if they expect me to answer them.*

Instead, however, the twin Hortas' delighted cries were echoed by similar screeches from all around. *That's right,* Odo thought, *call the others.* With any luck, the Hortas could communicate with each other across the entire length and depth of DS9. If so, maybe he could take care of them all with one trick. He slithered away from the infirmary, hoping to make himself more visible to the rest of the Hortas. His two squealing converts followed like ducklings behind him.

Other Hortas joined them. They poured out of the shops and vaults, shattering the air with earsplitting sirens. Thankfully, Odo no longer had ears, but he could feel the vibrations even through his imitation shell. Well, he thought, they certainly sounded loud enough to be heard from one end of the station to the other. Smaller Hortas soon surrounded him. It was difficult to count them all, especially in this unfamiliar body, but Odo realized with disappointment that he had attracted less than a dozen . . . so far.

Probably all that had invaded the Promenade, he concluded. Which meant that there were still more Hortas loose elsewhere on the station.

It was a start, though.

Like the an inhuman Pied Piper, or the legendary Marching Goddess of Daffodon IX, Odo led the Hortas back toward the habitat ring. He didn't have enough cells in the security office to hold them all, but there was a stretch of living quarters, on Level 16, that should have been evacuated by now. *Once I stow them there,* Odo thought, *Chief O'Brien can figure out a way to cage them indefinitely—if I pull off this impersonation long enough.*

Odo descended an inclined emergency ramp toward Crossover Bridge 3. Fluorescent guide lights mounted in the floor marked the way to the closest escape routes. Odo ignored them; he knew his way around DS9 before it was even called DS9. Behind him, a seething mass of Hortas screeched enthusiastically, attracting new additions every few meters. Odo wished like hell he knew what they were saying.

Several levels below the Promenade, in a dark and uninhabited turboshaft, having left Quark's holo-suites far behind, the firstborn Horta heard her siblings' cries of delight. The wild choir tugged at her instincts, tempting her to tunnel upward to join the rest of her family. Mother, she wondered; could it really be Mother at last?

Another compulsion called to her, however, touch-ing her on a level even more primal. She sensed food. *The* food. The tantalizing repast that had drawn her on ever since the two small carbon-beings had abandoned her. It was close now, she could tell. The smell and taste and feel of the food seemed to radiate from some nearby point, penetrating her shell and filling her with an irresistible hunger. She was almost there, and the roar of her aroused appetite came close to drowning out the urgent invitation of the other Hortas.

Crawling down the side of the vertical shaft, gripping the polished tracks with her tendrils, the Horta paused, uncertain which way to turn. *Mother,* she thought, starting to reverse her descent. Then another wave of hunger passed over her, driving all thought of anything but the waiting food from out of her mind. *Yes, yes,* she enthused. Digestive juices dripped from her hide, falling like acid rain down the long shaft. It was as if she could already feel the food seeping into her, hot and savory and invigorating.

Creeping as quickly as she could, struggling to hold on to the almost frictionless interior of the turboshaft, the Horta hurried down through the core of DS9.

Almost there . . .

CHAPTER
9

JULIAN ROSE and moved forward when the runabout decelerated. He made certain he stood well back this time—no sense getting in the way. Kira seemed even more on edge than before, if that was possible, and he had no great wish to distract her from her work.

As he watched, she brought the runabout down inside a deep, shadowy crater on the third moon. Velvetlike darkness covered them. Directly overhead, the gas giant filled half the sky like a painter's nightmare, its atmosphere a turbulent mass of swirling reds, fiery oranges, and dazzling whites. Five luminous gold rings circled it. Several moons hung to either side. In happier times, Julian thought, it would have been a spectacular sight.

He forced his attention back to the runabout. Major Kira shut down the runabout's engines, then started flicking switches. First the overhead lights went out, then the control panels, then the emergency lights. The walls suddenly began to close in, and Julian swallowed. The runabout felt like a coffin. Just a touch of claustrophobia, he told himself. Turning, he went back to his seat, picked up his medical bag, and sat with it on his knees. He hugged the bag to his chest. This could well be the worst part of the mission, he told himself.

Kira finished shutting down the runabout's primary systems, leaving only low-level life support, sensors, and the transporter functioning. Her anger had cooled; everything seemed to be going smoothly for once. She knew Dax would shut down the transporter after they had beamed onto the moon. After that, it would be nearly impossible for the Cardassians to find the runabout with any sort of routine scan.

She rose and hurried aft. The runabout seemed unnaturally quiet. She heard every cough, every rustle of clothing, every movement around her. At least Bashir had enough sense for once to sit down and shut up.

"Double-check your equipment," she called.

The five ensigns pulled out their weapons and checked them over. Only Dr. Bashir, futtering around with his small black medical bag, looked out of step. As if to apologize, he grinned at her in that annoyingly cheerful way of his.

"Everyone ready?" she demanded.

"Yes, Major!" the ensigns chorused.

"Uh, yes, right," Bashir said a second late.

"Excellent," Kira said. "If there are any last-minute questions, now is the time to ask them."

"How long till we can beam across?" Bashir asked.

"Twelve minutes," Dax called from the conn. "We will overtake the innermost moon in eight minutes, but I need at least four minutes more to find a safe place to beam you."

"From our first preliminary scan," Kira went on, "we believe there is an underground mining complex. If they're following standard Cardassian mining techniques, the labor will all be done by heavy automated equipment since there isn't a native population to enslave. That will work to our advantage. They won't be watching machinery as closely as they would people."

Dax added, "I will set you down as close to the main mining operations as I can. You will have to use a modified tricorder to find the Horta."

"Any more questions?" Major Kira asked. Nobody said anything, not even Bashir, so she nodded. They were as ready as they'd ever be.

"The moon is in range," Dax called. "Scanning now . . ."

Kira drew the phaser at her right hip and checked the setting. One of the Resistance's many slogans—*The only good Cardassian is a dead Cardassian*—came back to her.

"Best to set our phasers on stun," Bashir advised.

Kira glared at him and noticed that he was staring at her weapon. Then he met her gaze and his eyes narrowed ever so slightly. This was a more capable side of him, she realized, one that she seldom saw—or perhaps seldom took the time to see.

"Just in case," he said, "we need to question a prisoner. The stun setting *is* just as effective against Cardassians as humans and Bajorans, after all. I mean, uh, you can always shoot them later—I mean —if they still pose a threat—"

"I know what you mean, Doctor," Kira said.

Though she hated to admit it, he was right. Silently she adjusted her phaser's setting. "Set weapons to maximum stun, as the doctor suggests," she told the rest of the team. "We may want to question prisoners."

"I've found a safe location," Dax called back. "You're going to Level Thirty-five. Remember, signal me when you're ready to beam back up. We have a twelve-minute transporter window every one point nine seven hours from this mark."

"Ready!" Major Kira barked. Taking a series of deep breaths, she raised her phaser and prepared herself mentally for battle.

Around her, the cabin of the runabout began to disappear in a twinkle of brightly colored lights as she beamed deep below the moon's surface.

Ttan paced uneasily in the cell the Cardassians had brought her to. It had clearly been designed for humanoid prisoners: three walls, the floor, and the ceiling had been carved from solid rock. The fourth wall consisted of reinforced tritanium plating. The single doorway, in the middle of the tritanium wall, had force beams running across it.

Ttan could have tunneled out with no trouble, of course. Gul Mavek and the others must have known she could escape whenever she wanted to. Clearly that wasn't the point: they also knew she couldn't leave. She feared for the safety of her children.

Suppose they've begun to hatch by now, she fretted. *Without me there to watch them, to coo for them, to make them sleep in their shells, they will be unhappy. They will come looking. Will they find me, or has Gul Mavek suspended them in midair as he did with me? Will he leave them in the dark? Will he talk to them?*

For a second she let her acids etch into the floor, carving out a meter-deep hollow, and she sank into it. She found little comfort in the surrounding rock, however.

She wept tears of acid.

Julian materialized behind Kira and next to Ensign Parks. He felt a moment's dizziness as he grew used to the lessened gravity and almost fell when he tried to turn too quickly. Parks caught his elbow for a second, and he exchanged a quick glance with her as he caught his balance.

"Thanks," Julian whispered, meaning it. He didn't want to look like a clumsy cadet in front of Major Kira.

"You're welcome." She released him and trotted up the tunnel, her phaser drawn. Kira, Julian saw now, faced the other way with her own phaser out. She seemed to be standing watch, which made perfect sense, since they didn't want Cardassians sneaking up on them.

Julian didn't see any immediate signs of danger, so he took a moment to survey everything around him. He stood in a long, high tunnel that curved gently out of sight thirty meters in each direction. Light came from glowing cylinders jutting down from the ceiling every few paces. The tunnel walls had a wet, oily look, and they gleamed a dull green-gold.

Best get to business, he thought. Kira would have his head on a platter if he didn't have Ttan located by the time the rest of the team made it down. As if on cue, the hum of a transporter beam sounded again behind him.

He raised his tricorder and began scanning for Ttan's readings. Odd, he thought. Rather than a single silicon creature, he seemed to be picking up hundreds, if not thousands of them. Could there be a colony of Hortas here? The walls all but crawled with silicon life. No, he finally decided, the tricorder had to be wrong. He shook it. Surely Dax hadn't made a mistake—

"Doctor?" Kira called. "Where is she?"

Julian didn't glance up. "Still scanning, Major." *Perhaps it needs some minor adjustments,* he thought.

"How long?"

"I can't tell. I'm finding it difficult to pick up Ttan's readings. Something is causing interference." His fingers darted across the tricorder's controls, trying one setting after another. *Come on, come on,* he thought frantically.

The transporter beam hummed again. Julian looked up to find ensigns Muckerheide, Wilkens, and Jonsson standing there. The whole team had beamed down. They were all staring at him. He swallowed, not liking the attention.

"I'll assume it's going to take a while, then." Kira turned to the others with her usual brisk military efficiency. "We need to secure this passage. You and you, you and you." She gestured Ensign Aponte and Ensign Wilkens to the left, then Ensign Jonsson and Ensign Muckerheide to the right. "Find any cross tunnels for a hundred meters each way. Check them out, then report back. You have five minutes."

Julian took another try at finding Ttan, but again picked up thousands of silicon life-forms. *Think,* he told himself. *You're doing something wrong. What would Dax do? What would O'Brien adjust?*

He looked up again, still pondering the problem, as both teams left. The four ensigns moved in long, low leaps covering four or five meters at a step, almost like ballet dancers. Though the drawn phasers in their hands somewhat marred the image, he thought.

He ran a quick diagnostic and discovered nothing wrong with the tricorder. It *should* have worked. He should have been able to spot Ttan from a thousand meters away. Maybe the machine really *did* hate him.

What could he possibly be doing wrong? He moved to the exact middle of the tunnel. The silicon readings lessened a little. Perhaps he could decrease the sensitivity, he thought, adjusting the settings with one thumb while continuing to scan.

Julian turned once more, and suddenly he wasn't picking up any silicon at all. Then it hit him.

"What a fool I am!" he said. He glanced up and found Major Kira frowning at him. "These tunnels," he continued, taking them in with a grand gesture, "were carved out with high-powered phasers. The glassy look to the walls *is* glass. Slag, to be precise."

"What does that mean?" Kira demanded.

"Slag. Glass. *Silicon,* just like Ttan. The tunnel walls are causing the interference with my tricorder. That's why I'm having trouble spotting her."

"Great," Kira said sarcastically. "We're here, but we can't find her."

"I didn't say that," Julian said with a modest little cough. Of course he could find her; it was just a matter of time. He took another step down the tunnel. "Just that it's difficult. Give me a few more . . . aha!" he said. A blip had appeared on his tricorder. He adjusted the settings, trying to get a better reading.

"You have her?" Kira asked eagerly.

"I *think* so." He studied the display. The mass was correct, and it seemed to be moving back and forth, like a caged animal. "Yes, definitely a silicon-based life-form. It must be her."

"Where?"

"Five hundred meters east and down fifty meters. Fourteen levels above us." He met her gaze again. "Everything is calibrated properly now, Major. I won't lose her."

"Good," Kira said.

Then, over Kira's shoulder, sudden movement caught his eye. It was Ensign Wilkens almost flying down the tunnel in long, low bounds behind Major Kira. Something had gone wrong, he realized.

"Major!" he said, "I think we have trouble."

Kira whirled. "What's wrong?" she demanded of Wilkens.

Wilkens tried to stop, but couldn't in the low gravity. Julian braced himself and grabbed the man's arm. Kira grabbed his other arm, and together they managed to stop him.

"The mine ahead's in use—" Wilkens gasped. "There's a big cavern—slave labor—lots of people in chains—"

The news stunned Julian. So much for Dax's automated mine, he thought grimly. He had a strange feeling things had just become complicated. It posed a certain moral dilemma, too—how could they leave those people here? They'd have to inform the Federation when they got back to DS9. Perhaps a rescue mission could be mounted in time to save them.

"How far away are they?" Kira asked Wilkens.

"Two hundred meters, around the corner then straight."

"Did they spot you?"

"No." He stood straighter, his breathing slowing to normal. "Ensign Aponte stayed to watch them."

"I'll take a look," Kira said. She turned to Ensign

Parks. "Wait for Jonsson and Muckerheide, then fill them in. We'll be back as soon as possible."

"What about me, Major?" Julian asked. If there was going to be any action he wanted to be part of it. "What if you need a doctor?"

"Keep an eye on that Horta!" she said. "Ttan is our first concern. I don't want the Cardassians moving her without my hearing about it first."

"Major," Wilkens said. "There's one other thing. Those prisoners—they're all Bajorans!"

Great, Julian thought. Just when he thought things couldn't get more complicated, they took a horrible turn for the worse.

"What?" Kira exclaimed. "Show me!"

"This way." Together, they sprinted up the tunnel like terrestrial gazelles. In seconds they vanished around the curve of the tunnel.

Julian could only shake his head. Why did things have to be so difficult?

Swallowing nervously, Major Kira crept forward on her hands and knees. She had a bad feeling inside. *Bajoran slave labor.* The Cardassians were cruel in the best of times. They had no respect for prisoners' rights and only showed mercy and compassion when it suited some greater plan. Prisoners here would have the worst of all possible worlds.

The tunnel ended in midair roughly ten meters above the floor of a large cavern. As she neared the edge, she dropped down on her belly and inched forward until she could see everything below without being seen herself.

Her breath caught in her throat. Below, literally dozens of Bajoran men and women moved about what would have been backbreaking tasks in normal gravity. Some swung picks; others broke rocks with sledgehammers; still more shoveled gravel into a train of huge six-wheeled carts. All of the prisoners wore metal shackles around their wrists and ankles. All of them looked half-starved and badly abused. Most had blue-black bruises on their faces, and many had half-healed whip marks across their backs and arms. It was one of the most heart-wrenching sights she'd ever seen, as bad as any of the Cardassian prison camps on Bajor had been. The only difference was with the prisoners. They had no hope. She could see it in the emptiness of their gazes, the stoop of their backs, the shuffle of their steps. These people had been utterly crushed by the Cardassians. She could have been watching the walking dead.

As she watched, one woman in a tattered gray jumpsuit collapsed. Her shovel fell to the ground with a loud ringing noise, attracting an overseer's attention. As the Cardassian strode purposefully toward her, his whip raised to strike, another Bajoran dropped his pick and dashed over to help the woman. That made Kira feel a little better—they hadn't managed to kill the spirit in all of these people. The man pulled the fallen woman back to her feet and got her shoveling again before the overseer could beat her.

Kira drew in her breath. That Bajoran—she knew his face. It took a minute to place it because of the dirt, bruises, and stubble of a beard, but when she did, she knew with certainty who it was: Anten Lapyn. They'd fought together in the Resistance. If she remembered correctly, he'd been reported dead several years before the Cardassians pulled out. If he was a Resistance fighter, that probably meant the others had been, too. This whole camp must be some sort of special punishment for Bajoran prisoners of war. Just like the Cardassians, she thought bitterly, to single out the best and the bravest for special humiliation.

She began counting the overseers. Two of them lounged behind a high curtain, drinking what looked like Soonian ale from large tankards—probably off duty or on a break, she decided. Four more swaggered among the Bajoran workers. They didn't seem to have much trouble keeping to their feet. Probably wearing gravity boots, she decided. They also had stunguns of some sort at their belts—nothing more lethal than that, she thought, so the prisoners wouldn't be any threat if they seized weapons and attempted a rebellion. No doubt real soldiers somewhere deeper in the complex had more lethal weapons close at hand.

Every few minutes, as if to make a point, one or another of the overseers snapped his whip—usually across a Bajoran's back. It happened twice while Kira watched, the second time to the woman who'd collapsed. She screamed and fell, clawing at her back. The overseer laughed.

Kira curled her fingers into a fist. *We can take them,* she thought, *I know we can. There's only six. We'll have surprise on our side.*

She itched to draw her phaser, but managed to restrain herself. She had a responsibility to the others under her command. It would have to be a team effort—as Dax had so succinctly put it—when they acted.

She pushed back from the ledge, then rejoined the others where they waited. Aponte was scowling angrily, her cheeks flushed a bright red. Wilkens looked sick. Kira didn't blame him.

"What do we do?" Aponte asked in a strangled voice.

"I don't know," Kira said. To her surprise, she discovered she really *didn't* know. A year ago, she knew, she would have had the three of them charge in to save the prisoners with their phasers blasting. Was she getting old and slow, or had Benjamin Sisko's careful planning and measured responses begun to wear off on her?

"Major, they're *killing* people in there!" Aponte protested. "I saw one of those Cardie pigs whip a man till he couldn't walk, then drag him away like so much garbage!"

"They're my people," Kira said hotly. She had felt more for that one felled woman than Aponte ever would. "But we're not going to get anywhere by rushing in. Things have to be done carefully. Plans have to be made—" She broke off. *Now I'm sounding like Dax and Sisko,* she thought. "Come on," she said. "Back to the others."

Turning, she loped purposefully down the middle of the tunnel. She made a special point of not looking back, but felt relieved when she heard Aponte and Wilkens fall in behind. She couldn't get the image of the screaming woman out of her mind.

Bashir, Parks, Muckerheide, and Jonsson were talking in a little knot when she bounded around the curve in the tunnel. They looked as surprised and anxious as she felt.

"Why isn't anyone on guard?" Kira demanded, slowing. It was a serious breach of security. Not that she didn't understand it; she would have been just as anxious if someone else had gone off to investigate the report of prisoners.

"I—" Muckerheide began.

She waved him to silence. "Just don't let it happen again," she said. From his expression, she knew it wouldn't.

Dr. Bashir's brow was furrowed with concern. "Are you all right, Major?" he asked. "You look—"

"Doctor," she interrupted, "I have just seen fifty Bajoran prisoners being worked to death. Many of them are badly in need of medical attention. Some will probably die without it." She quickly filled in the rest of the details, leaving nothing out, not even the woman who'd fallen. From his expression, she knew he was as shocked and appalled as she was. "There's more," she went on. "I recognized one of them. He served in the freedom fighters with me. He was reported dead several years before the Cardassians pulled out from Bajor. They have to be political prisoners."

"It's like something out of a twentieth-century Earth history tape," Ensign Aponte added. "If I hadn't seen it, I wouldn't have believed intelligent beings capable of inflicting such pain in this day and age. They've actually got those Bajorans using picks and sledgehammers to break rocks!"

Kira gazed coolly at her. "The Cardassians had work camps almost exactly like that one all over Bajor for decades."

Aponte swallowed, but grew silent. Kira sighed inwardly. These people were her allies here; making them feel guilt over the Federation's failure to liberate Bajor wouldn't help.

Dr. Bashir cleared his throat. "I know what you're thinking, Major," he said. "Our mission is to rescue Ttan, not lost Bajoran nationals—not even friends."

Kira looked at him. "Would you leave them here?" she asked. *"Could* you? You heard how they are being treated, Doctor."

"We can't help everybody," he said. "There are only seven of us, Major. This is a bigger matter than we can handle, one that calls for diplomacy. The Federation can make a formal protest on behalf of Bajor—"

Kira snorted. "You've seen how Cardassians operate," she said. "They would deny all knowledge of this place. By the time a diplomatic mission got here to investigate, there wouldn't be a shred of evidence left—let alone Bajoran prisoners of war."

"But—" Bashir began.

"These are my people," Kira said, "and at least one of them is a friend. I can't leave them here. I intend to free them—or die trying."

"Major," Ensign Jonsson said. "With all due respect, I agree with your sentiments, but Dr. Bashir is right. A rescue is impossible. For one thing, the runabout won't hold us all. If there are fifty Bajorans working in there, who knows how many more are scattered throughout the moon? The runabout will only hold twenty. And that's not leaving any room for Ttan."

"You didn't see them," Ensign Aponte said, her eyes dark with anger. "If you did, you'd know we can't abandon them!"

"Major," Bashir said. "Perhaps we can come back for them."

"That's not an option," Kira said firmly. "As soon as the Cardassians know their security is breached, they'll pack their prisoners up . . . if they don't kill them." She looked at each of her team in turn. "I'm not asking you to do anything I won't do myself. You knew this mission would be dangerous when you accepted it. Nothing has changed; the project has just gotten larger. Somehow we'll find a way to take them all with us—or we'll leave them in charge while we go back for help. If anyone wants to back out now, speak up. You can wait here while the rest of us proceed. Well?"

Aponte and Wilkens met her gaze and nodded. Muckerheide studied the ground, but nodded too. Parks and Jonsson agreed more slowly. That only left Bashir.

When she looked at him, he drew his phaser. "I'll be at your side, Major," he said to her surprise, "whatever the outcome."

CHAPTER
10

VIEWED FROM SPACE, the weapon sail towers resembled fangs arching outward from three locations on the habitat ring. Each tower, which extended both above and below the ring, covered a 120-degree segment of the surrounding void. Smaller and less impressive than the huge docking pylons, they nevertheless carried a lot more punch; the sails could direct either phasers or photon torpedoes at any vessel or entity that dared to threaten *Deep Space Nine*.

From within, O'Brien mused, they were the usual mishmash of sinister Cardassian designs and unreliable, jury-rigged equipment. He waited, one hand on his phaser, in the stark gray hall outside the phaser monitoring room, flanked by two Bajoran security men in matching brown uniforms. Otherwise the passage was silent and empty; this level was off-limits to all but authorized personnel.

More security stood on guard at the other two weapons towers. O'Brien wasn't sure why he'd chosen

Tower 2 to defend personally, but he'd learned, after many years in Starfleet, to trust his hunches. Or "educated guesses," as he called them in official Starfleet reports.

One of the Bajorans, Gaysd Tel, stared nervously at his phaser. He seemed uncomfortable handling it. Must be used to working the Promenade, O'Brien figured; Odo didn't allow weapons of any sort in that area. "Chief?" the Bajoran said. He was a young man, in his mid-twenties probably, with slicked-back black hair.

"Yes?" O'Brien asked. He kept his eyes on the walls and floor before him. He almost hoped every single Horta would converge here. That would mean Keiko and Molly were out of immediate danger. The sooner he heard they were safe, the better he'd feel.

"It's about Hortas, sir," Gaysd said. "I've heard that they're completely impervious to phasers."

"Not exactly," O'Brien reassured him. He noticed that Battes Ang, the other Bajoran, was listening closely to the conversation, while trying hard not to be too obvious about it. Battes was an older, harder character whose grizzled face still bore the scars of years fighting in the Bajoran Resistance. "They're tough, but they're not invulnerable. According to the computer, high-intensity phaser fire at close range can knock a real chunk out of them. Maybe even kill them." His words appeared to bolster the Bajorans' spirit. Maybe too much so, he worried.

"Listen," he said firmly. "That's not why we're here. Besides, that's an adult Horta I was talking about. These are youngsters; their shells may not have hardened completely. We don't know how much phaser fire they can take. The last thing we want to do is kill them, or even injure one severely. So set your phasers on stun, and hope that's enough to turn them back."

"But what if it's not?" Gaysd asked.

"You got kids, mister?" O'Brien snapped. His temper felt strained to the breaking point. First that miserable computer, now this wrinkly-nosed stooge had to give him flak. *I should be with Keiko and the baby,* he thought.

"Uh, a niece, sir."

"Well, pretend this is your niece you're gunning for." Easier said than done, O'Brien realized, but hopefully both men got the point. He surveyed the corridor, detecting no signs of life, humanoid or otherwise. Quiet for the moment, he concluded. Time enough to check in with Ops. He patted his comm badge. "O'Brien here. Status report?"

To his surprise, Sisko himself replied, curtly voicing the words O'Brien had been dreading: "More trouble on the Promenade, Chief. Odo's gone into action; I can't talk now. Hold your position."

Sisko broke the connection, leaving O'Brien alone with his fears for his family. Despite himself, every moment of Molly's short existence replayed itself on the monitor of his memories, from her birth on the *Enterprise* (assisted by Worf, of all people!) to his kissing her goodbye this morning before he headed for Ops. The possibility that he may have seen her for the last time was too terrible to imagine. *I should have spent more time with her,* he thought, torturing himself. *I should have made sure she knew how much I loved her.*

His grip tightened on his phaser. At that instant he agreed totally with the Cardassian computer; he wanted to eliminate all the Hortas as fast as possible.

"Chief O'Brien?" Battes asked hesitantly. "Are you all right?"

"Yes," he lied. Taking a deep breath to calm himself, he opened his mouth to further reassure the Bajorans. Before he could say anything, however, a rumbling noise came from the end of the corridor. The security team snapped to attention and held out their phasers. The rumbling grew louder by the second, as if drawing nearer, but O'Brien could see nothing in the empty hall. He sniffed the air, and thought he detected the smell of melting plastic. The lights dimmed overhead. Glancing upward, he saw the ceiling sag, if only by a centimeter or so. Instinctively he placed a palm against the wall—and felt a growing vibration rattle the bones of his hand.

"They're in the ceiling!" he said as the realization hit him. Estimating that the Hortas were only a few yards in front of him, he took one step backward, upped the setting on his phaser, and fired directly overhead. The red-hot beam cut through the rhodinium sheeting and the kelinide foundation above. O'Brien adjusted the phaser to emit a wide-angle beam less than a centimeter thick, hoping to set up a "firewall" between the Hortas and the weapons tower. He tried not to think about the damage he was doing to station itself. Time enough for repairs later, he thought.

Shrill, grating cries greeted O'Brien's action. Wincing at the sharp, painful sounds, he smiled grimly. *Well,* he thought, *at least I'm getting a response.* Then, abruptly, the ceiling ahead of him erupted in a spray of steam and molten metal. A tiny globule of white-hot steel splashed against his leg, raising a blister underneath his uniform. Ignoring the stinging pain, he threw himself backward, hard against the sealed door to the phaser monitoring room. The Bajoran officers backed away as well, a second before the frustrated Hortas dropped into sight. They landed heavily upon the floor, crashing like thunder.

There were two of them: shapeless brown masses, spotted with orange and yellow warts, that quivered with anger or hunger. As the lead Horta edged toward him, O'Brien had to fight an urge to vaporize it with the phaser's full power. Instead he shouted at the two Bajorans: "Phasers on stun! Drive them back if you can!"

Gaysd stepped forward and hit the oncoming Horta with a direct blast from his phaser. On the opposite side of O'Brien, Battes targeted the other Horta. The creatures' wails made O'Brien's teeth ache, but they showed no sign of retreating. They seemed more annoyed than stunned; O'Brien wasn't sure whether to be relieved or distressed. "Keep pouring it on," he commanded. He aimed his own phaser at the floor, ready to keep the Hortas from tunneling under them.

The Bajorans held their posts. Unbroken streams of scarlet energy washed over the Hortas, breaking apart in flashes of faint blue light wherever the phaser beams intersected with the Hortas' armored plating. The Hortas' cries diminished in volume, as if, having been startled at first by the phaser fire, they were now growing used to it. If boulders could shrug, O'Brien thought unhappily, eyeing the Hortas, this is what they'd look like. Overcoming the phasers' force, the Hortas pushed forward against the beams.

"Up settings," O'Brien ordered. "One notch only." The red glow of the beams grew brighter, and he had to squint to shield his eyes, but the Hortas, unafraid now, pressed on. The closest Horta was now only a yard away. Lifting his arm, O'Brien added his own phaser to the assault on the Hortas. Indigo flashes burst and crackled over the creatures' shells. The hum of active phasers competed with the muted grinding of the Hortas. Slowly but surely, though, the unstoppable little juggernauts kept inching forward. "Hell," he muttered under his breath. Gradually, by fractional degrees, he upped the power on his phaser—to no noticeable effect.

How much was too much? He had already set his phaser for just short of what would have been a killing blast for humans, yet the Hortas treated the beam like a heavy wind and kept right on going. The faces of Keiko and Molly, possibly already dead because of monsters just like these ones, flashed through his mind. He seized that anger, tried to use it to strengthen his will enough to set the phaser on its maximum setting. His arm trembled. His fingers tightened around the weapon until his knuckles turned white. The Hortas came toward him, only a few feet away now.

Suddenly, he remembered the massacre on Setlik. The children—the babies—murdered by the Cardassians. And the first time he had been forced to kill.

Not again, he thought.

Switching off his phaser, he let his arm drop to his side. "Back off," he told the Bajorans. He'd seen what the Hortas' acid could do to solid rhodinium; he had no desire to watch it go to work on Bajoran flesh and bone. O'Brien stepped aside and let the Hortas proceed. They trundled toward the tower door, passing within a few feet of O'Brien. He could feel the heat radiating off their rocky bodies. Instinctively, he backed farther away, as if he'd been standing too close to a blazing fire. He activated his comm. "Tower personnel, evacuate Tower Two. Do not, repeat, do not engage alien life-forms. This is Chief O'Brien. Out."

Gaysd and Battes ceased their fire, and joined O'Brien behind the Hortas. They watched in silence as the creatures burned through the heavy metal door protecting the phaser station. *There go our defenses,* O'Brien thought. He prayed he had made the right decision, and hoped that the other two weapons towers were still safe.

Frankly, he doubted it.

"Careful," he told the two security men. "Watch the holes up there. Something else might fall on our heads."

"The towers are under attack, Commander," Lieutenant Eddon reported. An Andorian recently assigned to DS9, her blue antennae twitched nervously as she spoke. "All weapons systems reported inoperative."

Damn, Sisko thought. He paced back and forth on the causeway overlooking Ops. And less than twenty-four hours after an attack on a Federation vessel. Aside from the weapons built into the remaining two runabouts, DS9 was a sitting duck for any other raiders who wanted to try their luck against the station.

"Shall I notify Starfleet?" Eddon asked.

"No," Sisko told her. "Gul Dukat may be monitoring our communications, and I don't want to tempt our Cardassian neighbors." He paused to consider all possibilities before issuing new instructions. He didn't wait long, however; half the trick of good leadership, he'd decided long ago, was making decisions, right or wrong, and sticking to them. Then you hoped for the best.

"Order maintenance teams to the towers are soon as security reports them safe. I want at least one tower up and working as soon as possible. Priority on Tower Three." That was the one, Sisko knew, that faced Cardassian territory—and the direction into which Kira and the others had headed.

"Second," he said. "I want both runabouts manned and ready to depart on a moment's notice."

"For evacuation purposes?" Sanger asked. He was a young human, fresh from the Academy, who usually assisted Dax in her research. He'd clearly realized that a runabout could only transport an insignificant percentage of DS9's total population.

"For battle," Sisko explained. If the Cardassians, or anyone else, attacked the station while the towers were down, the runabouts would have to carry the fight to the enemy. As warships, they were nowhere near the class of an *Enterprise*-model starship, but, for now, they were the only game in town.

"What about the *Puyallup?*" Sanger asked.

Sisko shook his head. "No time," he said regretfully. "Divert all repair crews currently working on the *Puyallup* to the weapons towers as well." In an ideal world he would have liked to have had a Starfleet cruiser at his disposal in this crisis, but his first priority had to be the station itself. As usual, DS9 was on its own.

"Warning," the computer blared suddenly, interrupting Sisko's musings. "Direct sabotage of military facilities. Regulations call for immediate execution of alien saboteurs. Recommend death by teleportation."

Some programs never give up, Sisko thought. "Computer," he said harshly. "Bite your tongue."

"They're leaving, Chief," Gaysd told O'Brien. The Bajoran officer stood outside the tower doors, directing his tricorder toward the smooth, circular hole the Hortas had left behind.

"What?" O'Brien said. Preoccupied with his concerns for his family, as well as his failure to protect the towers, O'Brien was caught off guard by the Bajoran's remark. Had he heard what he thought he heard? "Report," he ordered, snapping to attention.

"The Hortas," Gaysd explained. "They're leaving, both of them. Motion sensors detect two large moving objects tunneling away from the weapons station."

"Where are they heading?" O'Brien asked. "The Promenade?" His fist tightened around his phaser. *I should have disintegrated them when I had the chance,* he thought.

"No, sir," Gaysd said, and O'Brien breathed a sigh of relief. "They're staying on the habitat ring, heading toward Level Sixteen."

O'Brien nodded to Gaysd. "Report to Ops. Update them on the situation, if they aren't already aware of these Hortas' movements. Tell them we need a repair team here immediately." O'Brien didn't know yet how much damage the Hortas had done to DS9's defensive capabilities, but he knew Sisko would want the towers functioning again as soon as possible, if not before. He turned away from the two Bajorans, and rested his back against the wall of the corridor. Level 16, he thought, scratching his curly red hair in puzzlement. What were the Hortas up to now; surely they couldn't have consumed all the inorganic goodies in the towers so quickly? This tower's supply of photon torpedoes alone would constitute a banquet by Horta standards. Something must have lured them away from their feast.

But what?

He needed a mouth, Odo realized, to communicate with his security team. Still disguised as a Mother Horta, he formed a tongue, a larynx, and a pair of human lips on the underside of his shell, conveniently near his comm badge. The flock of smaller Hortas trailing faithfully behind him did not notice or react to the extra orifice their "mother" had suddenly developed. Good, Odo thought. Speaking in low tones, he whispered terse instructions to security.

So far everything had proceeded even better than he'd planned. He had led the Hortas all the way from the Promenade out to the habitat ring, accumulating more and more Hortas as he drew nearer to his destination. The noisy parade following him seemed to be attracting the destructive creatures from all over the station, or so he hoped. And, almost as good, this sector of the habitat ring was blissfully devoid of civilians, who were presumably crowded like Terran cattle elsewhere. He glided down the empty hall, listening to the hungry babies chirp and scrape in his wake. A ghastly idea forced its way into his thoughts: What if Hortas nurse their young? He should have checked that point with the computer earlier. Fortunately, he recalled, they were an egg-laying species, so he'd probably escape that embarrassment. Thank goodness for the consistencies of parallel evolution! Still, the Hortas were bound to catch on to his imposture eventually.

Damn it, he cursed silently. *I'm a security chief, not a baby-sitter.*

On Odo's orders, a large suite had been cleared out and prepared for the Hortas. A Bajoran woman stood at attention outside the suite, ready to open and close the doors that Odo could not easily operate in his present form; he recognized Lieutenant Moru, the same officer who had led O'Brien's family to safety. Fine, Odo concluded; if he'd had a head, he would have nodded it in approval.

Moru unsealed the door as Odo approached. His tendrils wiggling in what he hoped was a convincing manner, Odo rumbled into the luxury-sized accommodation. A window on the opposite wall displayed a view of the Bajoran system. A large Cardassian bed had been removed to make room for the growing Hortas; in theory, Odo mused, we should be able to contain all twenty here. Then Sisko, not to mention the Bajoran government, could figure out what to do with them until Kira returned. *If* Kira returned.

Odo didn't like to think about the latter possibility. Curiously, despite her past as an outlaw and terrorist, Kira was possibly his closest acquaintance on DS9. (*Well,* he admitted grudgingly, *I spend more time trading barbs with Quark, but that is strictly business!*) He respected Kira and understood her, as much as he understood any humanoid. For that reason, however, he refused to waste too much time worrying about her; like him, she was a professional and she knew the risks. Odo also knew that Kira could take care of herself when the going got rough.

Bashir was another story altogether, although Odo had to concede the young doctor was more than competent within the narrow parameters of his medical practice. Too bad the fool had to keep sticking his eager nose where it didn't belong, in pursuit of some ridiculous, romantic notion of "adventure."

And Dax? The Trill scientist remained something of an enigma to Odo. At times she seemed admirably mature for a humanoid. On other occasions, she struck him as alarmingly frivolous, even going so far as to willingly fraternize with Quark and his kin. It was puzzling, but he had reserved judgment on her. Sisko thought highly of Dax, which counted for something. Odo had come to respect Sisko, even if he often disagreed with the naive Starfleet policies Sisko felt obliged to promote. *That's one more thing,* Odo acknowledged, *Kira and I have in common. Maybe the most important thing. . . .*

Gradually, the baby Hortas entered the suite, jostling and crowding against each other in their determination to follow their mother. They would have all made it inside already, Odo noted, except for their tendency to bunch up in the doorway, locking their bumpy hides together so tightly that they were, momentarily, unable to pass through the entrance. With much squeaking, and the occasional playful spray of acid, they managed to work their way into the suite, one by one. They were, he had to admit, significantly cuter than the average humanoid infant; was this what his own people's offspring looked like?

In all, Odo counted about twenty real Hortas, although it was hard to keep an accurate tally with their constant milling around; like a litter of newborn razorcats, the baby Hortas tended to crawl over and under each other. They scraped together like miniature tectonic plates in a museum diorama until it was hard to tell where one Horta ended and another began. Assembled in one place, they made an impressive pile.

Got them all, Odo concluded smugly. *That wasn't so hard after all.*

As soon as the last Horta wriggled its entire body into the chamber, the door slid shut at once. A turquoise light flashed over the door, indicating that the door had been locked from the outside. Lieutenant Moru at work, as instructed. Besides the door itself, forcefields should be in place throughout this sector. *Mission almost accomplished,* Odo thought with satisfaction. He'd make sure the Hortas were settled, then have Ops beam him back to the Promenade. With any luck, the rest of the station had not gone completely to hell while he'd been occupied with the Hortas.

Maybe he'd even look into Quark's missing furniture, but not before he rewarded himself with a much-needed nap in his bucket.

Screeching like rusty buzz saws, the baby Hortas crowded around Odo, surrounding him and almost smothering him in their desperate need for attention or whatever. *I wish I knew what they needed from me,* Odo thought, as his inundation in Hortas became increasing oppressive. Time to get out of here, he decided.

Then he heard a sizzling, slurping sound directly behind him, from the far end of the suite where the window looked out on the stars. Turning his senses in the direction of the noise, Odo saw a single Horta, apparently too hungry to even look to its mother, melting away the several layers of wall that separated the suite from the deadly vaccum of space. A warning siren pierced the room, drowning out the cries of the Hortas. Already, the Horta's voracious appetite had excavated a terrifying hole in the structure. Microwave nodes and life-support systems flared briefly, then fell dark, the sparks and energy surges almost lost amid the incandescent red glow generated by the tunneling Horta. Odo's Horta-like body stiffened in alarm. From the look of the damage, they were only seconds away from a blowout.

"Emergency," a computerized voice announced overhead. "Hull breach imminent. Isolating endangered sector now. Emergency . . ." The voice dissolved into a hail of static as another bank of circuitry vanished, fueling the glow and the rising steam.

Odo tried to shake off the Hortas clambering over him, every one of them clearly panicked by the siren and the static, but they seemed to be everywhere, hampering his movements and obscuring his vision. Swiftly, he abandoned his pose, dissolving into a thick viscous liquid and oozing around the mass of Hortas, who collapsed upon each other, shrieking in fear and confusion. Like a cascading wave of golden mucus, he flowed after the renegade Horta, unsure how to stop it, but knowing he had try something, for all the Hortas' sake, not to mention his own.

But it was already too late. A sudden wind of hurricane strength tugged fiercely at him, alerting him that the outer hull had been penetrated, as all the air in the suite rushed toward open space. He saw a glimpse of stars directly ahead of him, and watched helplessly as the baby Horta was sucked into the void. The wind grabbed his liquid substance, almost shredding him into a splatter of drips and flying streaks of gold. He felt the temperature dropping by the instant. He found himself flying helplessly toward the deadly hole that had already consumed the careless young Horta. Instinctively, he struggled to maintain cohesion. If he could solidify fast enough, add enough mass to weigh him down . . . ! But the icy torrent of air carried him onward, tumbling toward the blackness of space.

Somehow, he could still hear the rest of the Hortas screaming.

CHAPTER
11

"DO WE ATTACK in one wave or two?" Julian asked softly. He felt his pulse quicken at the thought of combat. "What about setting up a cross fire—"

"Slow down, Doctor," Major Kira said. "I have no intention of rushing in and attacking blindly. First we're going to need a plan. This is a team mission. I need a map of the tunnels on this level and the level below. Wilkens—"

"Let me take care of the map," Julian said quickly. That was one thing he could do quickly and easily.

"I hardly think you're qualified to scout—" Kira began.

He raised his tricorder. "I can find the walls faster and more accurately with this. Remember the interference? The walls are fused silicon. My tricorder is already calibrated to pick it up."

"Good idea. Sketch a big map on the floor," Kira said. "Something easy to see."

"Right." He opened his bag and rummaged around, looking for a marker of some kind. Silicon plaster, neurostimulator, there had to be something he could use—

"Major," Ensign Parks said. "I'm picking up an internal communication." Julian glanced up at her. She had her tricorder out and had plugged in some kind of earpiece. Her gaze grew distant as she listened to whatever they were talking about. "Something called 'Central' is talking about ore quotas," she reported slowly. "They have Cardassian freighters due sometime today."

"How many freighters?" Kira asked.

"They didn't say."

"Great." Kira turned and gazed up the tunnel. Julian could see a range of emotions playing across her face. "Hurry with that map, Doctor," she said. "I think we may be running out of time."

He bent back to his bag. The tube of antiradiation jelly would probably do best for a marker, he finally decided. It had a thick, oily texture. Squeezing a little onto his index finger, he took an experimental swipe at the floor. It left a greasy black line.

Nodding, he adjusted the sensitivity on his tricorder again. The reflections from silicon in the walls showed plainly now that he knew what he was looking at. Bending, he quickly sketched the level they were on, then the one under it. According to his tricorder, there were eight entrances to the cavern on the ground level, plus six on their current level. It should be possible, he thought, to completely surround the overseers.

Major Kira and the others ringed him as he worked. When he finished, he stood and offered the radiation jelly to Kira. "You might want to add details of the cavern," he told her.

"Right," she said. She squeezed out a bit of the

jelly. "This is the supervisor's area, curtained off," she said, adding a small square against the far wall. "This is the work area. Six-wheeled carts here. Tools here. Workers pounding boulders to gravel here."

Julian asked, "Where were the guards?" They would be the biggest problem, he knew. They had to hit them before they could raise any sort of alarm.

"Two were behind the curtain. The others were walking among the prisoners." She looked up. "We'll split into three groups," she said. "Jonsson, you're coming with me. We'll take the entrance behind the gravel dump. Aponte, you take the entrance by the carts with Parks. Muckerheide, Wilkens, and Bashir can take the entrance we already saw. As soon as everyone is in position, I'll give the order to attack. Shoot the Cardassians nearest the doors first. We can't afford any sort of warning to the rest of the complex— at least not until we know how many soldiers are stationed here."

"Let's go," Julian said to Muckerheide and Wilkens, rising. *Well,* he thought, *I did want adventure.* He took a deep breath, then started up the tunnel in long gliding steps, with Muckerheide and Wilkens at his heels.

Ten minutes later everyone was in position. Julian had only taken the barest glance at the cavern below, but what he had seen sickened him. That sentient beings should be worked so hard, so savagely, and for such a purposeless task as breaking larger stones into smaller ones loaned new depth to his understanding of Kira and her hatred for the Cardassians. When he tried to imagine growing up in a society not only used to, but expecting such treatment from their rulers— he could scarcely imagine the long-term psychological effects. Perhaps it was a miracle Kira had turned out as well as she had.

His communicator chirped, and though he'd been expecting it, he almost dropped his phaser. *Get a hold of yourself,* he mentally ordered.

He tapped his badge communicator. "Ready, Major!" he whispered.

"On the count of three," Kira said over the communicator. "One . . . two . . . three!"

And on the count of three Julian gave a war-whoop and leaped forward, phaser ready. His heart was pounding like a sledgehammer. He reached the end of the tunnel and leaped out into the cavern, a ten-meter drop suddenly yawning below him.

The world seemed to be slowing down. He scanned the crowds below for Cardassian overseers and spotted one gaping up at him, whip in hand. Julian fired and saw the Cardassian stumble. Around him other phaser shots rang out.

He scanned the crowds below. All the Bajoran workers had paused to stare in confusion. The remaining overseers were dropping their whips and grabbing at their stunguns. Someone began to scream.

Julian's forward momentum only carried him so far. He started to fall toward the ground. He fired again, but the Cardassian he had targeted ducked behind an ore wagon just in time. Two more bright phaser beams hit the Cardassian where he cowered, and Julian was pleased to see the fellow collapse, arms and legs jerking spasmodically.

More Bajoran prisoners had begun screaming. Others ran frantically this way and that, adding to the confusion. More phasers fired. Another Cardassian fell. The last two Cardassians had their stunguns out and were firing back. A bright green bolt zipped past

Julian's nose and struck Ensign Aponte behind him. He turned as she tumbled from the tunnel mouth where she'd been standing. She probably wouldn't be hurt in the low gravity, he thought in a moment of strange, almost clinical clarity.

He had almost reached the ground by then—and when he hit, tucking into a roll, he came up fast on his feet. The low gravity made him a natural acrobat here, he realized; he never could have done that on Earth.

He glimpsed movement to his left and saw a Cardassian with a stunner pushing through a clump of Bajorans. The Cardassian was firing blindly at anyone and everyone around him.

"Get down!" Julian shouted, then he gave another war-whoop and charged straight at the overseer. "He's mine! Everyone *down!*"

Bajorans dove toward the floor, covering their heads. The Cardassian whirled, stunner ready, but before he could take fire, a phaser shot caught him from behind.

Julian looked up. Kira gave him a quick wave.

"Thanks!" he called.

But Kira had already turned and fired at another target. Julian followed her shot. The phaser beam struck an overseer in the foot. The Cardassian stumbled and fell, but limped through the cavern into a tunnel.

Julian fired, but his shot went wide. The Cardassian vanished from sight.

"Bashir!" he heard Kira shout. "Go after him!"

Julian didn't hesitate. He plunged after the Cardassian, using his momentum to swing through the doorway and down the tunnel after him.

The Cardassian hadn't gotten far. His right leg dragged, and he seemed to be struggling to stay conscious. Loping forward, Julian calmly aimed, fired, and brought him down with a shot to the center of the back. Which brought the attack to a successful close, exactly as planned, he thought a little proudly.

He caught up to the fallen Cardassian. When he bent to pick the fellow up, he found his hands were shaking. His heart was pounding and his head suddenly ached. *Get a hold of yourself, Doctor,* he thought. It had to be post-combat-induced stress fatigue; he recognized the signs, though he'd never experienced it before. But then he'd never been in an organized attack quite like this one, either—and that stun beam had almost hit him in the face back there.

There was only one thing to do—wait it out. He folded his legs under him and sat, his phaser in his lap in case any more Cardassians wandered past.

Five minutes later, feeling drained but strangely exhilarated, he rose, slung the overseer over one shoulder, and headed back for the cavern. His legs felt weak and only the low gravity kept him going—that and the fact that he had work to do. From the glimpse he'd had, he knew many of those Bajoran prisoners needed of medical treatment.

He entered the cavern with his burden and stopped in surprise. The Bajoran prisoners seemed to have found new life. They had already queued up to have their shackles removed. Parks, Wilkens, Aponte, and Muckerheide were burning through the rhodinium chains with their phasers.

"Over here, Doctor!" Kira called. "Hurry!"

Her voice came from a knot of Bajorans. A lump came to Julian's throat. Unceremoniously, he dumped his prisoner on the floor and hurried over. If the Cardies had shot her—

The crowd parted for him. He was strangely relieved to find Kira kneeling on the floor cradling a Bajoran woman's head in her lap. The woman had a nasty gash across her cheek, nose, and forehead, and blood streamed from her lips.

"She's not breathing!" Kira said. She looked up. "Come on, Doctor! Do something!"

"My bag—" he began, looking around frantically. He'd had it just before the attack.

"Here." Ensign Jonsson pressed it into his hand.

Julian tore it open and pulled out a portable medical scanner. He ran the scanner over the woman's head and torso, then checked the readings. All her vital signs were at zero. The body had already begun to cool; she'd been dead for ten, perhaps fifteen minutes. He might have been able to revive her aboard a starship, but even there her chances wouldn't have been good. She probably would have suffered irreversible brain damage.

"I'm sorry," he said in a half-choked voice. "There's nothing I can do." When he looked up, to his amazement he saw tears in Major Kira's eyes.

Kira let the woman go. "Thanks anyway," she said. Turning, she strode off toward the overseers' curtain.

Something's wrong, Julian thought. He took a few quick steps and caught up with her. "Major," he said, "did you know her?"

"No," Kira said bitterly, not looking at him. "I didn't know her. She's one more statistic in the Cardassians' record of butchery."

"Then why . . . ?" He left the sentence unfinished.

"Why am I so upset?" She glared at him. He could see tears glistening in her eyes. "Why? Because it's my fault she's dead! I should have been faster. I shouldn't have waited. If I'd followed my instincts and taken the cavern with Aponte and Wilkens—"

"Major," Julian said softly. "One casualty—not even caused by our attack—is not a bad statistic."

"You don't understand, do you, Doctor?" Kira's voice had a razor's edge. "If I hadn't waited to bring everyone in on the plan, if I hadn't tried to play team leader by your damn Federation rules, that woman wouldn't be dead now."

"But *you* might be," Julian said.

"I'm a soldier—"

"So are they!" he pointed out. She couldn't blame herself for this woman's death. He couldn't let her do that.

"Well—" she finally said. "That's not the point!"

"Come on, Major," he said softly. "You know better than that."

"You're not a soldier. You can't understand."

"I may not be a soldier, but I've trained as a psychotherapist. I know you can't allow yourself to get lost in what-ifs. These people are depending on us now. They're alive, they're free, and if we don't get moving soon, all that could change."

Kira didn't meet his gaze. "Give Parks and the others a hand with the shackles," she said.

He grinned. "You don't have to say thanks. That's what doctors are for."

"Hey!" Kira's eyes suddenly widened, focusing on something over Julian's shoulder. "Stop right there!" she shouted.

Julian whirled. A Bajoran woman sat astride the chest of the Cardassian he'd stunned in the tunnel outside. She held a large rock high over her head, ready to bring it down on his skull.

Kira pushed around him and walked slowly toward

the woman, her inner conflict seemingly forgotten. "Put that rock down!" Kira said again.

Julian followed, adding, "Please, I know what you've gone through, but violence isn't—"

With all her strength, the woman slammed the rock onto the Cardassian's forehead. Bone shattered. Blood and a gray-green glop that had once been brains sprayed out in all directions.

"It's down," the woman said.

Julian ran forward, seized the woman by the arms, and shook her. "What in the name of heaven is the matter with you?" he demanded.

"He liked to rape me," she said, staring up into his face. "I can't tell you how long I've waited for this day."

"Leave her alone," Kira said. She touched Julian on the arm. "I'll take care of this."

"But—" Julian began. He still couldn't believe what he'd seen the woman do.

"I said I'd take care of it!" Kira insisted.

Julian took a deep, calming breath. *They don't view it as murder,* he thought. *They view it as war. All they've known is combat and suffering. It's going to take years for them to learn compassion again.*

Against his will, he forced himself to say, "Yes, Major," and watched Kira lead the woman toward the curtained area.

Aboard the *Amazon,* Dax monitored the rapidly increasing number of coded communications beamed back toward Cardassia from the moon. Suddenly voices came in on a low-band subspace frequency . . . two Cardassians talking privately.

This could be important, Dax thought. She activated the runabout's Universal Translator as she called the transmission up on a split screen on her monitor. For a second, bursts of white noise obliterated the images, but when she hit the side of the control panel with her fist as she'd seen Kira do with equipment on many occasions, the image jumped, then steadied. Possibly some feedback left over from the Van Luden radiation belt, she thought. Hopefully it hadn't done any permanent damage to any of the runabout's systems.

A Cardassian man and a Cardassian woman, each dressed in standard issue gray uniforms, were talking in quiet voices. She could see them, but they couldn't see her.

"—ready when you arrive," the man was saying from the moon. "I've been waiting for our duty shifts to overlap for days!"

"Oh, Yakkan," the woman said. "I've brought some body oils. I'm looking forward to rubbing them into your scales this evening." She leaned forward and gave him a seductive smile. "They're extracted from arboreal slugs on Malvestia IV."

"That sounds wonderful!" Yakkan said.

Dax tried not to gag. She considered herself open-minded and certainly experienced, but the thought of slug oils hit a nerve somehow.

"Better news, lover," the Cardassian woman went on with a seductive smile. "Our convoy has fifty new guards for permanent assignment at your base. You'll be able to take your leave this cycle after all."

As the conversation degenerated into sickening Cardassian verbal foreplay, Dax—feeling partly ill and partly embarrassed—muted the sound. It didn't look as though she'd learn much more from these Cardassian lovebirds anyway. But she had learned all she needed to know: a convoy of Cardassian starships was due to arrive any time now.

She had to warn Kira and the others. Dax calculated the orbits of the two moons and realized they would be in communication range again in less than an hour. She'd have to risk a transmission.

During the occupation of Bajor, Kira thought she'd seen everything bad that a Cardassian could do. They had murdered not just individuals, but whole families. They had raped countless thousands of Bajoran women. They had elevated physical and psychological torture to a perverse form of art.

The woman, who said her name was Corporal Naka Tormak, managed to add a few new vices to the list. The stories she told of the murdered overseer's "love-making" made Kira's skin crawl.

If she hadn't killed him, Kira would have done it herself. She felt violated—as a woman, as a soldier, as a Bajoran—just from hearing about what he'd done.

Corporal Naka had been tough, though. She'd endured, and her chance for revenge finally came. Kira hoped she would be able to sleep at night now that this particular demon had been exorcised.

"Rest for now," Kira told her. The overseers had a couple of cots set up, and she helped Tormak lie down on one. In seconds the woman was asleep, the corners of her mouth tucked ever so slightly upward as though satisfied in a job well done.

"Nerys," a man's voice said. "I thought it was you."

Major Kira glanced up to find Anten Lapyn standing by the edge of the curtain. Her old friend smiled, the weathered lines of his face breaking into unexpected planes and angles beneath a week's growth of beard and dozens of blue-black bruises. It was still a pleasant smile, but sad, marred only a little by two missing front teeth.

"Lapyn." She gave him a brief hug. "I was about to call you over."

Lapyn emptied out a tankard of pale green ale and refilled it with cool water from a jug; it seemed the Cardassians hadn't provided replicators for the overseers, let alone the prisoners. He drank long and deep, and she took the chance to study him. He looked forty pounds lighter and twenty years older than when she last saw him—how long had it been, perhaps six years before?

"You have no idea how good it is to see you," he said slowly. "I thought we'd spend the rest of our lives on this godforsaken rock."

"We don't have time for that now," Kira said. "This rescue has taken too long as it is. I need information fast. How many more prisoners are there?"

"You mean the whole moon isn't being liberated even while we speak?"

"No. We're it."

He paled. "By the prophets, Kira! Are you insane?"

"This was supposed to be a quick raid," she said. "We had no idea what we were getting into. How many others are here?"

"As far as I know," he said, "we're it."

"Do you know the layout of the mining complex?"

"Just from here to the slave pens and back again. The Cardassians did not reward curiosity."

"What about the Horta—Ttan? Have you seen her?"

"A Horta? Here?" He gave a quick bark of a laugh. "That's what this is about, isn't it? You're not here to rescue us at all."

"If we'd known you were here—" she began.

"I know, I know." He made a reassuring gesture. "We weren't expecting rescue. Davonia is a death camp. The Cardassians took great pleasure in telling us they'd listed us as dead when they sent us here, and that we'd spend the rest of our lives breaking rocks for their amusement."

"Davonia? Is that what they call this place?"

"Yes," he said. "One of the worst hellholes in space. There's pergium, latinum, nickel, iron, cadmium, uranium—you name it, it's buried here somewhere. They let heavy equipment dig for the good stuff and use us to break rocks into gravel." He laughed bitterly. "That's the price of being a troublemaker in a prisoner-of-war camp. I escaped one time too many."

Kira leaned forward. "How many Cardassians are on Davonia?" Much as his story interested her, she had to get back to the problem at hand.

"I've counted seventeen overseers," he said, "on rotating shifts. We have another four or five hours before this lot will be relieved. I've also seen a handful of real Cardassian soldiers, right down to the battle armor and heavy-duty assault weapons, and several officers." He shrugged. "And there's probably a small support staff. I'd say no more than fifty or sixty total. Now, what's this about a Horta?"

"They kidnapped her from a cruiser en route to *Deep Space Nine*. We trailed their ship here."

"What's *Deep Space Nine?*" the prisoner asked, looking puzzled.

Kira blinked in surprise. "Don't you know?" she said. "The war's over. The Cardassians withdrew from Bajor. DS9 is what we now call the old Cardassian space station. It's run by Bajorans . . . with a little assistance from the Federation."

He stared at her; then a huge grin split his face. "Well, I'll be damned. The bastards never bothered to let us know." He stood, cupped his hands to his mouth, and shouted, "The war is over! The Cardassians have withdrawn from Bajor!"

Cheers rang out from all sides of the cavern. Naka Tormak stirred happily on her cot.

Kira sprang to her feet and ripped the curtain aside. "Quiet!" she cried. "Yes, they withdrew—but that doesn't mean a thing here! Davonia isn't secured! They'll kill us all if they catch us! Now keep quiet!"

A hush fell over the crowd, but nothing could hide the jubilant expression on every Bajoran's face. The news seemed to give them new life, new hope. Perhaps, Kira thought, it would be enough to carry them even further beyond their normal breaking point. Most looked on the verge of collapse.

"What sort of transport do you have for us?" Lapyn asked. "How soon can we beam up?"

"You don't want to know."

He pursed his lips, then nodded. "I should have figured. Since you weren't looking for us, you didn't come equipped to carry us away. There isn't enough room on your ship, is there?"

"We'll make do somehow."

"Don't be foolish. We'll have to take Cardassian transport."

Kira paused. "You know, I hadn't thought of that."

"It won't be easy," Lapyn said, a far-off look in his eyes. "We're going to need real weapons, and a lot of them, plus twice as much luck as you've already had."

"You said there were sixty of them."

"There's that many of us, now, too."

Kira tried not to laugh, though she didn't think he'd

be insulted. "I hardly think you're up to it. And we only have seven phasers."

"Plus the guards' stunners," he said. "Plus picks, sledgehammers, and our bare fists, if it comes down to that."

"It won't," Kira promised.

"We're already dead," he told her. "We'll be fighting for a chance to live again. We *will* fight with whatever we have. Just like the old days."

"Just like the old days," she agreed. Perhaps they really could do it, she thought. Perhaps they really could take the whole damn moon. Wouldn't that put the Cardassians in their place. "What about guard stations?" she asked.

"I know of one," he said. "They marched us past it once to show us off to some visiting officials."

"Where is it?" Kira asked.

"Three levels up."

"We'll start there," she said, the decision coming easily. It was their best hope for now. "You'll have to come with us as a guide. The others can wait down here and gather their strength while Dr. Bashir treats their injuries. We'll be back with weapons . . . or we won't be back. Tell them while I brief my team."

CHAPTER
12

As THE VACUUM OF SPACE sucked Odo toward the breach in the hull, the beckoning black cavity seemed to widen like the expanding pupil of an enormous eye. The lost Horta's passage had left a cylindrical tunnel with smooth, rounded edges, but Odo, hurled helplessly forward by the explosive decompression, was in no position to appreciate the clean, cauterized nature of the wound. In fact, he would have preferred something jagged to grab on to.

Behind him, he heard the remaining Hortas tumbling after him, bouncing and crashing against the tunnel wall. His mind coolly assessed the danger at something close to warp speed. Hopefully, he thought, the Hortas would obstruct each other's progress, just like they had when they'd first crammed into the suite. At best, however, that gave him an extra second or two; unless he acted immediately, they would all be blown into space before Ops even knew they were gone. Odo knew *he* could survive outside the station for short periods of time. He doubted the newborn Hortas could.

It was a race, then, between the gale-force wind and his own shapeshifting abilities. He stretched urgently in all directions, while hardening his substance from the inside out. The hole filled his vision now, growing larger and closer as he flew to meet it. Beyond it, he glimpsed distant stars amid the icy blackness of space. He tried to match the hole's shape and size. The gap rushed toward him; he felt as though he were falling horizontally into a bottomless pit. This is it, he thought. Ready or not, here I come.

Odo currently resembled a huge pancake, black as carbon at the center but still moist and yellow around the edges. The tunnel ended abruptly, and his wet, sticky tendrils seized onto the rim of the hole and refused to let go. The cold became an advantage now; it helped him freeze himself solid over the entire breach, forming a patch in the ruptured hull. His grip started to slip, but Odo strained to hang on.

Then the first Horta collided against him, jarring him with the sudden impact. Another rocklike body slammed into his midsection, followed by several more blows. He'd heard of an old human punishment called "stoning." Now he knew what it felt like. The Hortas almost knocked him loose, but Odo focused on his current form, concentrating as hard as he could, until his entire body grew as stiff and unyielding as the strongest tritanium alloy. He fit over the breach like a dense, disklike, darkly colored scab. Only after he had anchored himself securely, however, did a horrific image blaze to life in his imagination: What if the Hortas burned right through him? He waited anxiously for the searing pain to begin.

Nothing. Odo counted to ten, but nothing happened, no acid came to eat away at him. With the breach sealed, the sucking wind had ceased, and the baby Hortas began crawling back to the remembered security of the suite. Doubtless they wondered where their adopted mother was, Odo guessed, but perhaps they'd learned a hard lesson from their sibling's demise: Don't burrow away from the station! He wondered if enough air remained in the chamber to keep the Hortas alive; then he remembered that the atmosphere on Janus VI had been artificially created by its human colonists. Presumably, the subterranean Hortas did not require oxygen.

Now if the automatic safety mechanisms operated the way they were supposed to and sealed the breach, he could slip out of this awkward position and get the hell away from here. Of course, he grumbled silently, that was probably too much to ask.

"Hull breach in the habitat ring," Lieutenant Eddon announced abruptly. "We're losing atmosphere."

"Get it closed, Lieutenant," Sisko ordered. He hoped desperately that the weapons towers had not been affected, and that Jake was nowhere near the rupture.

"I'm trying, sir," the Andorian said, "but the automatic safety mechanisms are refusing to activate . . . wait!" She looked up from her monitor in surprise. "Something has sealed the breach, but it's not one of the backup mechanisms." Slender blue fingers scrambled over the controls. Eddon's eyes widened as they absorbed the flowing streams of data. "Commander, sensors indicate that the seal is *organic*. Or something close to it."

Odo, Sisko realized, just as Sanger called out more information. "The breach is—was—in an evacuated sector. Security reports, though, that Constable Odo, and several of the Hortas, may have been caught in the area."

"Thank you, Ensign, but I already figured that out." Sisko leaned against the guardrail. *If this was a starship,* he thought, *I'd have a command chair to sit in.* "Eddon, reroute the sealing mechanisms through the adjacent levels. We have to assume the Hortas have consumed the circuits in the immediate level. As soon as the breach is closed, lock on to that 'organic' seal and beam him directly to Ops. I assume the transporters are working?"

"So far," she said grimly.

"Launch the runabouts," Sisko told her. Both ships had limited transporter capabilities; he wanted them out of range of the Hortas' appetite. *Those shipboard transporters may be all I have soon,* he thought, *unless I can figure out some way to get Ttan's children under control.* "Instruct the pilots to stay within beaming range of DS9." He took a deep breath, then continued to plan for the worst.

"N'Heydor," he instructed the Centaurian technician, "order DS9 evacuated of nonpermanent personnel. I want all visitors back on their ships, and those ships away from the station, in forty-five minutes. If the Hortas block anyone's passage, have them beamed directly to their vessels."

"Yes, sir," N'Heydor said. Like all Centaurians, he looked like he'd been born and raised on Earth, perhaps somewhere around Greece or Italy. He was a dependable and reliable officer who had been assigned to DS9 from the moment Starfleet took possession of the station.

"The Cardassians are bound to notice any emergency evacuation," Sanger pointed out. *He'll make a good first officer someday,* Sisko mused, *if he doesn't annoy the wrong admiral.* He wondered whether Kira had been giving the young man lessons in second-guessing his superiors.

"I think the Horta is out of the bag at this point," Sisko said wryly.

"Safety seals in place," Eddon stated. "Beaming the organic patch—I mean, Constable Odo—now."

Sisko looked toward his right. The small transporter pad hummed with energy. He squinted his eyes against the sudden glare as a column of white light appeared above the base of the transporter. Then the light vanished, leaving a black, metallic disk flopping awkwardly on the pad like a beached jellyfish. The disk oozed upward into the more familiar form of Odo. The security chief glanced quickly around him, taking in his new surroundings. "About time," he said gruffly. "I assume the suite is secure?"

"We're relieved to see you, too," Sisko replied. "Did the Hortas survive as well?"

"All but one," Odo told him. "A single Horta was sucked out into space before I was able to close the breach." His scowl softened into a look of genuine regret. "I should have reacted faster."

"I'm sure you did the best you could," Sisko said softly. He knew how seriously Odo took his responsibilities. Then, in a louder tone, he gave an order to the Andorian lieutenant. "Eddon, see if you can lock on to the missing Horta. It should be drifting somewhere in the immediate vicinity of DS9. Beam it directly to the infirmary. Notify Nurse Kabo she may be getting another patient."

"Do you think there's really a chance the Horta might have survived?" Sanger asked.

"With a Horta, who knows?" Sisko said. "Nothing else seems to hurt them." He joined Odo by the transporter. The shapeshifter looked none the worse for his unplanned excursion outside the station. Then again, Sisko reminded himself, Odo could smooth over any cuts, scrapes, bruises, or even torn clothing with a moment's thought. Presumably, he didn't even need to comb his hair. "Constable, what about the other Hortas?"

"They're confined in an unoccupied suite. I believe I rounded up all of them, although I can't guarantee that. My circumstances were not ideal for counting heads."

"Understood," Sisko said. He started to tell Odo about the damage to the weapons towers, but Sanger spoke first.

"I'm afraid they're not confined at all," he blurted, then blanched in the face of Odo's fierce, disapproving glare. "The Hortas are on the move again."

"But the shields . . . ?" Odo began.

Sanger shrugged nervously. "They don't seem to be stopping them, sir."

Sisko clenched his fists, but maintained a controlled, masklike expression. "Where are they now?"

N'Heydor answered first. The Centaurian kept his gaze glued to the screen before him. "All the remaining Hortas are heading straight from the habitat ring to Crossover Bridge Three. Commander, I believe they're coming back to the core. En masse."

I've never been face-to-face with a hungry Horta

before, Sisko thought. *Looks like I'll get my chance sooner than I planned.*

Damn.

Miles O'Brien hated jogging, but he rushed back toward Ops at something between a walk and a run. Huffing roughly, his broad face red from exertion, he felt a pain growing in his side. Still, with the Hortas wreaking havoc on DS9's already none-too-reliable innards, he didn't feel like trusting his molecules to the station's transporters. The problem in working so closely with transporters, as he had on the *Enterprise,* was that you learned too well what can go wrong. Doctors must feel the same way about major surgery, he figured.

Caught up in his gloomy ruminations, interrupted by spikes of hot agony under his ribs, he didn't see Keiko and Molly until he nearly collided with them.

"Miles!" Keiko cried out. Wearing her favorite tan jacket over a tasteful violet jumpsuit, with a thin belt cinching the jacket around her waist, she clutched little Molly to her chest. Despite the anxious look on her face, O'Brien thought she'd never looked more beautiful. Suddenly, he forgot all about the ache in his side. He enveloped his family in an immense bear hug that nothing short of a disruptor blast could have torn apart.

"Thank God," he gasped, still short of breath. "When I heard that the Promenade had been attacked . . . !"

"We're fine," Keiko assured him, stroking her baby's hair. "Molly saved the day, actually. She kept a Horta at bay by feeding him everything in sight."

O'Brien laughed out loud, feeling, for the moment,

an astronomical quantity of tension slip away. "I told you she needed a dog," he joked lamely.

A tiny smile lifted the corners of Keiko's lips. Then, reluctantly, her expression grew grave. "Oh, Miles, what now? Where should we go?"

"Just stay in our quarters until you hear otherwise." He tried to look more relaxed than he felt. "I'm sure Commander Sisko has the situation well in hand."

His badge beeped, and O'Brien forced himself to release his grip on his wife. He took a few steps backward. "O'Brien here."

Sisko's voice seemed to fill the corridor with foreboding. The commander did not sound happy. "Time to make our last stand, Chief. Report to the core entrance of Crossover Bridge Three. Odo will meet you there."

"Right away, Commander," O'Brien said, signing off. He gave Keiko a pained, apologetic look, while automatically unbuckling his phaser.

"Your last stand?" she asked anxiously. In her arms, Molly slept soundly, apparently untroubled by dreams of rampaging Hortas.

You shouldn't have heard that, he thought. *Sisko didn't know you were standing by.* "Stay in our quarters," he said. "Everything will be fine. I promise."

Bridge 3 was not far away. He jogged away and, for his own sake, didn't look back.

"Onscreen," Sisko ordered. A horizontal cross section of DS9 flashed onto the viewer, appearing as a sequence of concentric circles with the core at its center. A single cluster of red triangles, indicating the current locations of the baby Hortas, stood out sharply against the pale blue schematic. Sure enough, Sisko noted, the triangles were heading for one of the radial tunnels connecting the habitat ring to the core.

Why were they all moving toward the center of the station, as though something was drawing them on? Their current trajectory seemed too consistent, almost coordinated; he would have expected a more random pattern from a litter of unsupervised infants. Sisko wished he knew more about growth and development of Hortas. Was it possible they were communicating with each other? And, if so, to what end?

Sisko stared at the viewer, tracking the Hortas' relentless approach. "I only count eighteen Hortas," he observed aloud. "Allowing for the one casualty we know about, that still leaves us one short. Are we sure we have them all onscreen?" He wondered briefly if the missing Horta was somehow directing the others.

N'Heydor shrugged apologetically. "Maybe. Maybe not," he admitted. "We have systems failures all over the station, including the sensors. Entire levels are flooded with microwaves from damaged energy receptors. I can't guarantee we have a solid lock on every Horta."

"Understood," Sisko said. It was also possible, he thought, that one of the eggs hadn't hatched yet, or that the missing Horta had been stillborn. "Have someone check out Habitat Suite Nine-five-nine. I want an inventory on those eggs—or what's left of them."

"All security personnel are currently defending the core," Sanger pointed out.

"Then send a technician," Sisko said impatiently. "I assume we have one that can count to twenty."

"Absolutely!" the young man said hastily. Gulping nervously, he opened a comm line hurriedly. Sisko had more important things to worry about, however, than one green officer's embarrassment. He contemplated the determined onrush of Hortas apparent on the viewer. *Even if there is one more Horta on the loose,* he theorized, *the overall pattern is clear. The extra Horta is almost surely zeroing in on the core as well.*

But why?

Lieutenant Eddon interrupted his thoughts. "I located the Horta that Constable Odo saw sucked outside," she said. "It's still within range of our transporters. I'm beaming it to the infirmary now."

"Very good," Sisko said. He contacted Bashir's nurse immediately. "Do you have the Horta?" he asked her.

The voice of the Bajoran woman emerged from his badge. "It just arrived, but, Commander, I think it's dead."

Sisko's heart sank. First the mother, now the child. "Are you sure?" he asked.

"Well, it's hard to tell," Kabo conceded. "But it's not moving, and I'm not detecting any life signs." She paused. "By the Prophets, if I didn't know better, I'd swear this was just a stray meteor and not a living thing at all."

"Thank you, Nurse Kabo," Sisko said. "Please continue to monitor the . . . the body. Report any changes in its condition. Sisko out."

A terrible feeling of weariness came over Sisko as he stood in Ops. He refused to slump in front of his crew, but, at the moment, he felt as old as an admiral. He ran a hand over his scalp, unconsciously checking to see if he still had all his hair. Twenty Hortas, he thought. And now one was missing, and another probably gone forever. Up on the screen, scarlet triangles worked their way across the bridge, where his people, including Odo and O'Brien, waited to stop them once and for all.

How many of Ttan's children will I have to kill to save DS9, he thought grimly, *assuming I can even hurt them at all?*

CHAPTER
13

KIRA CREPT FORWARD to where the tunnel ended and a normal-looking hallway began. This, she thought, had to be the way to the crew quarters and administrative sector—what the Cardassians called Central. She found she was holding her breath and forced herself to exhale. *Treat it like a training exercise,* she told herself. *Keep moving. Don't hesitate. If you see anyone, shoot because you know they're going to be hostile.*

She glanced back. Lapyn nodded once. The rest of her team—minus only Dr. Bashir and Ensign Wilkens, who had stayed behind to help with the liberated Bajorans—gripped their phasers and tensed for action.

"In groups of two," Kira called softly. "Wait for my signal."

Bending almost double, she sprinted from cover. In low gravity it was almost comical—she bounded five meters at a step and almost overshot the adjoining corridor.

Take it easy, she told herself. She scrambled back

into position, then pressed herself flat against the tunnel wall. For a second she strained to listen, but didn't hear anything beyond the pounding of her heart. Phaser ready to fire, she swung out and stared down the long gray corridor.

It was deserted, as she'd expected. Gray walls, glowing white ceiling panels, and a smooth gray floor stretched far ahead of her. She could see closed doors to either side. Any of them might hold hostiles, and what appeared to be a second corridor intersected the one she stood in about forty meters farther down.

She signaled the others forward, and when they had all joined her, she stepped up onto the floor tiles.

For a second the universe swam drunkenly. She reeled to one side and leaned against the wall, gasping. Something's wrong, she thought, fighting panic. She weighed a ton. She was going to fall—

"Major?" she heard Ensign Aponte say. "Major!"

The dizziness began to pass. Kira forced herself upright, staggering a bit. Her center of balance was off, she realized, but it rapidly returned.

Then she called herself a fool for not realizing what was going on. "They're using artificial gravity in this section," she said over her shoulder. "Watch your step. I moved too quickly and the blood rushed from my head."

She hefted her suddenly leaden phaser and moved forward as stealthily as possible. She felt huge and clumsy, and her footsteps seemed to echo unnaturally loudly. A trickle of sweat ran down her neck.

She touched the first room's handpad, and the door sprang aside. Its lights flickered on. It was a storage room—food concentrates, according to the boxes. She motioned the others forward.

"That's what they feed us," Lapyn said softly,

looking over her shoulder. He made a face. "Awful stuff, but supposedly balanced for a Bajoran's minimum nutritional needs."

"I imagine the rest of the rooms along here are for storage too," Kira said, "but check the others just in case." She motioned Parks and Wilkens forward, and they began opening door after door with similar results.

Leaving them to that task, she advanced to where the next corridor intersected theirs. The guard station, according to Lapyn, lay just around the corner. She paused and listened intently for a moment, but didn't hear anything, not a voice, not a footfall, not a sigh or a snore. She had no way of telling what lay around the corner.

She wished she could use a tricorder, but couldn't risk it. There might be security monitors that would pick it up. It was down to old-fashioned tactics. She stuck her head out and took a quick glance up and down the corridor.

This corridor ended to her right in some kind of control room, with a series of two-meter-tall glass windows that looked out onto the corridor. Lapyn must have taken it for the guard station, she thought. Several Cardassians in gray uniforms sat inside watching monitors. At least one was speaking into an intercom.

Kira eased back out of sight. Luckily none of them had seen her. Motioning for Lapyn and the others to follow, she led the way back to one of the storage rooms, ushered everyone inside, and shut the door. Quickly she told them what she'd seen.

"I think we can take them," she said, "but I wonder if we should. It wouldn't gain us any more weapons. Any thoughts?" *I started out trying to make this a team effort,* Kira told herself, *and I'm damned well going to finish it that way.*

"They'll know where the weapons are kept," Lapyn said.

"We'll need to keep at least one prisoner awake," Muckerheide offered. "And persuade him to talk."

"Or use their computer," Aponte said. "There are bound to be complete maps for the complex." Everyone else seemed to agree with that. Kira nodded; it seemed like a sensible plan.

"They might not be able to see us if we crawl there," she said. "They're all seated, and their attention seems occupied with whatever they're monitoring. We'll try it that way. Let's move!"

She opened the storage room's door cautiously, peered out, then led the way back to the intersection. Dropping to her hands and knees, she peered around the corner. In the control room, she could see the back of one Cardassian's head, but the rest were out of sight.

We can do this, she thought. *We can take them.*

Cautiously, careful to make no more sounds than the barest shuffling noise on the floor tiles, she moved forward. The others followed. She reached the room's door and crouched to its left, below the window. Aponte took the other side of the door, with Muckerheide behind her. Lapyn and Jonsson stationed themselves behind Kira.

Kira reached for the door's handpad, but before she could touch it, the door whisked open on its own and a Cardassian in a gray uniform sauntered out.

Kira stunned him before he could react, then scrambled over his unconscious body and into the room. Her timing was off, but she had to make do, she knew. She couldn't let an alarm go up.

The Cardassians gaped at her. "Hands up or I'll shoot!" she cried. She motioned with her phaser. "Up. Now."

The Cardassians stood slowly, raising their hands over their heads. There were five of them, Kira counted, plus the one in the doorway.

She let the others file in before speaking again. "What is this station?" she demanded.

"Tell the Bajoran slime nothing!" the tall Cardassian on the left snarled.

"Wrong answer." Kira calmly stunned him. He collapsed, arms twitching.

None of them would talk, she knew, if they believed she wouldn't do more than stun them. She had to put some real fear into them. She turned to Aponte.

"Take the bodies out," she said, "and kill them."

Ensign Aponte paled. "Major, you can't mean—"

"That's an order, Ensign. We'll do it just like Sisko would do."

When Aponte smiled and gave a quick nod, Kira knew she understood. Ensign Aponte dragged first one, then the other out. A second later Kira heard two phaser blasts—doubtless her firing harmlessly into the wall or floor, she thought.

Kira smiled and turned back to the other prisoners. "I do so hate the sight of blood," she said. Then she hardened her voice. "Now, you!" she demanded of the next Cardassian in line. "What is this station?"

"I—uh—can't—" he whimpered.

"Wrong answer," she said, and she calmly shot him, too.

Aponte appeared in the doorway. "Another one?"

"Yes. But he almost cooperated . . . just maim this one."

"Yes, Major."

Kira swept her gaze down the line of Cardassians to the one who looked the youngest and, therefore, most gullible. His face had turned a very pale green. "Well?" she demanded. "You know the question."

"We're just technicians. We're in charge of the mining equipment on the twenty lowest levels. We don't know anything, really—"

"Too bad," she said. "I guess you've outlived your usefulness." She raised her phaser.

"Wait!" he cried. "Please! I have a wife and child—"

"Traitor!" the Cardassian next to him hissed.

"I'm trying to save all our lives," he snapped back. "Do you want to die here like the others?"

Kira stunned the fourth Cardassian, then the fifth one for good measure. The young technician backed up against a control panel, a look of fear on his face. Softly he began to whimper.

"Shut up!" Kira barked. "Pay attention, do what you're told, and answer promptly. If you do, you'll live through this to see your wife and child again. Understand?"

"Y-yes!"

She pushed him down into one of the seats. "Call up a schematic of this whole mining complex," she said. "I want to see where we are in relation to Central."

The technician turned and punched a few commands into his console. Kira leaned close to see the monitor. Rather than a detailed schematic, though, another Cardassian's face filled the screen. Kira pulled back, startled and confused. She'd been tricked. She should have known no Cardassian soldier would betray his station so easily.

The Cardassian on the screen appeared to be an

officer of some kind. "What's going on there—" he began.

"We're under attack!" the technician blurted out. "Help us!"

Kira shot the computer before he could say another word. Even as she did, she knew the damage was done; the Cardassians had been warned.

Sparks jumped as circuits shorted and couplings fried. She had to leap back and cover her face to avoid being burned. In the confusion, the technician tried to run for the door.

Aponte grabbed for him and missed, but Kira had been half expecting his break. She stepped forward and shot him in the back of the head. He slumped to the floor, unconscious.

Damn him, she thought. Feeling a helpless, frustrated rage, she kicked him in the ribs as hard as she could. It didn't help.

So much for having surprise on their side.

A moment later, a loud, shrill alarm began to blare.

The runabout's chronometer chimed softly, signaling Dax. The Trill rose from her meditations and hurried to the pilot's seat. At last, she thought, it was time to call Kira.

When she opened the communication channel, however, a surge of white noise almost deafened her. She pounded the side of the console again.

The screen went black. Dead.

She stared for a second, horrified, then hit the control panel once more. So much for Major Kira's technique, she thought grimly.

Quickly she called up a computer diagnostic. The program ran through a quick series of tests and, for once, came up with an immediate answer: the phase inverter crystal had burned out. No doubt the Van Luden radiation belt had overloaded it, Dax thought. She'd been lucky it hadn't gone dead the first time she tried to use it.

A quick check of the *Amazon*'s onboard stores revealed a spare. All she had to do was install it and she'd be set. Now, where was the emergency tool kit? It wasn't clipped in place on the rear bulkhead where it should have been.

Then she remembered that Julian had been using it to recalibrate his tricorder. She'd left him to clean up and put the tools away after she finished the job for him. Everything had been secured after the card game ended—where the hell had he put it?

She turned slowly. The tool kit wasn't anywhere in sight. With a sinking feeling inside, she realized she'd have to tear the runabout apart to find it. She started with the sleeping mats, then the table—

Julian had studied battle injuries in school and treated hundreds of patients during his tenure on DS9, but had never run into anything on the scale of what these Bajorans had suffered on Davonia. He mentally compared it to the first doctors rushing into the Nazi death camps on Earth or the dilithium mines on Konnoria V. There was so much to do, you scarcely knew where to begin. Between malnutrition, broken bones, bruises, cuts, gouges, scrapes, and general ill health and their mental state, he was amazed so many of them seemed capable of functioning at any level at all.

While Ensign Wilkens, under Kira's orders, posted lookouts in the tunnels and organized the two dozen able-bodied Bajorans into fighting teams, Julian worked on the injured. He set half a dozen broken bones, dispensed vitamin shots until his limited supplies ran out, and sealed literally dozens of cuts, gouges, scrapes, and sores. None of the Bajoran men and women were in a life-threatening state, but none were fit for any sort of strenuous activity, either. To a great degree each of them suffered from years of malnutrition, neglect, and in a number of cases, outright abuse.

He finished treating a woman with severe whip-scars across her back as Wilkens ran in from the tunnel.

"Sir," Wilkens gasped, "there's an alarm being raised outside."

Julian paused and strained to hear. "I can't hear anything—" he began.

Wilkens shook his head. "It's very faint and coming from the upper levels."

Julian wondered briefly whether they should wait where they were or try to find a safer place. That was the sort of decision Kira made best. Still, he was in charge now, and he couldn't very well waffle until Cardassians found him. And this would be the first place they looked.

"We'd better move," he said. "Get the squads together. They can help the sick or injured. We'll retreat into the tunnels."

"No," said one of the Bajorans whom Julian had just treated. He stood, flexing his arm. The patch of synthetic skin Julian had applied to a bone-deep cut seemed to be holding. "We'll fight," the man said. "I won't hide in this hole another day!"

"You're not in any shape—" Julian began.

"Hah!" He seized a pick that had been lying on the

floor. "Just show me a Cardassian! We'll see who's in shape!"

The others around him echoed his words. In seconds the whole cavern was stirring. Julian looked from one determined face to another. Six Bajorans held the guards' stunners over their heads. The others took up sledgehammers, picks, shovels—everything at hand that could serve as a weapon.

Perhaps we can help Kira, Julian thought. If there were alarms ringing, they must have been detected, but not caught. If they'd been caught, there wouldn't be any need for alarms.

"Very well," he said. "We fight. Get the carts. We're moving out of here right now."

The six-wheeled carts might prove invaluable if they ran into Cardassians, he thought. And they'd provide transport for the wounded.

He just hoped he wasn't making an awful mistake.

"So much for secrecy," Kira said, glancing around at the various control panels. "Everyone out of here. Move!"

When everyone had cleared the room, she turned her phaser up to maximum power and raked its beam across the equipment. Flames leaped and more sparks flew as delicate machinery melted. She hesitated a moment, looking at the six stunned Cardassians, but decided she didn't have the will to kill them where they lay—she wasn't a Cardassian. Besides, she thought, the Cardassians would stop to rescue their own kind, gaining more time for her and her team.

The others were waiting in the corridor. "This way," she called, darting straight ahead. She passed the first corridor, turned left at a second, and right at a third. The alarm continued to blare. Finally she came to a lift of some kind. She pushed the call button.

"Get ready!" she called, lowering the setting on the phaser to stun once more. "As soon as you see them, start firing!"

The others spread out in a semicircle, weapons raised. Kira kept one eye on the lift's readout. *Almost here,* she thought, tensing.

Even before the lift's huge double doors had whisked open, she started firing. Five blue phaser beams strafed across the lift's occupants. The uniformed Cardassian soldiers inside didn't have a chance to move, let alone fire back. They fell in a tangle of limbs, assault phasers, and drab gray uniforms.

Kira braced the door open with her shoulder. "Get their weapons," she said, "and their communicators."

One communicator in particular was already squawking, its tinny little voice all but lost beneath the mass of bodies. Aponte and Lapyn dragged the Cardassians out one at a time while the others stripped them of weapons. The ambush yielded a surprising number of knives, stun grenades, paralysis darts, and small energy weapons. In all, they now held ten Cardassian prisoners with full battle gear.

Lapyn used one of their shirts to tie up most of the weapons. Kira kept the twenty stun grenades for her own use.

"Get these back to Bashir and the other Bajorans," she said. "They're going to need them soon, I expect."

"Right," Lapyn said, and he headed back at a trot the way they'd come.

Kira picked up the communicator that was still squawking. She activated it. "Hello," she said.

"Who is this?" the Cardassian on the other end demanded.

"Major Bata Huri of the Bajoran Liberation Front. Do I have the pleasure of addressing the base commander?"

"This is Gul Mavek, yes," he snarled.

"Listen to me very carefully, Gul Mavek," Kira said. "My assault team is currently sweeping through the lower levels of your base, placing dilithium bombs with timers for later detonation. We will be beaming our fellow freedom-fighters back to our fleet very shortly. I strongly recommend your immediate evacuation of this base, unless you want a bad case of radiation poisoning. Bata out."

Kira smashed the communicator, then tossed the bits into the lift. Its doors were trying to close; Muckerheide and Aponte had to brace themselves to hold them open.

"A second more . . ." Kira said, examining two of the stun grenades. They had timers, exactly as she'd hoped. She adjusted them for thirty-second delays, activated them, and set them in the front corners of the lift. Now they couldn't be seen until you were actually inside.

Dancing back, she motioned for the two ensigns to release the doors. They did so, and the lift closed with an almost audible snap. It headed up.

"They'll send more soldiers down," Aponte said.

"I know," Kira said, her thoughts racing, "but I think they're going to be moving very, very slowly, especially if they think we've been booby-trapping the tunnels. It should buy us more time."

Ttan felt herself go rigid. That high-pitched vibrating noise that made her cilia tremble and set her silicon blood surging—she'd only heard similar sounds twice before.

Once had been on Janus VI, when a reactor had overloaded, flooding a sector of the mines with human-killing radiation. The humans had used that sound as an alarm.

The second time had been aboard the *Puyallup,* when the Cardassian ship had attacked. It had sent all of the Federation officers scrambling to their stations.

Ttan guessed this sound—so similar in many respects—also meant something had gone wrong. Had the Cardassians lost their reactor, too? Were they even now dying at their stations as they tried to stop radiation from flooding through their little underground complex?

For a half-second Ttan began to tunnel deeper into the rock, but then one of the Cardassian guards appeared in front of her cell.

"Creature," he called.

"What do you want of me?" Ttan answered.

"Gul Mavek orders you to remain here, in your cell. There is a minor security problem on another level. Do not let the alarms concern you. He reminds you that your children will suffer if you fail to obey his commands. Do you understand?"

"Yes," Ttan said bitterly. "I understand."

A beam of crimson energy blasted the wall above Julian's head, showering him with jagged bits of stone. One stung his cheek, and he jerked back. Raising a hand to his face, he felt blood.

"Just a small cut, Doctor," Wilkens assured him.

"Get those carts up here!" Julian called. He stuck his hand around the corner and fired a quick salvo from his phaser, trying to keep the Cardassians back a little longer. Six Cardassian soldiers in battle armor had been advancing steadily up the tunnel for the last five minutes. Their superior weapons coupled with armor gave them a decided edge, Julian thought. He'd already retreated half a dozen times. He didn't know how much longer his men would be able to hold them off.

Five of the six-wheeled carts rolled up. Bajorans with control boxes arrived right behind them. The carts were his last hope.

"I want you to line them up across the tunnel," he said. A blockade might well slow down the Cardassians, he thought.

"Right away, Doctor," they assured him.

As Julian watched, first one, then another rolled around the corner and lined up facing the attacking Cardassians. Phaser beam after phaser beam struck their cargo bins, punching through the rhodinium like knives through paper. The Cardassians were firing at people they assumed were hiding in the carts. There weren't any—he had known better than to leave them inside.

Suddenly inspiration struck. "Advance them!" he said. "Keep the line of carts even. Push the Cardassians back!"

He didn't know if it would work, but it was worth a try. He eased forward to see what happened as the carts began to roll down the corridor, gaining speed. Side by side, the five of them took up the entire passageway. Nobody could get by them . . . or shoot around them, which was what he'd originally had in mind when he'd ordered them brought forward.

As he watched, Cardassian phaser fire continued to strafe the carts from the other side. The soldiers seemed to be holding their positions, firing blast after useless blast. Julian sucked in a sudden horrified breath when he realized they had no intention of retreating—that they'd be killed.

He winced as startled screams and several yelps of pain came from the six unseen Cardassians. Two carts veered to the side as bodies jammed under their wheels. Still the line continued to roll forward. When they cleared the spot where the Cardassian troops had stood, Julian noticed the rather unpleasant mess they'd left behind. Not only had the carts run down the six Cardassians, the treads on their wheels had done a pretty good job of chewing them up into so much mulch.

Cheering, the Bajorans stormed out to search the remains. Perhaps something was still useable, Julian thought. He suddenly felt a little dizzy and had to sit down. *I should be getting used to battles,* he told himself.

"Doctor, you're losing blood," Wilkens said. "I think you might want to let me treat that cut on your cheek."

Julian glanced up at him. "You said it was just a scratch."

"I, uh, may have underreported it, sir. It didn't seem like the right time—"

"Yes, quite right," Julian assured him. He understood entirely. You don't tell the commander he has a bad cut in the middle of a battle.

He pressed one hand to the wound to try to stanch the flow of blood. "Get my medical bag, will you?"

"Right, sir." He hurried to get it

"Captain Dyoran!" Julian called. The tall, gaunt man stalked over, looking strangely satisfied. Like many Bajorans, Julian thought, Dyoran seemed to have a thirst for Cardassian blood that bordered on mania.

Dyoran snapped to attention and gave him a Bajoran salute. "Two working phaser rifles, six vibroknives, and fifteen stun grenades recovered, sir," he said. "And Lapyn just showed up with still more weapons. He's currently handing them out to the most able-bodied. About half of us are going to be fighting-fit."

"Great," Julian said.

"May I add, sir," Dyoran continued, "that was a brilliant move."

"Routine Federation training," Julian said with a self-deprecating little shrug. When in doubt, improvise. He'd seen Sisko do that more times than he liked to think about.

Dyoran still looked awed.

"Now," Julian told him. "I have a feeling Major Kira is stretching their security forces rather thin up above. I don't think we have anything to worry about for the time being. Send out scouting parties. I want to find a way onto the upper levels . . . an unguarded way."

"Yes, sir!" Dyoran saluted, then turned and sprinted back to the others. Minute by minute, second by second, the Bajorans seemed to be gathering their strength, Julian thought, like professional athletes gaining a second wind. In seconds, Dyoran had teams out to explore neighboring tunnels.

For a moment Julian considered trying to contact Kira, but ultimately he decided against it. She'd given him strict orders to maintain communicator silence so the Cardassians wouldn't be able to pinpoint their locations. Still, he couldn't help but wonder what was happening with her up there.

Alarms were still ringing; he could hear them in the distance. If nothing else, he knew it meant Kira was still alive and fighting. That, or the Cardassians were about to focus their complete attention on rounding up their escaped prisoners.

"A one-second delay," Kira told her team, "can be more effective than anything else, if you do it right."

She ran a trip wire across the corridor, with one end tied to the pin of a stun grenade. *What I wouldn't give for a couple of plasma bombs right now,* she thought. The next Cardassian who came down this corridor would get far more than he had bargained for, but he'd live through it. A plasma bomb, on the other hand, offered a far more permanent solution.

Rising, she checked the trip wire for proper tension, then set off up the corridor. She'd instructed Ensign Aponte to take tricorder readings for Ttan. Now that the Cardassians knew they were there, it didn't make sense for them not to use the tricorder. A Horta, Kira thought, might be more than enough to equal the odds.

"She's two levels up and a hundred and forty meters ahead," Aponte said.

"What's above us?"

"A room . . . no occupants, Major."

"Stand back." Kira raised her phaser, adjusted its setting, and began cutting into the wall. The wall-board came off easily, revealing rock. She quickly cut handholds into it. When she reached the corridor's ceiling, she sliced a very neat hole through it.

Then she holstered her phaser, tested the handholds

she'd cut for temperature, and when she decided they wouldn't burn her, began to climb. She popped up into a Cardassian's rather spartan living quarters. It had a bed, a closet, a small table, a single chair, and a replicator. The weapons rack next to the door held a phaser rifle and a pair of hand weapons.

She climbed out and helped Muckerheide and Aponte up. Muckerheide appropriated the weapons while Aponte took a quick tricorder scan of the area around them. "Two Cardassians running in the corridor outside," the ensign said. "Wait . . . they're passing us."

Kira relaxed a bit. She didn't want to fight the Cardassians on two sides at once. Having them close on her tail was bad enough.

A dull *whump* of sound echoed from the opening in the floor. Someone had just set off the first of the booby traps she'd left behind, she realized with some satisfaction. The others would be coming more slowly now. Perhaps she'd gained them a few more minutes.

"How is the corridor outside?" she asked.

"Empty," Aponte said.

Kira opened the door. "Out," she said. "Keep watch. I want to set another booby trap here." She pulled out two more stun grenades and set to work.

One more level to go, she thought, *and we'll have you free, Ttan. Hold on a few more minutes.*

"Sir," Captain Dyoran said to Dr. Bashir, "we've found a freight lift. Apparently they use it to transport raw materials to the surface. It's currently in use, but the whole process appears to be automated. I think we can override its positronic controls and have it take us to any level we choose."

"Excellent," Julian said. He patted the plastic patch on his cheek; it had been an easy matter to seal the cut, but he'd taped it anyway to make sure it stayed clean. He had a feeling he'd be doing a lot more jumping around before they escaped from the Cardassian base. "We'll move everyone up higher. There must be plenty of places to hide. When we get everyone settled, we'll find Major Kira and the others."

"Right." Captain Dyoran moved off, calling orders, and to Julian's eyes a rather motley procession soon assembled. He took his place at the head of the line of Bajorans, with Dyoran at his side, and when he judged everyone ready, he started for the freight lift. When everyone was moving, he stepped to the side to watch, lending a hand here, keeping the Bajorans' spirits up, keeping everyone to a steady pace. He wanted no stragglers. The lookouts watching the side tunnels would report it if more Cardassians appeared. In the meantime, they had to find a more secure place to hide.

Dyoran had the freight lift's doors open by the time he got there. Inside, huge cargo containers of raw ore had been stacked nearly to the ceiling.

There wasn't enough room for a single person, he saw, let alone the fifty-two now assembled. There were disappointed moans from everyone around him. Clearly they couldn't get on . . . and they didn't have hours to unload the lift. Its hijacking would be noticed fairly quickly.

"Close the doors," Julian finally said. That was the only logical decision he could make. "Send it up to the surface."

"What?" Captain Dyoran demanded. "Are you crazy?"

"I'm not up to shifting all that ore, and you're not, either," Julian said. "They'll send the lift back down when it's empty. We'll take it then."

"Right!" Dyoran said, grinning. He motioned to his men, and reluctantly it seemed to Julian they let the huge doors close with a boom that shook the tunnel.

Julian took out his tricorder and wandered a few meters up the tunnel. When he had cleared the others, he took a quick reading, searching for Ttan. He spotted her easily this time, twelve levels up and two hundred and eighty meters to the right. *That's the level we'll try for,* he decided. If nothing else, he might be able to help Kira rescue the Horta.

CHAPTER
14

SIDE BY SIDE, the Hortas resembled a range of craggy, stone hills mysteriously given the power of independent movement. Three Hortas led the pack; the width of the corridor forced the others to follow closely behind. From several yards away, the Hortas looked to be almost full grown now, about the length and width of Ops transporter pad. Any larger, O'Brien thought, and the mountains would indeed be coming to Mohammed. "What *are* they after?" he asked.

"How should I know?" Odo replied brusquely. The shapeshifter stood directly in front of O'Brien, flanked by a team of security men and women. Looking over Odo's shoulder, O'Brien saw the lead Hortas moving hesitantly, but irrevocably, onto the bridge and toward the core. Unlike his failed defense of the weapons tower, the site of which he had selected more or less arbitrarily, this time he knew he was at the crucial battlefield. Even still, skeleton forces were posted at the other two bridges in case the Hortas, despite appearances, scattered and attacked the other bridges as well. All three locations awaited his instructions. As long as their communications held out, any success here could be mimicked immediately by teams elsewhere on the core. O'Brien hoped a solution existed.

"They're moving slower than before," Odo volunteered. "I think perhaps they learned something from the disaster in the habitat ring. They don't want to end up in space, so they're more cautious in their tunneling."

"But not scared enough to stay put?" O'Brien said.

"No," Odo said. "Unfortunately, they're like humanoids in that respect. They don't know when to stay home."

And where is your home, Odo? O'Brien resisted the temptation to respond aloud. "Constable," he asked instead, "are you ready to play the 'mama' trick again?"

Odo grimaced through flattened features. "If I have to," he said. "Prior experience, however, indicates that my influence over them has its limits; even disguised as their mother, I could not keep that one Horta from tunneling to his death—and nearly killing the rest of them. Frankly, the situation calls for a better, less personal strategy." His stern blue eyes challenged O'Brien. "I thought you Starfleet types specialized in pulling technological fixes out of the air."

"If I have to," O'Brien said, bristling a bit at the sarcastic tone of Odo's comment. *Okay,* he thought, *I'll throw the first ball then.* "Shields in place," he ordered. "Maximum strength."

The oncoming phalanx of Hortas intersected with the first shield right away. Blinding flashes of turquoise energy erupted wherever the Hortas' rocky exterior came into contact with the invisible barrier. The Hortas rumbled in protest, but did not retreat. Before O'Brien's disbelieving gaze, they pushed forward against the field. Acrid white vapors rose from the Hortas' lumps and crevices. The bursts of blue light escaping the violated forcefield became diffused in a thick, roiling fog. Even from a safe distance away, the acidic fumes stung O'Brien's eyes and nose. He blinked the tears away, wiping his cheek with his sleeve. "More power," he demanded. "Divert everything to the forward shield."

A Bajoran technician raised her hands helplessly. "That's all we've got, Chief. Half the power conduits on this level are fused, melted, or otherwise inoperative."

"Steal some juice from Quark's Place if you have to." O'Brien told her. "I don't care if every holographic floozie on this entire station goes to her eternal reward, give me more power!"

"I'm trying, Chief," she said. A silver-haired woman in a gray uniform, she had pried open a control pad in the wall. Now her fingers raced through a series of operations, approaching the problem from one avenue after another. O'Brien glanced nervously at the Hortas. They were less than a third of the way across the bridge, but they were making progress. God, he thought, horrified, there seemed to be dozens of them.

"There!" the Bajoran said triumphantly, looking eagerly toward the bridge to witness the fruits of her efforts.

For a second, her exuberance seemed justified. The coruscating sparks of blue flared brighter while, simultaneously, the Hortas' low rumbling gave way to a angry, crystalline squeal that made O'Brien's ears ache. One of the aliens even appeared to bounce back a few feet, repelled forcibly by the unexpected surge in the field's strength. *Hah,* O'Brien thought, *maybe we'll put these snappers in a playpen yet.*

Then the Hortas regrouped and confronted the shield again. The crimson veins running irregularly over their armored shells pulsed with exertion, glowing redder by the moment as the Hortas visibly strained to force their way through. And, inch by inch, as O'Brien's heart pounded and his mouth grew dry as dust, the Hortas came closer. "They're not babies," he protested loudly, "they're bulldozers!"

A cry from the Bajoran woman tore his attention away from the advancing Hortas. She jerked back her hands in time as the control pad exploded in a spray of glittering electrical fire. With a quick command into his badge, O'Brien ordered the display off-line. "Are you okay?" he asked the woman.

She nodded affirmatively. There were carbon burns on her sleeves and collar. "I'm sorry, Chief. Feedback from the field caused an overload."

"Is the shielding still in place?"

"Barely," she said. She rubbed at the burns on her uniform, but only succeeded in smudging the ashy black marks.

That was all O'Brien needed to hear. *Damn it,* he cursed silently. *This hellhole barely works at the best of times, let alone when it's being nibbled to death by Hortas.* "Odo," he called out. "Your turn."

To O'Brien's relief, the security chief refrained from any caustic remark. He saw Odo roll his eyes, then watched as those eyes, the face they were lodged in, and every other part of Odo disappeared into the flux of his transformation. A breath later, a full-sized simulacrum of a Mother Horta glided down the bridge to meet its "children." *If only,* O'Brien thought, *the real Hortas find Odo's disguise as convincing as I do. . . .*

"Deactivate the shield," he said, as Odo approached the midsection of the bridge. "Or what's left of it, that is."

Odo encountered no obstruction between himself and the Hortas. Chief O'Brien's work, he wondered, or a simple power failure? The Horta's shape was as cozy as he recalled; still, he wasn't sure how long he'd be able to maintain this form. The sixteen hours allowed his solid form was running out. Furthermore, too many transformations in too few hours, plus his recent battle against explosive decompression, had left him more fatigued than he cared to let on. Odo thought longingly of the comfort of his pail, wishing for a few minutes of untroubled rest, but settled down instead on the floor of the bridge, immediately in the path of the real Hortas. *A mother's work,* he thought bitterly, *is never done.*

The Hortas did not react to his presence as enthusiastically as they had before, although the lead Horta halted less than a foot away from Odo and greeted him with the harsh, abrasive sounds of stone against stone. As before, Odo did not know how to respond so he remained silent, noting how much larger all the Hortas were now. The one nearest him was almost as massive as Odo's current form, about the size of a snack kiosk on the Promenade. He hoped that he was still dealing with infants, and not a gang of rebellious adolescents.

The nearby Horta brushed against Odo. Its voice, loud and scraping, rose slightly, then died away. It backed away from Odo while, on both sides of him, rows of pitted, pulsating Hortas eased past the disguised constable and continued their trek toward the core. Their sibling was not really retreating either; it was preparing to circle around Odo, who briefly considered falling back and turning himself into a wall. But no, he realized, that would be suicide. He'd seen what a determined Horta could do to a wall.

Instead he abandoned the impersonation. Like a swiftly flowing river of gold, he streamed back to the core-side entrance, swirling around and past the more slowly moving Hortas, until he rose up on humanoid legs at O'Brien's side. Fortunately, the Starfleet man had witnessed Odo's shapeshifts too often to be taken aback by the security chief's rapid re-formation.

"No luck?" O'Brien asked, all business.

"Either they know I'm not Ttan or they don't care." Odo shook his head wearily. "Kids these days . . ."

Odo looked like he was ready to drop, or melt, or whatever, O'Brien thought. Despite the constable's gruff attitude, his face and hands had taken on the slick, moist sheen of a candle held too close to a flame. A slight, but perceptible, ripple seemed to run under the surface of his beige uniform. O'Brien hoped he wouldn't have to mop Odo off the floor anytime soon.

Looking away from Odo, he watched the Hortas draw nearer. The first two had nearly reached the end of the tunnel, with the others trailing after them. Memories of his failure at the weapons towers came back to him. He didn't bother to reach for his phaser. The Hortas looked larger now, and even more impenetrable, and they were getting closer by the second.

The ball is definitely in my court, he concluded. *Good enough. If nothing else, Odo's latest effort bought me time to set up one more trick. With any luck, it will be the last one I need.*

"Shields at both ends of the bridge," he demanded.

Odo shook his head; it swayed unnervingly at the end of an increasingly fluid neck. "They burn through shields faster than Quark slips through loopholes." Even his voice seemed less solid. He gurgled instead of barked.

"Trust me," O'Brien replied. "The shields are for our sake." He tapped his comm, establishing a link with the central computer. "Deactivate artificial gravity in all bridges to the core."

For once, the computer didn't argue with O'Brien. Perhaps, he speculated, the damn program was as anxious to yank the rug out from under the Hortas as he was. After all, a small army of Hortas was only minutes away from invading the heart of *Deep Space Nine.* And if the Hortas started to devour the core, how long would it be before Ops itself was on the menu?

"Gravity canceled," the computer announced. O'Brien watched with satisfaction as, one after another, the Hortas floated upward, away from the floor of the bridge. They hovered helplessly, suspended in a contained zero-gravity cell. The rustling filaments along their undersides whipped about uselessly, unable to achieve more than glancing contact with any other surface. A pair of drifting Hortas bumped into each other, then ricocheted away gently in opposite directions, where one of the Hortas knocked into a third, sending it spinning down the corridor back the way it had come while tumbling over and over in the air. Within seconds, all the Hortas were colliding in midair, bouncing back and forth along the corridor. It was like viewing a game of zero-g billiards played in slow motion.

Perfect, O'Brien thought. Nonlethal, but effective.

He'd guessed that the Hortas, adapted by centuries of evolution to life within the dense interior of a planet, would be ill-equipped to cope with a gravity-free environment. And the truly beautiful part of the trap was that it actually took *less* energy to cut out the artificial gravity than to maintain it. From an engineering standpoint, he couldn't help but appreciate the economy of his stratagem, especially considering the ravaged state of all the station's systems. Maybe they could manage without Dax's scientific expertise after all.

Then the Hortas began screaming: wild, ear-piercing screams that sounded like sirens blaring, or, O'Brien acknowledged reluctantly, like baby Molly in the grip of a nightmare. "They're panicking," he whispered to Odo.

"Yes," Odo agreed. Even across the massive species boundaries separating humans from Hortas, the sound of pure fear was unmistakable.

The keening tore at O'Brien's heart, but he could have lived with the screams if necessary. Better to terrify the poor babes than to annihilate them, or to let them take apart *Deep Space Nine,* bite by bite. The frightened Hortas did more than scream, though; they were spraying acid frantically in all directions. Jets of caustic liquid, orange as fire, spurted from every crack in the Hortas' lumpy bodies. Globules of acid pooled in the air, forming glowing puddles of death levitating throughout the bridge, but for every burst that fell short of the surrounding surfaces, another spray splattered against the walls and flooring, turning solid metal into a bubbling, dripping mess that quickly evaporated to form gaping holes in the structure of the bridge. The drifting globs of acid soon found the walls as well, digging beneath the gray plating to the delicate mechanisms underneath. White-hot sparks leaped from damaged circuits. Flames and dark black smoke merged with the white steam of the Hortas' corrosive secretions.

Through the sparking and the screaming, O'Brien could barely hear the desperate reports coming over his comm, but he got the gist of it right away. The acid storm created by the Hortas in their frenzy to escape their zero-g prison was wreaking havoc on systems on every level of the bridge.

O'Brien stared at the chaos and destruction. Not far away, one of the Hortas spun end over end as it sprayed blazing orange streamers all around it, like an antique pinwheel firework. But the desperate Hortas were much more dangerous, he knew, than any crude pyrotechnic device.

"Chief O'Brien," the silver-haired technician called out. She pointed her Starfleet-issue tricorder at the sealed bridge. "Microwaves are flooding the bridge. The acid must have consumed the transmission nodes. Radiation levels are rising."

Thank heaven the shields are still in place, O'Brien thought, *but for how long?* Smoking fissures and gaping scars marred the interior of the bridge, while the shrieking Hortas caromed through a sea of smoke, sparks, and flying acid. *Forget the radiation,* he thought. *What about the structural integrity of the bridge itself?*

"Computer," he said. "Restore gravity to all cross-over bridges immediately."

The Cardassian program did not want to let the Hortas off so easily. "Requesting confirmation from commanding officer. . . ."

"Bring that gravity back now," O'Brien barked angrily, "while we still can!" As an afterthought, he added, "And, computer, locate and deactivate all damaged energy junctions." Damn it, he thought, why couldn't the Cardies have built a safe, reasonable EPS system into the station instead of their usual, cheap microwave array?

"Acknowledged," the computer replied, surrendering to his authority. O'Brien felt a sudden humming vibration under his feet, and gravity returned to the corridor with a bang and splash. Eighteen Hortas crashed to the floor at once, while blobs of drifting acid fell like rain all along the bridge. The acid doused the Hortas, but left no marks upon their invulnerable shells. O'Brien watched, scowling, as the acid ran down the Hortas' sides to wreak terrible damage on the bridge floor. How many levels, he wondered, would the falling acid burn through? He took comfort in knowing that the entire bridge had already been evacuated.

The nearest Horta, who moments before had spun like an acid-spewing top, landed upside down. Its tendrils flapped ineffectually in the air and, for a moment, O'Brien let himself hope that the Horta, like an overturned tortoise, would be unable to right itself. In that case, he'd simply grab a stick and give them all a good flip over onto their backs.

This simple plan died almost before he finished conceiving it. Before his eyes, the inverted Horta sunk into the floor, disappearing from sight. A second later, and a few yards away, it reemerged rightside up. Obviously, all the beastie needed was an instant surrounded by solids to orient itself again. "I don't believe this!" O'Brien muttered. "Can't anything stop these things?"

"On Janus VI," Odo said with obvious difficulty, "they have no predators or crime. I checked."

O'Brien glanced at his companion, trying hard not to stare too obviously. It looked like Odo had put all his effort into keeping his face, and especially his mouth, more or less intact. By contrast, gravity had pulled his hands and fingers down, elongating them so that his digits were thin, attenuated things with drop-shaped bulbs at the ends. The ripple beneath his uniform was now a surging current; Odo's substance sloshed about audibly, driven by strange biological tides, barely contained by the anthropomorphic water balloon his body had become. Tiny beads of moisture dotted his imitation flesh; if O'Brien hadn't known better, he might have mistaken them for perspiration.

"For God's sake, man," he said softly, conscious of Odo's carefully maintained dignity. "There's nothing more you can do here. Take care of yourself before, well, you know."

Odo stared at O'Brien. His face no longer had definition enough to express any emotion. The look in his eyes might have been anger, or gratitude, or feelings O'Brien could not even guess at. Odo lifted one hand and watched it stretch like taffy toward the floor.

"You're right," he said quickly, then turned away. With his peripheral vision, O'Brien caught a glimpse of something gold and wet flowing away from the scene, in the direction of the Promenade. He hoped Odo would reach his office—and his pail—in time. But was any place on the Promenade safe, with the Hortas so close to the core? Deep inside, O'Brien doubted it.

"Eyes on the bridge," he ordered the assembled team, and not just to let Odo make a clean escape. The Hortas had shaken off the trauma of their adventure in zero gravity. A mixed blessing, to be sure: the screaming had stopped, but the Hortas were on the move again.

And O'Brien had run out of tricks.

Frustrated, he slammed his fist into a bulkhead. This was the weapons towers all over again. *You're an idiot and a failure,* he cursed himself. Even little Molly had handled the Hortas better than he had so far.

Molly . . .

With a start, O'Brien realized he still had one more card to play: Molly's solution. "Feed them," he said, softly at first, then louder and as an order. "Feed them," he commanded. "Bulkheads, struts, spare parts . . . I want everything that isn't nailed down brought to the Hortas pronto!" To demonstrate, he grabbed hold of the open cover of the fused control pad and wrenched it violently free from its hinges. He flung the thin sheet of metal in the path of the closest Horta. Bent and battered from O'Brien's attack, the cover clanged loudly when it struck the floor of the bridge. The noise, or perhaps some tantalizing mineral odor the humans could not detect, attracted the Horta's attention. It edged up to the cover, snuffling at it with its tendrils. Apparently the sheet was just what the doctor ordered; with an enthusiastic rumble, the rocky creature pounced upon O'Brien's offering, hauling its entire body over and atop the cover. O'Brien heard the hiss of boiling metal and glimpsed a flash of glowing red through the fringe of filaments along the bottom of the Horta.

The sheet was a mere tidbit, however, which the Horta consumed almost instantly. Fortunately, Starfleet and Bajoran officers came scurrying from all directions, carrying fresh food for the Horta and its siblings: guardrails, cabinet doors, beakers, desktops, data clips, scanners, fire extinguishers, consoles, padds, microscopes, mugs, stepladders, carrying cases, tricorders, stools, suits of security armor, decorative kelinide-alloy molding, metal charts and public notices, even a large obsidian bust of Gul Dukat that must have been tossed unceremoniously in a closet shortly after the Bajorans laid claim to the station. O'Brien saw two hefty Bajorans carrying an entire airlock door between them. The large, gear-shaped object surely weighed a couple hundred pounds. Behind them, a Tiburonian lieutenant, the scalloped lobes of her ears flushed with exertion, clutched an engraved map of DS9; someone had painted the phrase YOU ARE HERE over the original Cardassian characters.

All spare or inessential material, or so O'Brien hoped. Still it seemed to do the job. The Hortas fell upon this bounty with an avidity that reassured him that his scheme was working, but that also distressed him owing to the sheer speed and energy with which the Hortas devoured all that was brought before them. All along the bridge, DS9 personnel stepped warily around acid-formed pits and crevices while Hortas feasted eagerly on quickly assembled piles of supplies and debris. For the present, a state of equilibrium existed, with his people adding to the piles about as quickly as the Hortas ate away at them, but how long could they keep up with the Hortas' seemingly insatiable hunger? Staring at the creatures as they burned and burrowed into the heaps of junk, O'Brien felt like the manager of an all-you-can-eat flea market, and one that was rapidly running out of stock.

To his surprise, he saw Jake and Nog among the workers ferrying material to the Hortas. The commander's son had an armful of genuine aluminum baseball bats, while Quark's nephew struggled under the weight of what looked like a cheap cast-iron treasure chest. O'Brien worked his way through the busy line of Starfleet and Bajoran officers until he caught up with the boys only a few yards away from the great Horta barbecue. He dropped one meaty hand apiece on the boys' shoulders. Nog squealed in fright, dropping the treasure chest onto the floor. The latch holding the chest's lid shut snapped open upon impact, and the contents of the box spilled out before Nog's feet. Glancing down, O'Brien saw a pile of jointed toy figurines, representing various sentient races: Vulcans, humans, Klingons, and many other types of males and females. Every figure was nude, he spotted instantly, and anatomically correct.

"Erotic action figures," Nog explained, shrugging. "Kid stuff." O'Brien realized with a start that chest had to be Nog's old toy box. Nog looked embarrassed, but only slightly, like a teenager forced to show someone his baby pictures.

Ferengi, O'Brien thought. He shook his head to clear his brain of the ghastly image of tiny Ferengi toddlers at play with these obscene little models. "Look, lads," he said, "you shouldn't be here. It's dangerous."

"But, Chief," Jake Sisko protested, "we have to help out somehow. We *have* to." Nog nodded in agreement, although O'Brien thought the nod lacked both enthusiasm and sincerity.

He was struck, however, by the intensity in Jake's voice, and the terrible yearning in the boy's wide brown eyes. This was important to Jake, O'Brien knew, although he couldn't begin to guess why. He considered the sports equipment in Jake's arms; the commander and Jake had brought those bats all the way from Earth, O'Brien recalled, and if Jake was that eager to sacrifice his own precious possessions for the sake of the station, who was O'Brien to say him nay? For an instant, O'Brien recalled his first Starfleet assignment, and how vital it had been to prove himself back then. True, Jake was younger now than O'Brien had been then, but O'Brien thought he recognized the look in the boy's—no, he corrected himself —the young man's eyes.

Sisko may never forgive me, O'Brien decided then and there, *but I don't have the heart to send him away. Besides, it's not like any place on DS9 is truly safe from the Hortas.*

And as for Nog? O'Brien averted his eyes while the Ferengi youth gathered up his scattered "playthings." Well, he conceded reluctantly, any Ferengi who was willing to throw away anything, no matter how disgusting, deserved some credit.

"Okay," he told them both, "you can stay for now, and scrounge for provisions. But I don't want you getting anywhere near the Hortas, understand? And you'll head for shelter the minute they get past the bridge. Got that?"

"Yes, Chief," Jake said. The seriousness, and the desperation, in his voice was positively heartbreaking. Then he turned away quickly, as if terrified that O'Brien might change his mind at the last minute. "C'mon, Nog, let's go lend a hand!"

Nog hesitated, gazing wistfully at a tiny replica of a green Orion slave girl. He held the figure up to his eyes and twirled it between his fingers.

"Nog!"

The Ferengi hastily stuck the doll into his boot and chased after his friend. "I'm coming," he hollered. "I'm coming! What's the rush?"

A red-suited crewman bustled past O'Brien, blocking his view of the boys. He carried a globe of Bajor that had most of its borders redrawn with bright green, erasable ink. Nobody, O'Brien noted, was sacrificing their weapons yet. Not far away, two Hortas happily shared an oval conference table. The stacks of melting Horta fodder glowed like bonfires.

"Security," he instructed, hoping to bring some semblance of order to the scene, "continue bringing food for the Hortas. Maintenance and engineering, try to . . ." He paused and shook his head wearily. "Hell, try to repair the damage security is doing."

This is not *a long-term solution,* O'Brien reminded himself firmly. The Hortas' progress toward the core had been stalled temporarily, but not for long. Did he have to dismantle all of DS9 in order to save it? He prayed that Commander Sisko could pull some sort of rabbit out of his hat, as he had before, while there was still something of the station left.

In the meantime, he threw another console onto the bonfire.

"Gangway!" Quark grunted. "Let us by!" He scurried toward Crossover Bridge 3, shoving his way past teams of station personnel coming and going with heaps of Horta fodder. Behind him, Rom tried to keep up with his brother, even though he was laden with a stack of steel carrying cases, piled up past the top of Rom's head. Quark looked over his shoulder. Why was Rom dawdling at a time like this? "Hurry, you dolt. There's no time to waste."

"Perhaps, brother," Rom stuttered, "we would waste less time if you would help me carry these boxes?" His arms were wrapped around the bottom crate and his whole body swayed with the effort to keep the piled cases from tumbling over.

Quark merely hissed in reply. Some questions were not worth answering. He darted around a tall Coridan officer lugging a foot-long silver rod. He briefly considered informing her that the artifact in her hands was in fact a sacred Bajoran relic, which it was, but why bother? There was no profit in it. Besides, she was too skinny for anything else. He started to hurry past several more Starfleet flunkies, then heard a too familiar voice pipe up to the rear.

"Oh, excuse me. I mean, you don't want to feed that to the Hortas. The Bajorans would be very upset. . . ."

"Rom!" Quark snapped. He ground his molars together in frustration. Sometimes he wondered if his brother had been purchased in a discount offspring sale; if so, Quark bet that Rom had been marked down considerably.

Unsolicited helpful advice, offered free of charge! Quark marveled at the sheer magnitude of Rom's foolishness. *Next,* Quark thought bitterly, *he'll be offering* refunds!

As he drew nearer to Bridge 3, the activity around Quark increased. He navigated through the commotion, frequently looking backward to make sure Rom hadn't fallen too far behind. Then, for a second, his eyes widened as he saw two unexpected sights heading down the corridor in the opposite direction: an immature male Ferengi and a dark-skinned human youth. He stroked one ear thoughtfully as he hurried on. What were Nog and Sisko's son doing here? Those two had to be up to something. Quark resolved to look into the matter at the first opportunity. After all, as the Rules of Acquisition so wisely counseled: One person's secret is another person's opportunity.

First, however, he had to get by Miles O'Brien. The human spotted Quark as soon as the Ferengi neared the bridge. He placed himself directly in Quark's path, his arms crossed atop his oversized human chest. "Hold it right there, Quark," O'Brien barked. "What in blazes are you doing here?"

Quark scoped out the scene before answering. As far as he could tell, Odo was nowhere nearby. Of course, the problem with Odo was that you never could tell for sure. It would serve that sanctimonious shapeshifter right, he thought, if Odo were to turn into a chair or some such—and find himself fed to a Horta by an overeager Starfleet cadet. Quark cackled at his little private joke, then turned his attention back to Chief O'Brien.

"Doing my part as a public-minded citizen to help preserve *Deep Space Nine.*" Quark gestured toward Rom and his heavy load. "I understand you're having a scrap drive of sorts."

"Right," the human said dubiously. "Whatever you're selling, Quark, we're not buying, so you might as well be on your way."

"Selling?" Quark exclaimed, clutching his chest as if shocked by the very notion. "Who said anything about selling? I am donating these, my own personal possessions, for the greater good of all concerned."

"Right," O'Brien said again. The Starfleet officer had obviously been spending too much time with Odo, Quark concluded, and had been contaminated by Odo's relentless suspicion. It could be worse, though; Odo would have figured out this entire scam already.

"Look," Quark cajoled O'Brien, "do you want all this or not? Frankly, from what I've heard, you're in no position to be picky." Quark looked beyond O'Brien's looming form to where dozens of uniformed officers were energetically feeding bits and pieces of DS9 to the approaching Hortas. The cries of the feasting monsters echoed off the increasingly bare and skeletal walls.

O'Brien sighed loudly. His eyes were tired and bloodshot. "Okay," he said. "What have you got?"

"Kamoy syrup!" Quark declared, ignoring the way O'Brien's face wrinkled at the very thought of the noxious stuff. "Gallons and gallons of delectable, irresistible, Cardassian kamoy syrup. Just the thing for a hungry Horta!"

And all of it completely unsalable, Quark gloated, but thoroughly insured. And who knew? Despite that blather about "donations," maybe he should file some sort of claim with the Federation as well? He could conceivably be compensated twice for the loss of the same useless merchandise. A venal grin threatened to break out over Quark's features. Modesty be damned, he thought; this is a stroke of genius.

"Oh, go on with it then," O'Brien said grudgingly. He stepped aside and let Quark and Rom pass. "God knows there's little you can do to make the situation worse." Then O'Brien strode away and started shouting orders to workers who were patching holes in the bulkheads with plastene sheets. Quark caught snatches of O'Brien's directives, something about "infrastructure" and "babies out with bathwater," but he really didn't care about any of that. The lure of easy profit drew him on.

Various security officers looked warily at Quark as he and Rom scampered and staggered, respectively, toward the waiting Hortas. "Fresh supplies," he called out by way of explanation. "Top priority. Chief O'Brien's orders." At the very edge of the bridge he found a team of sweaty Bajorans passing materials hand-over-hand, like an old-fashioned bucket brigade, to the Hortas on the bridge. Quark felt a twinge of alarm when he saw how close the creatures were to the core and, by extension, to his bar. Still, there was nothing he could do about that now. He snatched the uppermost case from Rom's pile and handed it over to the feeding team. Standing on his toes to get a better view, he watched gleefully as the case was transported by a succession of busy hands to a craggy rocklike entity even larger than the ones who had attacked his bar earlier.

The Horta, upon reducing a redundant air filter to a blackened smear on the floor, approached Quark's donation with inhuman enthusiasm. Its questing forward tendrils stripped away the metal casing. Kamoy syrup, pink and oily, leaked from the perforations in the container. The Horta lurched forward suddenly, consuming the entire box in one acidic gulp.

Then, without warning, the Horta backed away abruptly. It made a peculiar retching noise, then spewed out a revolting stew of shiny melted metal and pink slime. The Bajorans threw another case to the Horta, but this time the creature gave it a wide berth, and so, as Quark watched in horror, did its assembled siblings. The security officers had to feed the nearest Hortas a partially dissembled diagnostic unit to keep the distraught beasts from tunneling away into the very floor of the bridge.

A Starfleet ensign grabbed Quark by the upper arm and began to escort him away from the scene. Quark barely noticed. His gaze kept going back to the regurgitated pink-and-silver mess the Horta had left behind.

I don't believe it, he thought. It was too terrible to accept, but there was no way to deny the awful truth.

Even a Horta wouldn't eat kamoy syrup.

CHAPTER
15

KIRA FINISHED RIGGING the booby traps over the hole in the floor, then stood back to check her work. Everything looked perfect—the slightest pressure on the trip wire would set off the grenades. Let that be a lesson to the Cardassians: even one Bajoran could hold an army at bay.

Turning, she jogged out into the corridor. It was still deserted. The alarm shrilled more loudly than ever out here, a blaring *wheep-wheep-wheep* noise that grated on her nerves and made her want to cover her ears. If it affected her that way, she knew it would be bothering her pursuers as well.

"This way," she said, turning left. She headed up the corridor at a dead run. Rounding the corner, she came face-to-face with a Cardassian technician in a one-piece blue uniform. The Cardassian dropped a data board and dove toward a nearby room.

Kira stunned him, then paused and looked back at Ensign Aponte. "I need more warning, Ensign." She didn't add, *If he were a soldier, we'd all be dead now.*

"Sorry, Major." Aponte looked at her tricorder somewhat sheepishly. "We're being followed," she said. "About fifteen Cardassians. I don't think they set off the last trap you left, either, Major."

"Damn," Kira said. Well, she thought, they couldn't fall for the same trick forever. "What's ahead?"

"A lift . . . wait! There are people aboard it. A lot of them, too."

Kira glanced around frantically. Where could they hide? She didn't see any cover, just the door the technician had dived for. Pressing the handpad didn't work; it chirped at her. Locked, she thought.

She took a step back, thumbed her phaser to full power, and fired. The locking mechanism disintegrated, and the door whisked to one side, revealing a laboratory of some kind. Three Cardassians in blue smocks stood behind a table littered with half-assembled equipment. One of them snatched a phaser from the table and fired, but Kira ducked out of the way. If the Cardassian had been a soldier with a soldier's quick reflexes, she'd be dead now, she thought.

Heart pounding, she pressed herself flat beside the door and drew a stun grenade. This had better work. She set it for a two-second delay, then tossed it into the room.

In answer, a phaser blast nearly took off her hand.

"Two . . . one . . ." she counted.

The grenade went off with a satisfyingly loud *whump* of sound. The corridor shook, and dust shot out from the laboratory.

Kira didn't wait. She whipped around and dove through the door, then rolled up into a crouch, swinging her phaser around to cover anyone still moving. Dust settled; the three Cardassians lay on the floor in an unconscious heap. Most of their equipment looked like it had shattered beyond all repair.

Quickly she circled the room, stepping over broken tables and shattered equipment. Just her luck—the room proved to be a dead end, with no other exits or entrances. She'd have to cut another exit for them.

"Watch for the soldiers," she told the two ensigns. "Keep them back as long as you can. And I want constant reports."

"Right, Major," Aponte said.

Kira moved to the back of the room and used her phaser to cut a hole in the floor. This time she dropped a couple of stun grenades through first, to get rid of any possible resistance below, but rather than descend to the next level, she raced back out into the hallway. No sign of their pursuers yet, she was relieved to see.

"This way," she said, heading up the corridor once more. "I cut a hole in the floor," she called over her shoulder. "Hopefully they'll think we moved down a level. It may gain us a few minutes while they check it out. How far is Ttan now?"

"Another sixty meters ahead," Aponte said. "Still one level up. She hasn't moved."

"What about the Cardassians behind us?"

"Moving slowly. I think they're checking for traps as they go. I'd say we have four minutes at most before they find that room. A bigger concern is that lift—its doors just opened."

Great, Kira thought. She'd forgotten about it. "How many aboard?" she demanded.

"Fifty-two. Major—" She looked up in surprise. "I'm reading them as Bajorans!"

"No," Kira moaned. It couldn't be Bashir—she'd told him to stay put.

"Yes," Aponte said, studying the tricorder's readings. "I think there are also two humans among them."

"That idiot!" Kira raged. "Why couldn't he follow orders and stay where he was? Why—" She broke off suddenly. This wasn't the time or the place. What was done was done; she'd hash it out with Bashir later, and he'd better have a good excuse. For now, she'd make the best of things.

"Come on," she said. "We'll join them, then set up a real ambush for the Cardassians behind us." She tapped her badge communicator for the first time. "Doctor, are you there?"

"Here," her badge chirped. "We've moved up a few levels—"

"I know where you are," she said. "Stay there. We will join you in three minutes. Make sure you don't shoot us. Out."

Julian stepped forward and waved when he saw Kira appear with the rest of the team at the end of the corridor. Now that they were back together, they could get on with rescuing Ttan, he thought.

Kira sprinted toward him. "Get back in that lift!" she shouted. "Hurry!"

The way she sounded, half the base had to be on her heels, Julian thought. He groaned inwardly, but turned and began giving orders. Luckily Captain Dyoran was there to help.

He helped carry on several of the sickest, whose strength had given out on the trek to the lift. They had no weapons and couldn't defend themselves. When they were safely aboard, he hopped out and began counting heads as the Bajorans filed aboard. Fortunately they seemed to know how important speed was. In record time they had all scrambled aboard, leaving just enough space at the front for Kira, the ensigns, and him.

He stuck his head out and looked up the corridor. Kira had stopped halfway to the lift while the others sprinted ahead. They brushed past him as they got on board.

He turned to Muckerhcide. "What level does she want us on?" he asked.

"The next one up," the ensign said. "Get ready to go. There are Cardassians right behind us."

"The level is punched in," Captain Dyoran called. "I'm holding the doors open. Tell her to hurry up."

Julian stepped out. Kira had been backing up slowly and was only four or five meters away. Now he could see what she was doing—setting the timers on what looked like Cardassian grenades of some kind. As he watched, she lobbed them down the corridor as far as she could. When she had set the timer on the last one, she turned and darted toward him.

As he stepped out to help Kira into the lift, a pair of Cardassian soldiers ducked across the far end of the corridor. Two more leaped out, knelt, and raised their phaser rifles. Julian whipped up his own phaser to fire, but before he could, an explosion rocked the far end of the corridor. Kira careened into him. Thrown off balance by the blast, he went down. Smoke and dust filled the air. Several ceiling panels fell, and the lights overhead began flickering out one by one. Julian's eyes began to sting. He blinked frantically, then began to cough. *Something's on fire,* he thought.

He rose to help Kira, but she dove at him, hitting his knees and knocking him flat as a sizzling bolt of energy zipped past his face.

"Keep down!" she cried. "We're going to have to crawl!"

"Right!" he managed to say. His chest felt like it was on fire and his eyes were tearing. A third and fourth blast shook the tunnel. The lights went out completely; the only illumination came from the lift. Julian struggled to his knees, but more phaser fire zipped past him. He dropped flat—and felt himself freeze up. He didn't know which way to turn.

Then he felt a hand on his arm. It was Kira, he saw. She pressed her face close to his ear. "Watch my feet!" she said into his ear. "Follow them!"

She turned and began to slide up the corridor on her belly, using her hands and knees to propel herself forward. Julian swallowed at a bitter taste in the back of his throat and tried to emulate her movement. It was more difficult than he would have imagined, and his legs and arms began to ache almost immediately.

He raised his head as they neared the lift and saw Kira make it inside. Tucking his head down, he crawled the last two meters, then rolled inside. The doors closed with a hiss and they started up.

"You idiot!" Kira snapped.

"What?" Julian looked up at her through a blur of tears and felt only confusion.

"This is no time for silly heroics! You should have waited aboard the lift with the others!"

He took a deep breath, coughed a bit, decided he was feeling better, and climbed to his feet. For a second he swayed, dizzy, and then he felt a dozen Bajoran hands reach out to help steady him.

"Major," he said. "Thanks."

Kira looked around. "You've been busy," she said. "I didn't send you this many weapons."

"We had a run-in with a Cardassian security team down below," he said. "I thought it best to join you here."

Kira nodded slowly. "As soon as we find Ttan, we'll head up and look for a Cardassian transport ship of some kind."

The lift suddenly jolted to a stop. Julian caught himself before he fell, then looked at Captain Dyoran, who was pounding on the controls. The doors didn't open.

Dyoran said, "They cut our power."

"What do we do now?" Julian asked. He looked at Kira. If anyone would have a plan, he knew it would be her.

Kira stepped forward, forced her fingers between the double doors, and heaved. They moved a few centimeters.

Julian saw at once what she had in mind. "Come on," he said, "help us." He grabbed the doors too, as did several others, and together they pried the inner doors open. They were half a meter short of the next level, Julian saw—it was just a matter of opening the outer door, the ones that sealed the corridor from the lift shaft.

He helped force the outer doors open. They slid aside more easily than the inner doors, and he found himself gazing out into another corridor exactly like the one below. The lights were still on here, though, and it was deserted.

"Major?" He made a step with his hands and offered it to Kira. Nodding, she stepped out; then he boosted Dyoran, then Muckerheide up.

"We'll find Ttan," Kira said.

"Right," Julian said. He handed her his tricorder. "You'll need this. I'll get everyone out of the lift and organized. Call if there's a problem."

Kira accepted his tricorder. He watched as she and Dyoran trotted up the corridor in search of the Horta.

Aboard the runabout, Dax surveyed the ruins around her. Piles of blankets, pillows, backup supplies, and combat rations littered the floor. After an hour's search she still hadn't found the emergency tool kit. She'd already missed the first window to contact Kira and the others, and if she didn't find the tool kit soon, she feared the Cardassian reinforcements would arrive before she could warn them.

If I were an immature human doctor, Dax thought, where would I put it? She sat in the seat where Julian had been, folded the table out of the wall, and tried to put herself into his shoes. It had been a long time since she'd felt quite that young and awkward.

Of course, she realized, he'd go for the fast and easy solution. He'd drop the tool kit into the first available space. Which happened to be the opening the table left when it was folded out.

She reached in and felt the smooth, cool plastic handle just inside and out of view, alongside a cup of cold replicated coffee and what felt like the remains of the ham sandwich she'd seen him eating. Yuck.

She pulled the tool kit out, unfolded it, and removed the three shiny metal instruments she needed: a spheroid diatronic calibrator, a boxlike phase inducer, and most importantly a standard Federation-issue screwdriver.

Returning to the communications console, she dropped to the floor and rolled underneath to get to work. Time was running out. Fortunately it wouldn't take long to swap out a single crystal. . . .

Kira thought she heard talking and motioned frantically for Dyoran to slow down. He drew up behind her.

Two? she pantomimed.

He nodded an *I think so.*

Kira took a quick glance, spotting two guards in front of a door. She regretted it when the guard closest to her suddenly whipped around and fired. The shot went wild, but it was enough to make Kira drop and roll back under cover.

"Just two?" Dyoran asked.

"Yes," she said, climbing back to her feet.

Her badge communicator beeped. "Major," she heard Dax's voice say.

Kira tapped her badge. "This really isn't a good time, Jadzia." She stuck her arm around the corner and fired her phaser blindly. Someone screamed.

"There's something I have to tell you," Dax said. "There's a Cardassian convoy about to arrive."

"I know, I know!" Kira snapped. "Kira out!"

She risked a quick glance around the corner and an energy beam almost took her head off. Damn cagey, she thought, pretending to be hit like that. She reached around the corner and fired blindly again.

"Cover me," Dyoran said. "I'm going to cross the corridor."

"Ready," Kira said grimly.

Ttan came to full consciousness with the noise of phaser fire echoing in her senses. She rose and went to the door to her cell. Through the force-bars she could see the corridor. Both guards had vanished.

Once more she heard sounds of phasers firing, and then the scream of an injured humanoid. She paused. Should she leave her cell? Gul Mavek might hurt her children if she did. But there was clearly something wrong. Had the Federation come to rescue her?

It was a possibility she hadn't dared consider until now. The sounds of battle were getting more intense. She knew she had to do something, and soon.

Finally she decided to take a look. If they had come to rescue her, she had to let them know about her children. Perhaps they already had them. Perhaps it was a matter of their finding her and beaming her back to their ship to join them!

She burrowed through the stone wall, then out into the corridor, right behind the two guards who had been watching her cell. One of them whipped his weapon around and shot her at point-blank range. The phaser beam traced a painful line across Ttan's back.

Ttan quivered all over for a moment, then leaped on top of him, acid pumping. In seconds his fragile carbon body had been reduced to a smoking black smear on the hallway floor.

The other guard was still firing at someone else up the corridor, but Ttan leaped on him, too, for good measure. As his flesh disintegrated under her, she felt a strange thrill of satisfaction. *It was self-defense,* she told herself. *That's what I'll tell Gul Mavek if he questions me.*

She surged forward. Two more humanoids were advancing down the corridor. They had smooth skins, like Captain Dawson of the *Puyallup,* but neither of them wore a Federation uniform. Clearly they weren't Cardassians. Who were they?

The woman in the lead raised her hand in greeting. "Ttan!" she said. "My name is Major Kira. We have come to free you."

Joy, joy! Ttan thought. It was true. The Federation had sent these people to rescue her.

She stopped in front of the female and asked, "Where are my children?"

The Universal Translator made a strange gurgling noise. Ttan hesitated, puzzled, then turned to examine it.

The Cardassian who had shot her moments before had hit her translator device, she realized with a gritty feeling inside. She tried again and got the same strange gurgling noise.

"I can't understand you," Kira said. "What's wrong?"

Slowly, very carefully, Ttan excreted acid in the exact pattern the Federation used for written communication. It was a clumsy method of communicating, but Ttan had been taught to use it in case of an emergency, and this certainly qualified as one.

When she moved back, large, blocky letters had been burned into the floor. They said: NO TRANSLATOR.

"Can you understand me?" the woman asked.

YES, Ttan wrote. She moved back and etched another line: SAVE MY CHILDREN.

"Your eggs?" Kira said. "They are safe on DS9— the space station you were traveling to. The Cardassians didn't take them. They only beamed you to their ship."

Relief flooded through Ttan—and then a cold rage like none she had ever felt before. Gul Mavek had lied to her. He had threatened her children when in truth he didn't even have them. It made everything else he had done seem all the more terrible. And she had believed him. Prime Mother, she had believed him!

Everything seemed to be coming together at once, Kira thought with little sense of satisfaction. But now they had to get out of here. She checked the time. They still had forty minutes before Dax would be in transporter range again . . . they had to hold out that long. Then perhaps Dax would be able to beam them a few at a time into whatever docking area this base had.

"Major!" Bashir called.

She jogged to the corner. With a sound like rolling boulders, the Horta followed.

"What is it?" she called.

"According to Ensign Aponte," he said, "there are Cardassians approaching from every side!"

"Bring the others here," she said.

When she turned back to the Horta, she found that Ttan had left a new message on the floor: I HELP. TELL HOW.

"Ttan," Kira said, hardly daring to hope. "We need transportation away from here. Our ship is not large enough to carry all of the prisoners we have rescued. We need to capture one of the Cardassians' ships. Do you know how to get to their docking bay?"

YES, Ttan wrote. FOLLOW.

Turning, the Horta touched the wall and seemed to melt into it. Her body turned almost sideways, leaving a tunnel large enough for a person to walk upright. The sides of the tunnel smoked a bit from the acid she excreted, but the acid became inert almost at once. Kira stuck her head into the tunnel. Yes, she thought, this would more than do. She could see Ttan burrowing upward at a rapid pace, and on a twenty-degree slope. Clearly the Horta knew exactly what angle humans needed to comfortably follow her.

Kira stepped back. The others were coming up the corridor in twos, with Dyoran and Muckerheide leading the way. Bashir darted around the marchers and trotted up to her side.

"We have about five minutes, Aponte says," he reported. "They think they have us pinned down here." He stared up the Horta's tunnel. "Amazing," he breathed. "Is she all right?"

"She's been hit by several phaser blasts, but she's a tough girl," Kira said. She wished they had a dozen more like her. "You can doctor her to your heart's contentment once we get aboard the shuttle. She's taking us to the docking bay now."

Julian jumped away from the tunnel. "She's coming back!"

"What?" Surprised, Kira leaned forward to see.

Sure enough, Ttan was on her way back down, enlarging the tunnel even more as she went. Two, possibly three men could have walked through it abreast. Suddenly Ttan veered to the side and disappeared from sight. She darted in and out several times, and when she was done, the first section of her new tunnel now had a large stone column standing in its center, supporting the roof.

Kira grinned. If they removed that column, she knew the roof would fall in—making pursuit impossible. Ttan knew what she was doing, all right.

"Why is she doing that?" Bashir asked. "I don't understand."

"She's left a booby trap of her own," Kira said, and she took a moment to explain. By the time she finished, most of the rescued prisoners had queued up.

Next came the hard part—waiting while everyone entered the tunnel.

"Aponte, Muckerheide," she called. "You and Captain Dyoran go through first, then Wilkens and Jonsson. Everyone else, follow in pairs. This tunnel leads straight to the docking bay. We'll find a ship there. Dr. Bashir and I will hold our position here, then seal the tunnel to keep the Cardassians from attacking our flank."

"Right!" Ensign Aponte said. She ducked into Ttan's tunnel, and the others followed, two at a time.

Ten, Kira counted, twenty, thirty. She could only stand and watch, tapping her foot and trying not to get too jumpy. *Hurry,* she breathed. The Cardassians would be there soon.

She glanced at Bashir. He was taking tricorder readings. "They're closing in!" he warned. "Both sides!"

Forty, Kira counted. Forty-two, forty-four. Come on, come on. Then she realized they weren't going to make it.

Tensing, she raised her phaser. "Get ready to fire," she said to Bashir. "As soon as you see movement. Then duck through the tunnel."

Forty-four, forty-six . . .

"What about you?" Bashir demanded.

"I can take care of myself," she said. Forty-eight—

Something rattled down the corridor toward them. It took her a half-second to focus on it. "Stun grenade!" she shouted, and instinctively she threw herself on Bashir.

She got Bashir to the floor just as the grenade went off—and just as the last pair of Bajorans were about to duck into Ttan's tunnel.

Then the walls were shaking and she felt the floor

heave under her almost like a thing alive. Lights flickered and died, and with a horrible metallic ripping noise, something fell on top of her from the ceiling.

She must have blacked out for a second, for the next thing she knew, she was inside the tunnel with Dr. Bashir. He was panting for breath in the semidarkness, and his eyes were wild.

"The last two—" she gasped.

He shook his head. "They didn't make it into the tunnel. They're both dead, crushed when the ceiling caved in."

Kira tried to stand and almost blacked out again from the pain that lanced through the whole left side of her body. She glanced down. Her left leg was folded back at an odd angle, against the joint. Oh, by the Prophets, no. Broken, she knew. She felt sick inside. She bit her lip. He must have injected her with painkillers, she thought, for her to be conscious at all.

Bashir gently turned her head to face him. "Easy, Major," he said, voice grave. "Do you have another stun grenade? Anything explosive?"

"No," she said. Her voice sounded small and distant. *I'm going into shock,* she realized. *This can't be happening. They need me too much.* Her gaze drifted down toward her leg again. She stared, disbelieving. How could it look like that? That couldn't really be her leg, she decided.

"Major?" Bashir turned her face toward him again. "Major! The column is still in place! Ttan's tunnel hasn't collapsed!"

"Yes," she said vaguely. She reached for her weapon, but it had vanished. "Give me your phaser," she said.

"I lost it in the blast," he said.

233

Kira drew a breath, then let it out with a gasp. Pain so intense she couldn't move, couldn't breathe racked her left side.

"Major?" Bashir said. "What should I do? Help me, Major. I'm counting on you."

She whispered, "Leave me. I've done what I had to. I'll slow you down. Get to a ship . . . get the others out of here. . . ."

"I can't do that," he said.

"It's an order!" she gasped.

"Whatever you say," Bashir said. "You're a real hero, Major. Never forget that."

For a second, Kira smiled. Then everything went black.

CHAPTER
16

AFTER SEVERAL TRIES, Sisko succeeded in going over the deputy secretary's head. Vedek Sloi, director of the Bajoran Council on Ecological Controls, appeared on the small screen in Sisko's office. It was not a clear transmission; her image wavered in and out of focus, and was sometimes distorted by waves of phosphor "snow." More evidence of the Hortas' destructive handiwork, Sisko knew.

"Vedek Sloi, thank you for responding to my inquiries." *Finally,* he added privately. The Vedek had been ducking his calls for hours, during which time the all-consuming Hortas had practically reduced the station to its bare bones.

The Bajoran cleric, her gaunt features framed by a headdress of folded red fabric, acknowledged his greeting with a nod. "I apologize for the delay," she said. Persistent static gave her voice an unnatural, crackling accent. "The work of the Prophets, and of the council, is never-ending."

Sisko was not surprised to discover that Secretary Pova's superior was also a religious leader. On Bajor, the line between church and state was often uncomfortably thin. He hoped Sloi was more like the Kai Opaka and less like Vedek Winn and her followers. Kira could have informed him, discreetly, on Sloi's reputation and politics, but Kira, of course, wasn't here. *Major,* he wondered, *where in hell are you? I need that Mother Horta back* now.

"I understand," he said. "Still, our situation is urgent. I assume you have been briefed on the emergency?"

"My respected colleague, Pova Lerg, has kept me apprised of the details. He has also shared his opinions on the matter, with which I am inclined to agree. The Hortas do not belong on or below the sacred soil of Bajor."

Damn! He'd half-expected this reaction, but Sisko refused to back down now. "With all due respect to your friend Pova," he said, deliberately letting some of his irritation creep into his tone, "perhaps he hasn't made our position perfectly clear. While we debate, the Hortas are on the verge of invading the core of DS9. Despite our best efforts, they are destroying this station and endangering the lives of everyone aboard, human *and* Bajoran. We have to transfer the Hortas to Bajor immediately."

The Vedek shook her head. "The Prophets created Bajor according to their divine plan, a plan which clearly does not include the Hortas. If such creatures were meant to exist on Bajor, they would have dwelt here from the beginning. What you are proposing is anathema."

Beneath his desk, and out of sight of Vedek Sloi,

Sisko's foot tapped angrily against the floor. Incredibly, he found himself missing Pova, who at least pretended to secular motivations. "But alien life-forms have visited Bajor before," he pointed out. Indeed, the Prophets themselves were far more alien than the Hortas, although this was not an argument likely to appease a Vedek.

"And our people have been the sadder for it," Sloi said. "Or have you forgotten the Cardassians?"

"The Hortas are not conquerors, Vedek. They're children!"

"Children who have brought your precious station to the brink of ruin. The more you speak of your own danger, the more I fear for my planet."

"It's not the same thing!" Sisko protested. "We're an enclosed environment sustained artificially . . ." Sloi tried to cut him off with a wave of her hand, but Sisko would not be silenced. "They can't destroy a planet. In fact, they came here to help Bajor."

"Not at my request," she reminded him, "or the provisional government's."

Sisko tried another tack. "Forget the Hortas' rights, then. What about the other lives at stake here? Bajoran lives?"

"Our people are accustomed to sacrifice," she answered coolly, apparently unfazed by the increasing heat of Sisko's tone. Another band of interference rippled across the screen, deforming the Vedek's face like a fun-house mirror. "There is another possibility, of course," she continued. The signal's distortion turned the straight line of her lips into a twisted grimace.

"Which is?" Sisko asked.

"Destroy the Hortas. Purely in self-defense."

Sisko no longer saw any point to controlling his anger. "That, Madame Director, is exactly what our Cardassian computer suggested as well."

Even through the snow and static, Sisko saw the Vedek's eyes flash with fury at his comparison. "Our conversation is at an end, Commander. The decision of the council is final. Any attempt to deposit the Hortas anywhere on Bajor will be considered an illegal invasion on the part of Starfleet. Bajor out."

The screen blanked abruptly. So much for diplomacy, Sisko thought. He stared at the screen as if he could beam his thoughts directly to the Vedek's office on Bajor.

"I'll find a way, Sloi," he said aloud, "to save the station and the Hortas. And to hell with you and your entire council."

Sisko stood up suddenly. He stepped away from his desk and marched toward Ops. There were other councils and committees that might be able to overrule or circumvent Vedek Sloi and her xenophobic brand of ecological protection, but he had neither the time nor the patience to wrestle anymore with the intricacies of Bajoran politics, not with a litter of feral Hortas breathing down his neck.

The double doors slid open automatically, selfishly depriving him of the pleasure of slamming them behind him. Sisko strode onto the upper tier of Ops. No one looked up to note his arrival; everyone appeared engrossed in tracking the Hortas or compensating for one of a hundred malfunctioning systems. The environmental controls were clearly in trouble, as well as the air circulators.

Despite the absence of Dax, Kira, and O'Brien, Ops was more crowded than usual. A bad sign, he realized. As they lost more and more territory to the Hortas, a larger percentage of his staff had crammed into Ops to assist however they could. Despite their injuries, Dawson and Shirar from the *Puyallup* had pitched in to help. Captain Dawson supervised the operations table while his Vulcan navigator scanned the surrounding area for transmissions from the *Amazon.*

Looking around Ops, Sisko was startled to see one young ensign wearing nothing but a blanket; at the moment, he knelt beside the science station, making rapid adjustments to the long-range sensor displays while his free hand struggled to hold the makeshift toga together. Sisko rolled his eyes wearily. There had to be a story behind the nearly naked ensign, but he didn't have the time to look into it. Neither did anybody else, apparently; it was a measure of how bad things were that nobody on the floor was giving the young man a hard time.

Sisko decided to get the news straight from the front. "Chief O'Brien," he said, activating his comm. "Sisko here. Report."

The Irishman's voice came through more clearly than the broadcast from Bajor. "We're losing ground, Commander, and in a big way. We've fed the ugly rock-rats damn near everything but the docking pylons and they're still coming."

"How far from the core?" Sisko asked.

"Commander, they're in the core already. They got past us on the bridge ten minutes ago."

Silently, Sisko cursed Sloi and Pova and their useless council to the darkest corner of the Bajoran netherworld. "Chief, I want you back in Ops now. Prepare to be beamed here directly."

There was a momentary silence on the other end of the line. "Chief?" Sisko inquired.

O'Brien's voice took on a slightly embarrassed tone.

"Er, if it's all the same to you, Commander, I'd just as soon take the turbolift."

"I can't risk you getting stuck in a shaft for the next three hours. There might not be a station left when you got out," Sisko said, hoping that he was exaggerating but not willing to bet on it.

"Right you are, sir," O'Brien conceded.

Sisko issued the command to the naked ensign, noting that the youth's blanket had drooped past his knees; nobody bothered to cover him up again. Almost instantly, Chief O'Brien's pattern formed over the transporter pad in a radiant aura of materializing energy. As soon as the glow faded, O'Brien stepped briskly off the pad. Sanger stepped aside to let the chief take his place at the engineering station.

Despite the unfolding crisis, Sisko felt reassured to see one of his senior officers back in Ops. "Where is Odo right now?" he asked aloud.

O'Brien looked up from his station. "Indisposed, if you know what I mean."

In his pail, in other words. Sisko nodded, and O'Brien returned to his work. *It's too bad,* Sisko thought, *that Odo can't split himself like an amoeba; I could use several more of him at the moment.* "What about the Hortas?" he inquired. "How far are they from Ops?"

O'Brien brought up a schematic on the main viewer. It was a vertical cross section of the core itself, with Ops located near the top, just below the communications cluster. Sisko spotted a flurry of red triangles spreading out a few levels below the Promenade, then starting to sink lower on the diagram. "That's peculiar," O'Brien commented. "They seem to be ignoring the upper core entirely this time. They're all moving into the lower core, but there's nothing down there except cargo bays, storage tanks, and"—O'Brien's eyes widened in alarm as he realized what he was saying—"the fusion reactors!"

Sisko was way ahead of him. Suddenly, everything came together. "Of course," he declared, "that's what they've been looking for all this time. The reactors. Think about it, Chief. The reaction chambers generate power which is then transferred to beds of liquid sodium and *silicon*. Silicon, that's the key; the Hortas' entire biology is based on it."

"My God," O'Brien said, as the full implications of Sisko's revelation sunk in. "Tanks of hot liquid silicon. It must seem like mother's milk to them!"

"That's right," Sisko agreed. "They've been confused and distracted up to now, but they must be able to sense it somehow. That's why they keep circling back toward the core, and that's where they're going now."

O'Brien's face grew pale. "But if they do to the reactors what they've done to the rest of the station, if they rupture the reaction chambers . . ." He didn't need to elaborate. *Deep Space Nine* could survive some torn-up living quarters and even an occasional hull breach, but if the reactors went the entire station would end up as a lifeless, uninhabitable tombstone drifting on the outskirts of the wormhole.

Sisko stared at the display on the viewer. The Hortas were still several levels away from the reactor, exploring the maintenance equipment and storage areas that made up most of the lower core, but the clock was clearly ticking toward a disaster that could kill everyone on the station. He couldn't wait for Kira anymore.

"Chief," he said in a firm, controlled voice. "I want you to set up as many shields as possible between the

Hortas and the reactors. Divert power from everything short of life support if you have to."

"But shields can't stop them," O'Brien said. "I wish they could!"

"The shields are just to buy time." Sisko tapped his comm. "Lieutenant Moru, get a full team of security officers, armed with the most powerful phasers you have, to the lower core. I want you to set up a firing line between the Hortas and the reactors." Sisko paused, thought of Jake and Jennifer and Ttan, then gave the order he'd been dreading: "Set phasers on maximum settings. Shoot to kill."

Forgive me, Ttan, he thought. *Forgive us all.*

BEEEEEEEP. A buzzing electronic siren suddenly activated at the science station, interrupting Sisko's guilty brooding. *Now what,* he wondered irritably. He turned his fierce, questioning gaze on Lieutenant Eddon.

"A proximity alarm," the Andorian explained. She deactivated the siren with a few deft movements of her pale blue fingers. "The Prodigal is coming as close to DS9 as it is going to get." She hastily consulted her screens, then added, "The station is in no danger, as long as our inertial fields compensate for the moon's gravitational pull."

"Chief?" Sisko asked.

"No problem so far," O'Brien assured him. "Frankly, that moon is the least of our troubles."

Thank heaven for small favors, Sisko thought. What with Ttan's abduction, the rescue mission, and the baby Hortas' subsequent rampage, he'd completely forgotten The Prodigal's scheduled flyby. Too bad, he thought ruefully. Under better circumstances, he would have liked to have watched the moon's approach with Jake. The sight was supposed to be quite impressive, with the moon approaching near enough that many features of its terrain could be seen with the naked eye. So close that . . .

"Chief," he asked abruptly, the urgent timbre of his voice catching the attention of everyone in Ops, hushing the hubbub of dozens of Starfleet officers at work. "Is the moon within transporter range of the station?"

"Almost," O'Brien announced after only a moment's calculation. "We should have a thirty-six-minute window of opportunity opening up in approximately ten minutes." The hope in O'Brien's eyes matched Sisko's. "Are you thinking what I'm thinking, Commander?"

"Lock on to those Hortas, Chief. Get ready to transport them on my command."

For the first time in hours, Sisko felt the danger might be coming under control. He opened a line to the security team posted in the lower core. "Lieutenant Moru, hold your fire until it is absolutely necessary. We may have a way out of this massacre." An encouraging smile formed on his face. *Take that, Vedek Sloi,* he thought. *And your little dog, too.*

Then, without warning, the lights went out, throwing Ops into total darkness. Sisko heard gasps of alarm and shouting, from the systems core two levels below. No screams, though, he noted with a touch of pride; his staff was trained better than that.

The emergency lights came on, as well as the main viewer and some of the monitors. The dim red illumination cast eerie scarlet shadows over the scene, but Sisko barely noticed. He needed to know what had happened immediately. "Chief O'Brien," he said loudly. "Report."

"Power levels are dropping in Reactor One,"

O'Brien told him. Pellets of sweat broke out on the Irishman's brow. "I think we have a Horta in the silicon bed."

"What?" Sisko was momentarily taken aback. The schematic on the viewer showed the Hortas still a few levels away from the reactors, nor had Lieutenant Moru reported engaging the enemy yet. He watched eighteen red triangles descending toward the bottom of DS9. They couldn't have reached the reactors already, unless . . .

"The missing Horta," he realized at once. Somehow it had gotten ahead of the others.

And their time had run out.

At last! The little Horta rejoiced, basking in a bath of warmth and satisfaction. Pure food, better than anything she had eaten since she escaped her shell, surrounded her on all sides. She had found what she was looking for. More, she was literally swimming in it.

All thoughts of the carbon-beings, of disappearing holoscenes, and of her long trek down the turboshaft were driven from her mind by the sheer bliss of immediate, unadulterated gratification. She sucked energized silicon through her cilia. She absorbed it directly through her hide. Rather than sating her appetite, the potent brew spurred her hunger on to even greater heights. She could not consume her tasty new world fast enough.

In the midst of her banquet, however, she remembered her brothers and sisters. She sensed that they were not far away and, in her joy, she was eager to share her bounty.

Come! Come! Come! the Horta sang out, beckoning

her siblings, extolling the treasure she'd uncovered. *Hurry*, she exhorted, and she thought she heard the other Hortas respond.

Soon they would join her, she thought happily. There was enough here for everyone. They could eat to their souls' content, or until the end of the world.

CHAPTER
17

TTAN HAD LEFT the end of her escape tunnel for last. As soon as she finished carving out a passage that her Federation rescuers could use, she bored her way through the rhodinium-reinforced slab of concrete that formed the floor of the docking bay.

When she emerged, she found herself surrounded by Cardassians with phaser rifles. She hesitated. Her back still stung where the guard had shot her. Clearly their weapons could do her serious damage on their highest setting . . . as they had to be set now.

"Don't fire," a familiar voice ordered.

Gul Mavek pushed through his men to face her. He crossed his arms and stared, his expression unreadable to the Horta.

"I am very angry, Ttan," he said in a low, menacing voice. *"Very* angry. So angry I have ordered all of your children killed in five minutes. If you help us capture the rebel slaves, I will stop that order. Your children do not have to die."

The blinding rage returned to Ttan. She began to creep forward very slowly.

"Ttan," Mavek said in a warning voice. "Have you forgotten your children? All nineteen of them are going to die if you don't obey me."

"Liar," Ttan said. The Universal Translator made a hopeless garbled sound. *Two meters. One meter.*

"Ttan—" For the first time, she saw a look of worry on Gul Mavek's face. He took a step back, then another.

"Liar," Ttan said again. She gathered her cilia under her body.

Gul Mavek screamed as Ttan leaped. The guards fired. Pain washed through Ttan's body, but she didn't stop, didn't hesitate. She had come too far now. She shot streams of acid from every gland in her body, shooting them not just at Gul Mavek, but in every direction.

The force of her leap bowled Mavek over, and she sat on top of him, letting acid pour from her body. The phasers around them had stopped firing, she noticed, but that didn't matter. All that mattered was Gul Mavek's frail carbon and calcium body now lying beneath, quickly burning away to nothing.

That is for my children, she thought, *and for the pain you have caused us all.*

When she looked up, all the other Cardassians had dropped their weapons and fled. Many of them were shrieking in agony—touched by the streams of acid Ttan had shot from her body as she launched herself at Gul Mavek.

The first few of her humanoid allies emerged from the tunnel, looking around in surprise. The ones with Federation uniforms took charge at once.

Content to watch for the moment, Ttan settled back as they stormed the *Dagger,* the late Gul Mavek's ship.

Thank goodness for small favors, Julian Bashir thought. He might have lost his phaser, but he'd managed to keep his medical bag. And in the suddenly lessened gravity, he could move like an acrobat in the peak of condition.

The hypospray that had put Major Kira to sleep snapped back into its holder. He pulled out two splints, emergency tape, and a tube of the silicon plaster he'd brought in case Ttan had been injured. He'd never thought he'd have to use it on a Bajoran.

Taking a quick medical scan of Kira's broken leg—a rather clean break on top of a dislocated knee, he discovered—he realized there wasn't a pretty way to do it. Taking a deep breath, he snapped her leg back into place. If Kira had been awake, he knew, she would have screamed in mortal agony. As it was, deep under a haze of painkillers, she moaned like a sick animal. This was one of the worst parts of being a doctor, Julian thought. He hated seeing people suffer.

Holding her leg fully extended, he taped the splints in place, then used the silicon plaster to make a cast. It was battlefield medicine at its most primitive, but it would do for now. He could move her without fear of killing her.

Rising a trifle unsteadily, he tucked the bag under one arm, picked Kira up with the other, and followed after the others. Thank goodness for the moon's low gravity here, he thought. Even burdened with Kira's body, he wasn't carrying more than two-thirds of his normal weight.

He thought he saw a little more light ahead and pressed on, feeling excited. Ttan, he soon discovered, had bored small holes into other levels of the Cardassian base, letting light spill through and illuminate the passage. Then he caught sight of the escaping Bajorans—or at least two of them. A man and a woman, looking to be in little better shape than he was, had paused to rest in a pool of light. They struggled to their feet as he approached.

"Let me take your bag," the woman said.

Julian handed it to her gratefully. In the process, though, he must have jostled Kira the wrong way because she suddenly stirred and moaned through the painkillers.

"Here," said the man, steadying Julian's arm for a second. "What can I do to help?"

Julian shifted Kira until he could hold her in one hand without fear of dropping her. Then he extended his other hand to the Bajoran.

"Grab my wrist—yes, like that—and I'll grab yours," he said. "We'll make a seat for her so there isn't any pressure on her leg." That was the best he could do for Kira right now, he thought.

With the Bajoran's help, he managed to balance Kira more easily. Following the woman holding his bag, he and the man had no trouble making it the last thirty meters to where the tunnel broke through a thick slab of concrete.

At the lip of the tunnel, he paused a second to gaze across the landing bay. Overhead, a forcefield shimmered, and beyond it Julian could see the black of interstellar space, sprinkled with glittering jewels of stars. This had to be the landing bay. Straight ahead, in the center of the open area, stood what looked like a Bruja-class Cardassian ship. He thought it was the same one that had attacked the *Puyallup,* but couldn't be certain. Its cargo hatch stood open, though, and

Bajorans were pouring through it as quickly as they could, as Aponte, Muckerheide, and Wilkens stood watch, phasers drawn and ready.

Then he spotted Ttan. The Horta sat on the ground next to the hatch as if on guard. The outline of a body had been burned into the concrete next to her. Was it a warning to the Cardassians? If so, it certainly seemed to work—Julian found it chilling.

The sound of phaser fire suddenly erupted behind him. Julian jerked his head around, trying to see down the tunnel. The Cardassians must have stormed the tunnel mouth, he thought. If only he'd managed to cave it in, he thought desperately.

"Hurry," he said to the Bajoran next to him. "They're right behind us."

The man nodded. "I hear them."

Julian eased forward onto the docking bay, carefully balancing Kira, and headed for the shuttle as quickly as he could. He'd only taken a dozen steps when he suddenly noticed blood dripping from the cast on Kira's left foot. Not a good sign, he thought. All the jostling must have cut something inside her leg. He'd have to treat it as soon as he could—but his top priority had to be getting her under cover. Stopping the bleeding wouldn't do a bit of good if the Cardassians got them.

As they neared the ship, to his relief Ensign Aponte came bounding down the gangway.

"Let me help—" she began.

Then a phaser blast hit her in the chest, knocking her back against the ship's hull with a thud. Julian drew up short, shocked. He couldn't believe what had just happened. Aponte had a hole the size of a dinner plate in her chest, he saw, and the flesh had been neatly cauterized so there wasn't any bleeding.

"Natalia—" he began. But he knew nothing he could say or do could possibly help. Not even the finest medical unit at Starfleet could bring her back from so severe a wound.

Swallowing, he forced his attention back to Kira. Unarmed, carrying a wounded friend, he couldn't turn and fight, much as he wanted to. *At least your death wasn't in vain,* he thought to Ensign Aponte. *You helped save all the others.*

Another phaser blast zipped past. It jarred something inside him. They had to get under cover as quickly as possible.

"Hurry," he urged the man helping him carry Kira.

"I am hurrying!" the man snapped back.

More crimson beams of energy lanced the air. Someone screamed what sounded like an incoherent warning to his right, and Julian paused for a heartbeat. Half a dozen Bajorans ran down from the cargo hatch and began laying down a covering fire for him.

He lugged Kira into the cargo hold and eased her to the deck. Blood slowly began to pool around her left foot, and he wondered if he'd missed something. When he took a quick scan of her leg, though, he realized it wasn't life-threatening, just a cut below her knee, which he hadn't noticed in the tunnel's dimness. He was free to take care of others first—just the way Kira would have wanted it, he thought a little wryly.

The Bajoran who'd helped him carry Kira aboard touched his arm. "You know we didn't have anything to worry about back there," the man said.

"What makes you say that?" Julian demanded. He'd almost been hit several times, after all. "The way those phaser blasts were flying—"

The man snorted. "I guess you didn't notice, but they were only shooting at people with guns. We were a secondary target. Now, how about going forward and seeing about getting us off this rock, will you? I'm a medic. I'll look after the wounded in here."

Julian glanced around, but the cargo hold seemed to be under control. There were several people with minor injuries, and a couple who seemed to be nursing broken arms, but that was it. The Bajoran could see to them. The Bajorans who'd stayed outside were boarding one by one, covering each other. Then, as he watched, Ttan surged up the gangway. She must've been guarding the rear, he thought.

"Everyone's aboard," Ensign Wilkens called to him.

"Close the hatch!" Julian called back, but someone had already hit the controls. As the hatch's huge doors swung shut, several phaser bolts made it through. Luckily they didn't hit anything important, just the rhodinium plating on the walls. Then the hold sealed with an audible hiss.

Julian took a deep, calming breath. *You're in charge here,* he told himself. *Act like it.*

He handed his medical bag to the Bajoran medic. "Everything you need is inside," he said.

"Thanks," the man said. He hurried off to see to the wounded.

"Wilkens," he said. "You're in charge down here. Get everyone settled in for takeoff. Muckerheide!"

"Here, sir," a weak voice called. Julian turned until he located the source. Muckerheide was propped in the corner. He looked like he'd taken a glancing phaser blast to his side. The fact that he was conscious at all was sign enough that he'd live.

"Take it easy," Julian called. "I'll be on the bridge."

He wove through the Bajorans sitting on the floor and made his way down a long, narrow corridor with tomblike cabins to either side. The Cardassians didn't build with human aesthetics in mind, he told himself, feeling a touch claustrophobic.

He pushed through a small hatch and into the ship's bridge. It was situated in the nose of ship, a semicircle-shaped room about twice the size of a runabout's main cabin. The captain's station was in the middle, six crew stations spaced equidistantly around it. Captain Dyoran and five other Bajorans he didn't know by name now manned all those stations.

The captain's seat was empty. Feeling a little bit out of place, Julian sank into it. The softness surprised him—one of the few comforts he'd yet found in the Cardassian military.

Now, he thought, *to get on top of things.* He studied the forward viewscreen, which showed the docking bay. Several dozen Cardassian soldiers seemed to be setting up an energy cannon. Doubtless they planned to use it on the ship. What would Sisko have done? Gathered information, then made the best decision he could based on available data.

"Report!" he snapped in his best impression of Sisko.

Captain Dyoran looked back at him a little oddly. "Engines up to full power. We can take off any time we want."

"Do so," Julian said.

"Doctor, there's a forcefield—"

"Then blast its controls. This ship has weapons, doesn't it?"

Dyoran grinned. "My thought exactly." He turned to the woman next to him. "Proceed, Cella."

She touched several buttons, and phaser fire lashed out from the ship.

The phaser shots struck the control booth. It vaporized. Abruptly the docking bay's lights went out. For a heartbeat Julian listened to absolute silence; then, even through the hull of the ship, he heard the vast sucking sound outside. Vacuum, he realized—the cargo bay had been exposed to the raw vacuum of space. To his horror, everything not bolted to the ground—Cardassians, papers, equipment, *everything*—blew out through the opening overhead where the forcefield had been.

It only took a few seconds to clear out the docking bay. But the sucking sound didn't stop. It dwindled to a whistle, a little like an old Earth train on an old tape. Why didn't the noise stop?

Ttan's tunnel. He felt a sudden flutter in his chest as he realized the effect must be spreading throughout the whole underground complex. Ttan had cut through the docking bay's floor into half a dozen levels, straight into the heart of the base. Every bit of air would be sucked out into space.

He'd condemned dozens, if not hundreds, of Cardassians to death. Never mind that they'd been trying to kill him and committing war crimes to boot—the magnitude of what he'd done staggered him. *His* orders had made it so. He'd never carried such a weight on his shoulders before, and the immensity of it staggered him.

"Captain?" Dyoran said. "Captain?"

It took Julian a moment to realize Dyoran meant him. "Uh, yes?" he said.

"All stations standing by."

"Then—lift off," he said. "Get us out of here."

He sank back, feeling sick and exhausted, and watched in a numb sort of amazement as the crew around him powered up the engines and lifted the ship on impulse power. They cleared the docking bay and reached open space, and the gas giant— with its swirling reds, oranges, and yellows—seemed to swing around. It took up most of the forward viewscreen.

It was done, he realized. They had succeeded. They'd not only rescued Ttan, but dozens of Bajoran prisoners.

Then his communicator hailed him.

"Julian?" Dax's voice said. "What in the seven hells is going on down there?"

Julian gasped. In the excitement he'd completely forgotten about her. He tapped his badge.

"Bashir here," he said. Hastily he filled her in.

There came a long silence when he finished. Finally Dax said, "We'll have to make the best of it. Go to this heading—" and she read off a series of numbers.

"Got that?" Julian asked Dyoran.

"Yes, Captain," Dyoran said. "New heading on this mark."

"Julian," Dax went on over the communicator. "I want you to listen to me very carefully. I'm picking up six large Cardassian vessels bearing down on your moon. Head for Federation space at impulse power for five more minutes. Be prepared to go to warp on my command."

"Roger," Julian said. He found himself gripping the arms of the captain's seat so hard his knuckles hurt. He forced himself to let go.

"We're being hailed," one of the Bajorans told him. "It's the lead ship—the *Ramoth's Revenge*. Should I answer?"

"No," Julian said. Then he bit his lip. If he didn't

answer, they'd know something was wrong. "Yes," he said. "Voice only—no picture."

"Coming through now."

"Dagger," said a chill Cardassian voice, "what is your status?"

"Davonia has suffered a major reactor leak," Julian said in what he hoped was an equally cool voice. "We are contaminated. Stand off, *Ramoth's Revenge."*

"Put me on visual."

"Negative," Julian said, praying desperately that the captain of the *Ramoth's Revenge* would believe him. "Our equipment is damaged." He caught his breath and waited for their response.

When none came for several heartbeats, he whispered to Dyoran, "Can we take them in a battle?"

"It would be difficult," Dyoran said. "There *are* six of them, sir."

"They're scanning us," another Bajoran called.

"Go to full impulse power." Julian tried to keep the tremor from his voice. "Keep us on course. Let's see what they're going to do." *And let's hope Dax has a plan,* he mentally added. *If only Kira were awake— she'd know what to do.*

"They're hailing us again," the Bajoran at the communications station said.

"Ignore it," Julian said.

"Sir," called a fourth Bajoran, "there's a small ship lifting off from the second moon. It's heading straight for the six ships. It's firing on them!"

"What!" Julian demanded. That had to be Dax. But she had to know her runabout would be no match for six Cardassian ships! "Put it on the viewscreen!" he said.

The view changed to show what was happening aft.

As he watched, the runabout fired a volley of phaser blasts, then its three remaining photon torpedoes. Abruptly the runabout swung around and sped toward Cardassian space. It went to warp before Julian's startled eyes.

Two of the torpedoes hit home before the Cardassians could raise shields. A series of brilliant explosions rocked one of the ships, and it spun away from the rest of the formation.

The five remaining vessels changed course to follow the runabout. They, too, went to warp speed in pursuit.

Julian swallowed. The runabout could barely do warp three without shaking itself to pieces. He knew the battle would be suddenly and savagely ended. Dax had sacrificed herself to save them.

Then the door to the bridge rolled open and Dax entered.

"Jadzia!" Julian exclaimed. "How—what—"

"I beamed myself aboard before the runabout went to warp on automatic pilot," she said. "I believe you're in my seat, Doctor."

"And glad to get out of it," he said, leaping to his feet. He'd thought he would never see her again.

"Go to maximum warp," Dax ordered. She sank into the captain's seat. "That won't fool them long. They'll be after us with everything they have."

The view switched to the front of the ship. Stars blurred into lines as they accelerated.

"Warp five-point-three," one of the Bajorans called. "That's about all we're going to get out of her."

"Will that be enough?" Julian asked. He wondered what speeds the Cardassian freighters were capable of.

"We'll see," Dax said. "I estimate their ships'

maximum speeds at somewhere between warp six and warp seven." She turned to Julian.

He grinned at her. Things were definitely back to normal, he realized.

"Now," she said, "I think I need a slightly more detailed report. Let's start with what happened to Major Kira."

CHAPTER
18

"FORGET THE OTHER HORTAS," Sisko ordered. "Lock on to the one in the reactor right away!"

At his engineering station, one level below the commander's perch in Ops, Chief O'Brien struggled with his equipment. Unfortunately, trying to lock on to a silicon-based life-form in the middle of a molten bath of liquid silicon was as tricky as it sounded, especially with many key sensors out and one of DS9's two working reactors in trouble.

Instructing Lieutenant Eddon to monitor the damage in the reactor, he tried to get some sort of decent readings on his transporter controls. "Contamination?" he asked her without looking up from his station.

"Minimal spillage so far, but rising. Something is curbing the flow of conductive fluid from the ruptured tank, and maybe even damping the radiation levels somewhat." The Andorian sounded confused. Once the silicon bed's container was ruptured, the resulting release of superheated liquid should have resulted in massive destruction in the reactor facility.

O'Brien knew what was saving them. "The Horta," he said tersely. Ironically, the little bugger was drinking up the radioactive fluid faster than it could spill into the rest of the station. The Horta's omnivorous tendencies would do them no good at all, however, once the creature found its way into the reaction chamber itself. There was no use crying over spilled radioactive waste, as they used to joke at the Academy, but antimatter was something else entirely. Somehow, he doubted that even a Horta could stomach an antimatter-induced fusion reaction. More likely, the resulting explosion would obliterate them all before the creature could take more than a bite.

It was too late to shut down the reactor, as well. Even though DS9 still had one more reactor in operation, the radioactive materials—and the antimatter—would not go away with the flick of a switch. Besides, O'Brien reasoned, it was better to keep the Horta happy and occupied at Reactor 1, rather than risk driving it over to Reactor 2. One rupture was enough.

"Prodigal within transporter range," N'Heydor announced.

"Visual," Sisko said.

O'Brien continued to concentrate on the transporter controls. Someone at the operations table could handle the commander's request.

He took a quick glance at the main viewer. Sure enough, the diagram had been replaced by a view of open space dominated by The Prodigal. Its rough surface looked like the product of centuries of volcanic upheavals, as well as several rounds of demolition derby with stray meteors and asteroids. No wonder, O'Brien thought, neither the Bajorans nor the Cardassians had ever tried colonizing it. The vagabond moon struck him as an ugly and inhospitable place—although maybe not to Hortas, he reminded himself.

Lord, though, it was practically next door. He'd have no trouble beaming the renegade Horta over there, if only he could get a lock on the damn beastie. He swiftly adjusted the transporter scans, trying to probe the ruptured energy bed, but fluctuating radiation levels caused his readings to shift constantly, beyond any reasonable margin for error. "Computer," he demanded, ready at this point to accept help from *any* quarter, "lock on to alien life-form in Reactor Bed One."

"Unable to comply," the computer replied. "Silicon life-form indistinguishable from silicon environment."

O'Brien couldn't believe it. He clenched his jaws together angrily. The bloody computer had been trying to beam the poor Hortas off the station since forever, it felt like—and now, the moment things got a little sticky, the stupid program was "unable to comply." The hell it was!

"Ignore chemical composition. Scan for concentrations of solid mass in the reactor bed."

"Insufficient capability to perform function. Seventy percent of primary sensors malfunctioning. Require immediate repairs to execute command."

Sisko appeared at O'Brien's shoulder. "Chief?" he asked softly. O'Brien felt rather than saw over a dozen pairs of eyes watching him intently. Everyone was counting on him now, he knew, and not just the assorted officers packed into Ops. The fate of the station and the Hortas and, especially, Molly and Keiko depended on whether or not he could execute Commander Sisko's last-ditch plan for their survival.

Is it just me, he thought, wiping his forehead, *or is it unusually hot in here?*

"I'm going to have to do this manually, sir," he explained, sounding a lot more confident than he felt, and doubting that he'd fooled Benjamin Sisko for one minute. He popped a latch on the side of his console and exposed the transporter sensors themselves. *The trick,* he assured himself, *is to skip past all the technological bureaucracy: the controls controlling the controls and so on. Bypass the computer safeguards, dispense with the voice-activated systems, skip the convenient buttons and touch controls . . . go straight to the parts that do the work.*

And, when all else fails, pray to whatever gods there be.

"Radiation levels rising," Eddon warned from the science station. Her antennae drooped alarmingly, although there was no sign of fear on her face.

"Remaining Hortas approaching reactors," Sanger chimed in. "There's only one layer of flooring between them and the security team."

O'Brien dug his fingers into the innards of the console. *All I really need to do,* he thought, *is recalibrate the subprocessor modules of the short-range sensors. . . .*

Unexpectedly, the floor of the station shook beneath his feet. O'Brien held on to his station and refused to let go. The entire chamber tilted about ten degrees to the left. Several officers lost their balance and fell to the floor. A Vulcan woman with a cast on her leg lurched against O'Brien, smacking into his side, but he managed to stay on his feet. With one hand clutched around a rail, Sisko grabbed the Vulcan and kept her from hitting the ground. A moment later a naked man landed hard on top of the operations table.

A naked man?

"The Prodigal's gravitational pull has overcome the inertial field," N'Heydor called out. Ordinarily, O'Brien knew, the moon would not have posed a problem; either a power loss or direct damage from the Horta had caused the field to fail. "The thrusters are compensating," N'Heydor said.

Ops righted itself, and O'Brien assumed they hadn't been knocked out of orbit yet. He heard Sisko take a deep breath behind him. "With all deliberate speed, Chief," he said, in the calm, emotionless voice he reserved for the direst of emergencies.

Hastily, O'Brien reprogrammed the subprocessors. He tuned out everything around him, including his own aches and bruises and rushes of fear, and focused on the machine and his mission. Estimate the mass. Filter out the radiation. Scan for life signs, but not according to standard parameters for carbon-based entities. . . .

"Got her!" O'Brien said triumphantly. But maybe only for a minute, he added silently.

"To The Prodigal, Chief O'Brien. Now!" Sisko commanded.

Via the transporter beam, O'Brien seized the rogue Horta, yanking her free of the reactor bed and throwing her onto the surface of the moon. He didn't realize he'd stopped breathing until the transporter released the Horta's signal and indicated that she had fully materialized on the satellite on the screen. Then he let out a sigh he figured could probably be heard on Bajor itself, if not back in Dublin.

"Done?" Sisko asked.

"Done," O'Brien told him.

"Long-range sensors are detecting Horta life signs on The Prodigal," Lieutenant Eddon informed them. "I believe it's burrowing into the interior of the moon." The blue antennae emerging from her white hair perked up even as she spoke, rising like sunflowers seeking the dawn.

Sisko smiled. The crisis had been averted, but the work wasn't done yet. "Lock on to the other Hortas, Chief. Send them after the first one."

O'Brien nodded. He closed the latch and restored the transporter to its standard settings. Compared to finding that single Horta in her silicon haystack, transporting her hatchmates would be child's play. It took him only a minute or two to beam all the remaining Hortas (except, he recalled sadly, the dead Horta now resting in the infirmary) over to The Prodigal.

Meanwhile, the commander fired off instructions to the rest of Ops. "Shut down Reactor Two," he ordered, "and place a containment field around the ruptured bed. Tell Lieutenant Moru and her people to stand down and get away from that radiation. I want a repair team down there at once." Sisko paused for a second, reconsidering. "Give the weapons towers top priority, though."

That last command gave O'Brien pause and muted some of the glee he'd been feeling since the Hortas left DS9. There was still a Cardassian raider out there somewhere, and after the Hortas' depredations the station was in no shape for a fight. Then, too, the Mother Horta remained missing, along with Kira, Bashir, Dax, and the others.

He hoped the rescue team had had an easier time than he had, but the longer they stayed missing in action, the less likely that seemed.

CHAPTER
19

DAX COULD FEEL the tension on the bridge. As the Cardassian ships closed in, she began to wonder if they were going to make it.

"They're energizing their weapons systems," the Bajoran at the weapons console told her.

"Raise shields," Dax ordered. "Prepare to drop out of warp. And prepare ready to hail DS9—we're going to need help fast."

The Cardassians hadn't been fooled for long by her trick with the runabout. They'd been in close pursuit for the last eight hours, gaining steadily. She'd used every trick she knew to try to slip away from them, but all she'd managed to do was gain a little more time. The Cardassians hadn't managed to get so much as a shot off at the *Dagger* yet, but she suspected that their luck was about to run out.

"Status?" she demanded again.

"Ready," one station after another reported.

A phaser blast hit the back of the *Dagger,* rocking it violently. Dax clung to the arms of the captain's chair, wishing Cardassians would equip their ships with safety belts like other intelligent races.

Another blast shook the ship. Only a few seconds more, she thought . . . according to the computer, they were about to enter Bajoran space.

"Deflector shields now down to seventy-eight-percent strength," someone called.

"Now!" Dax yelled.

The *Dagger* slowed to impulse power without warning. She'd hoped the Cardassians would overshoot them and have to come back, but it didn't happen. A third powerful blast shook the ship. The running lights flickered and died, then came back up at half power. Hopefully the passengers in the cargo hold had weathered the jolts without serious harm. Their section of the ship was taking the heaviest beating.

"Sir," the naked ensign called to Sisko. "I'm picking up a ship entering this system at high speed. Wait, make that six ships . . . all Cardassian!"

Sisko turned. "Cardassian?"

"The lead ship is a Bruja-class military vessel. The others are much larger. . . ."

Kira, he wondered, *what the hell have you started? And where was the Amazon?*

"Go to battle alert," Sisko said, striding toward the operations table. A klaxon began to blare. "Get Odo up here on the double if he's out of his bucket by now. Chief O'Brien, what's our status?"

O'Brien shook his head grimly. "Only one weapons tower is operational, sir. We have a single bank of phasers." He looked at Sisko apologetically. "My people are working as fast as they can, but those Hortas did a lot of damage."

Unfortunately, Sisko thought, six Cardassian attack

ships have enough firepower to make the Hortas' rampage seem like a bad case of mildew. "I want those phasers ready to fire," he told O'Brien. He was outgunned, but at least he wasn't unarmed. "Lieutenant Eddon, put me through to the Cardassians."

"Commander," Eddon announced. "The lead ship is already hailing us." She turned, surprise evident on her face. "It's Lieutenant Dax!"

"Well," Sisko said, "put her on."

A static-filled image lit up the main viewscreen. It was Dax, sure enough, and from what little Sisko could see of the bridge behind her, she had a Bajoran crew. He recognized Dr. Bashir, but nobody else.

A thousand questions rushed through his mind. Where had all these Bajorans come from? What about Ttan? And Kira?

"No time to explain, Benjamin," Dax said. "I've got a shipload of Bajoran nationals. We're in pretty bad shape. Our shields are down to forty-four-percent power and we've lost warp capacity. The Cardassians are getting ready to fire on us again."

"Hold tight," Sisko said. "I'll talk to their commander."

He turned toward Eddon at the communications station. "Hail those ships."

"Yes, sir," she said. "No answer."

"Put this through anyway. They'll be listening." He paused a second. "Cardassian pursuit ships, this is Commander Benjamin Sisko of *Deep Space Nine*. You are ordered to identify yourselves. Decelerate and stand by for more instructions."

"No response, sir."

"Then we'll send them a message they can't ignore." Sisko nodded at Chief O'Brien. "Give them a phaser volley across the lead vessel's bow."

"But, Commander," O'Brien protested, "that's all we've got! We'll be defenseless."

"I know, Chief. I know." He turned his gaze on a wounded man with a red beard. "Captain Dawson, if you'd like to do the honors . . . ?"

"With pleasure, Commander!" The captain of the *Puyallup* tapped decisively at a bank of controls, and half a second later three short bursts from the station's phaser banks split the distance between Dax's ship and the Cardassians.

"Sir!" Eddon addressed him. "I'm now getting a transmission from Gul Nogar of the *Ramoth's Revenge.*"

"Put him on."

The image of a Cardassian officer filled the viewscreen: black and silver uniform, corded neck, and an arrogant, supercilious manner that set Sisko's teeth on edge. Nogar leaned forward, lip curled back, and snarled: "Hold your fire, Commander Sisko. We are in pursuit of a criminal ship. Your assistance is neither required nor requested here. It is an internal Cardassian matter."

"That ship has requested political asylum here," Sisko lied, "and I'm afraid the provisional authorities have granted it." Sisko leaned forward over the Ops table. For a man facing an armada with no weapons to speak of, Sisko thought he must look remarkably unworried. "The ship is, as I'm sure you're aware, piloted by Bajoran nationals."

Captain Nogar stared at him without blinking. "I did not know that."

"You are, of course," Sisko went on in his most charming voice, "welcome to dock at DS9 and enjoy our shore-leave facilities while you plead your case to the Bajoran government. I'm sure they will be very eager to hear from you. I'm sure we can have a definitive answer for you in, say, six to eight weeks."

"That is not acceptable." Nogar's eyes narrowed as he peered at Sisko through the viewer. "My understanding was that your station had recently suffered certain . . . difficulties?"

This is it, Sisko thought. *Either he falls for my bluff or we're space dust.*

"Some minor disturbances, nothing more," Sisko said casually. "Kids acting up, you know how they can be. The entire station has never been in better condition, including our state-of-the-art weapons systems. If you fire again on that ship, I'm afraid I'll have no choice but to return fire on their behalf. Defending Bajor and Bajoran nationals is part of our charter here, as I'm sure you know."

"Hold," Nogar said, and the viewscreen went blank.

"Commander," Ensign Sanger said. "We're being scanned by the Cardassians."

"Block those scans, mister," Sisko ordered. "Your life depends on it."

"Yes, sir!" Sanger said, suitably inspired.

After a long, endless moment Nogar resumed his transmission. Sisko smiled calmly, despite the mounting tension in Ops. "Commander," Nogar said a trifle archly, "in the interest of furthering the spirit of friendship"—it seemed like an effort for him to spit out that word—"and cooperation between our people, we will let you have your Bajoran nationals, if that's what they are."

Despite the pounding of his heart, Sisko could almost hear the unspoken *"this time."*

"Thank you," he said. "And if you or your crew would like to visit our station—"

Captain Nogar disconnected with an audible snarl of displeasure.

Odo met Sisko at the airlock when the *Dagger* docked at DS9. Sisko was glad to see the constable solid again. Before their eyes, the huge clockwork door rolled aside, revealing a narrow passageway.

Julian Bashir was the only one waiting there. "Infirmary, I need fifteen stretchers down here, stat!" he called, darting around Sisko and Odo with a barely mumbled "Hello, sir." He sprinted down the corridor and vanished from sight.

Sisko exchanged a puzzled glance with Odo. "Perhaps we'd better go aboard," Odo suggested.

"My thoughts exactly," Sisko said.

Odo went through, then into the ship. The hatch led into an antechamber, which was empty, then into a corridor. Odo turned right, and Sisko followed on his heels. They could hear voices from ahead.

The corridor opened into a cargo bay, where literally dozens of injured Bajoran men and women lay waiting for treatment. The smell of blood thickened the air. Most of the prone bodies looked more bruised and shaken up than injured, but more than a few had serious wounds. Sheets covered what looked like half a dozen bodies off to one side . . . casualties?

And in the center of the room rested Ttan. Sisko nodded in relief. The mission had been a success more than a success, from the looks of things.

"Benjamin, over here."

Sisko followed the voice back to Dax. She was off to the side, bending over one of the injured Bajorans. Sisko joined her. The injured Bajoran turned out to be Major Kira, whose leg was in a splint. Kira looked as angry as a Denebian horned groat.

"Major?" Sisko asked, kneeling. "How are you?"

"Good," Kira said through clenched teeth. "Mission accomplished, sir. And then some."

"I see that. Very well done, Major. I'd be surprised if there aren't a few commendations in your future when news of what happened comes out. There's only one thing . . ."

"What's that?" Dax asked.

"What the hell happened?"

Dax laughed and began to fill him in. Kira scowled through the whole story, but obligingly filled in the parts Dax didn't know.

When they finished, Sisko nodded thoughtfully. "That's quite a story," he said. "But I still don't quite understand how you made it to the ship after you broke your leg, Major."

Dax said, "Julian told me she fainted from shock. He carried her aboard."

Kira snorted. "Fainted from shock indeed."

Sisko raised his eyebrows. "It sounds like you two make quite a team." Clearly there was more to the story than what he'd already heard. He'd have to worm the whole truth out of Julian later that week.

Then Julian beamed in with a dozen other helpers. He began giving orders, beaming the most seriously injured straight to the infirmary in record time.

"I think everything is in order," Sisko said, rising. "I'll expect full reports from everyone tomorrow. Odo, give them a hand getting off, will you? I have some calls to make . . . and a family to reunite."

"Yes, sir," Odo said.

Sisko crossed to where Ttan had been waiting patiently. The Horta shifted as he approached.

"I know you can understand me, but can't reply,"

he said. "I want you to know your eggs have hatched and all your children are safe except one."

The Universal Translator on Ttan's back made a garbled noise.

"If you'll follow me," Sisko said, "I'll take you to our chief engineer. If he can't fix your translator, he can fit you with a new one."

Turning, he tapped his communicator. "Chief O'Brien, report to the docking ring."

Under other circumstances, the Promenade would have fascinated Ttan. All around her, humanoids of various shapes and composition went about their business in a colorful, spacious environment very different from the caverns of Janus VI. Most were busy repairing storefronts and displays.

Ttan felt only a rising sense of apprehension as they neared the infirmary. The commander of the station had explained how he had beamed her children to safety on a nearby moon. Still, she dreaded the prospect of facing the remains of the one child who had not survived.

The human named O'Brien walked beside her. He seemed very sympathetic to her loss. "I have a child of my own," he confided. "I can only imagine what you must be going through. I wish we could have saved her."

"Thank you," Ttan replied. Her new translator worked perfectly, but could not convey all the sadness she carried inside.

"Here we are," O'Brien said. He stopped in front of a black door alongside the infirmary. "Dr. Bashir needed all the medical facilities for the wounded, so they moved your child into this holding facility." He touched a panel and the door slid aside.

273

The station's Place of the Dead was clean and spare, lacking even the most rudimentary etched ceremonial decorations. It was a place of no soul, without the comforting weight of tradition and history.

In the center of the chamber, atop a strange piece of machinery covered with controls and monitors, lay the child. A boy, she saw at once, so large and healthy-looking that she couldn't believe he was dead.

Oh, my son, she lamented silently, *why did you travel so far to come to such a barren place? Please forgive me. I never imagined my ambition and dreams of adventure would cost you your life.*

"Let me turn off the stasis field," he said, touching one of the controls. The golden glow around her son faded as the energized field dispersed. "Take as much time as you need. I know you'll want to say goodbye."

Ttan glided across the floor toward her child. The translator produced the unmistakable sound of sobs.

O'Brien cleared his throat. "I'll wait outside," he said.

Before the human could leave, however, an odd sizzling sound came from the medical equipment underneath the dead Horta. Sparks suddenly flashed from an array of burning circuits. Smoke billowed up to the ceiling.

Ttan froze. Was this some sort of malfunction, she wondered, or a bizarre human rite of cremation?

O'Brien rushed forward with a cry of alarm. Her baby twitched. Acid dripped from its cilia. "My God, it's eating the unit!" the human shouted.

Overcome with happiness, she lunged forward to embrace her son. She gripped him as if she would never let go. She felt him snuggle closer to her. The soft scent of his baby acids, so mild compared to her own, filled her with maternal pride.

"Commander," she heard O'Brien say. "I think you'd better get down here. I can't believe it, but . . . the baby's alive! The shock of the vacuum must have put it into a coma."

Mother? the baby asked.

That's right, she said. *I'm here.*

EPILOGUE

QUARK SURVEYED his bar proudly. The sightseers had gone, but the profit remained. Five days after the Hortas had been beamed to the rogue moon, things had almost returned to normal. No, not quite normal, Quark decided. Odo was worse than ever.

The constable, leaning on the bar, shook his head and scowled, as he'd been doing repeatedly over the last few days.

"What is it this time?" Quark demanded.

"I'm just remembering how agreeably amorphous the Mother Horta's shape was," he said. "Now I'm stuck back in this awkward humanoid form sixteen hours a day to deal with the likes of you."

"You can always turn into a gaming table," Quark said. "I'll put you to good use. The two hundred and forty-third Rule of Acquisition clearly states—"

"Or I suppose I could turn back into a Horta and finish this bar for lunch," Odo growled.

"Not necessary, not necessary!" Shaking his head,

Quark swaggered over to the table where Dr. Bashir was, as usual, flirting with Dax. Quark doubted the doctor's efforts would be any more successful this time. *After all,* Quark thought, *if I can't get anywhere with her, what chance does that eager puppy have?*

"Another bottle of this excellent vintage," Bashir called with a grand gesture.

"Coming right up!" Quark replied. "The Chateau Picard, right?"

"Uh, no, the good stuff," Bashir said.

As Quark fetched another bottle from behind the counter, Major Kira stormed in. Her leg had mended nicely, Quark thought, but her temper hadn't.

She stomped up to Bashir, snapped, "I have *never* fainted from shock!" Then she turned and stomped back out. Bashir blushed furiously. Dax looked amused.

Shaking his head, Quark brought a bottle of fifty-year-old Thunderbird back to Bashir and Dax, unscrewed the cap, and refilled both of their goblets.

"Anything else?" he asked.

"Not right now," Dr. Bashir said. He turned to Dax. "For a second there, I thought she was going to slug me!"

Dax rose, her face an icy mask. "I'm getting very tired of the slug remarks, Julian." She stalked after Kira.

Julian rose. "But Jadzia—!" He ran after her.

Yes, Quark thought, things were definitely getting back to normal. Wiping his hands on his apron, he calmly screwed the cap back onto the bottle and carried it behind the bar. No sense wasting it, though of course it would show up on Dr. Bashir's tab.

He went into the storeroom to check on his new

workers. Looking very unhappy, Nog and Jake were both on their hands and knees, laying a new tile floor.

Nog said, "We've almost finished fixing all the holes in the floor, Uncle."

"Good," Quark said. "Next you can start on the walls."

Jake groaned. Nog hissed in displeasure.

"Unless," Quark went on, "you want me to mention to your fathers how that first baby Horta got loose. Not to mention who deactivated the stasis field."

In reply, the two boys redoubled their efforts. Neither met his gaze. Quark cackled happily. With any luck, he could string them along for the next six months. He had a lot of repairs in mind . . . they'd save him a fortune in maintenance costs.

Actually, Jake had already 'fessed up to his father. He couldn't admit that to Nog, though; he knew his friend would lose all respect for him if he found out. *So,* Jake thought as he carefully affixed another tile to the floor, *I have to lie to my friend about telling the truth to my dad.* He groaned, and not just because of his tired muscles. Trying to deal with humans and Ferengi at the same time made his head hurt.

Not that it mattered in this case. His dad had still insisted that Jake help repair the damage he'd caused. And, as far as Jake knew, his father almost always got what he wanted, one way or another.

Benjamin Sisko had been refusing Vedek Sloi's calls for the last five days. Finally, in the sanctuary of his private office, he deigned to answer.

Her face was livid on the monitor. "This is an outrage," she began as her greeting. "You had no right to beam those Hortas to one of Bajor's sacred moons. I'm drafting a formal complaint to Starfleet requesting your removal at once."

"On what grounds?" he asked evenly.

"You were explicitly told to keep those unholy monsters on *Deep Space Nine,*" she snarled.

"Excuse me, but I believe you said—and I quote— 'The Hortas do not belong on or below the sacred soil of Bajor.' You said nothing about Bajor's moons. If you like, I can have the tape played for you."

"A shameless technicality, unworthy of you. You *knew* they wouldn't be welcome on any Bajoran territory."

"I'm sorry," he said. "I must have misunderstood. If you like, I can have them recalled. But that would probably prevent them from finishing their report."

"What report?"

"On the vast mineral wealth hidden below the moon's surface."

She paused. "Vast mineral wealth?"

"Oh, nothing you'd be interested in, I'm sure. Just some uranium, pergium, and quite a bit of latinum as well. But I know how your mind is occupied with spiritual matters, which are, of course, more important."

Vedek Sloi leaned back thoughtfully. The silence stretched between them.

"Vedek?" he asked.

"Perhaps," she finally said, "we have been too hasty. After all, a moon isn't *Bajor.*"

Benjamin said, "Then you don't want me to send the Hortas back to Janus VI?"

There was another long pause. Then the Vedek spoke again.

"Perhaps," she said slowly, "a compromise can be worked out after all. . . ."

Sisko smiled.